THE LEGACY OF FOULSTONE MANOR

J. C. Briggs

SAPERE
BOOKS

THE LEGACY OF FOULSTONE MANOR

Published by Sapere Books.

24 Trafalgar Road, Ilkley, LS29 8HH,
United Kingdom

saperebooks.com

ISBN: 978-0-85495-235-9

See this house, how dark it is
Beneath its vast-boughed trees!
Not one trembling leaflet cries
To that Watcher in the skies—
'Remove, remove thy searching gaze,
Innocent of heaven's ways,
Brood not, Moon, so wildly bright,
On secrets hidden from sight…'

Mute shadows creeping slow
Mark how the hours go.
Every stone is mouldering slow.
And the least winds that blow
Some minutest atom shake,
Some fretting ruin make
In roof and walls. How black it is
Beneath these thick boughed trees!

From *The Empty House* by Walter de la Mare

PROLOGUE

Foulstone Manor is on a rise above a little valley in which there is a derelict mill that had burned down years ago. There are a couple of cottages with gardens across the rutted lane where old apple trees still bear fruit. One of the cottages is empty. No one would want to live there now. It's dark with dusty windows, uneven stone-flagged floors, and a somewhat perilous narrow staircase — with water to be got only from the pump outside. Miss Goss lives in the other cottage. There is a light in the window, but the lane is dark and leads only to the old mill. No one passes that way. Who would want to live down there with that old house brooding behind the trees?

There are no lights in Foulstone Manor. No one lives there now. Its gardens are ruined and overgrown, too, with wild bushes, sprawling ivy and dank weeds. There is a glass house, now dangerously listing, its panes cracked and broken, its shelves sagging, and broken pots and glass scattering the brick floor. There had been stables and there are still one or two other outbuildings, some with broken doors showing the darkness within. Fields separate the house from the little valley, but the top of the house can still be seen in winter when the trees are bare. It is not possible now to tell where the woods end and the gardens begin.

There are strangers in the woods sometimes, grey, silent, oddly fragmented figures drifting in the mist and rain of autumn afternoons in the descending twilight, or just shifting shadows in the falling snow in freezing winter dawns when the light is only the colour of dim pewter. No one knows where they come from, or where they go. Homeless perhaps, but they never ask for anything. There is nothing at Foulstone Manor for them.

Fifty years of encroachment. Nature has taken over. The house dreams on — but restlessly — its sleep disturbed, perhaps, by the sound of a slate slipping from the sagging roof, or the wind in the empty corridors, or water dripping in an attic room, another pane of glass cracking under creeping black mould, a strand of ivy tightening its stealthy grip on a chimney, another spot of lichen sticking secretly to a rotting window frame, mice in the kitchen, rats in the cellars. And the smell of decay and damp and something else — something rotten. The house shifts in its sleep. Timbers creak and mortar crumbles from stone.

A whisper in the shadows. A footfall on a stair.

PART ONE: 1970

1

Joan

I left Foulstone Manor when I was a child. My aunt took me away to Kendal. I say aunt because that's what I called her. Let's get the truth out. She was Mrs Goss, really, who had been housekeeper to my father, but I called her Auntie Mary. That was what I was told. 'Easier, lovey,' she'd say, 'if folk ask.' And folk did, looking at me sympathetically, having heard the story of Auntie Mary's sister, Margaret, who'd died young, and who had been widowed, too. It wasn't that long after the first war so that was enough said. Auntie Mary told a good tale — brief, but with telling pauses and nods returned — so good, I came to believe it myself. I was only three years old when they took me away. Joanie, she called me at first. Then I became Joan. I forgot that it wasn't my name.

I didn't know Foulstone Manor was mine until just before my uncle died. Uncle William — not, of course, my uncle, or anybody's. I never heard of any relative. He was ninety years old. Auntie Mary had said it was a cursed place, but she never said why. It was what she said to keep me from asking questions. My uncle never spoke of it, but when he was eighty-nine and my aunt was long dead, he told me that she had been right. It had brought nothing but misery to those who owned it, and it should be left to rot. 'Leave it,' he said, 'leave it. You've this house now — your home.'

And I did. I believed my uncle for he was a good, kind man which my father was not. My aunt said that he was a troubled man, Gerard Revell, not meant to be a father. The war, she said, had made him bitter and bad-tempered. Nothing to do with me, but best to forget him. But I heard her. 'Madman,' she muttered to herself, banging a pan down onto the range, before telling me that things were as they were. 'No use thinking about what's gone. Me an' William are your parents, good as. 'Twere us as brought you up, lovey, an' you've naught to complain of now, have you? We're all right as we are.'

I accepted what she said. I really didn't have anything to complain of. My life was very ordinary. I worked in the bank. I went out with some boys. The girls I knew got engaged, married, and had children. I stayed at home with auntie and uncle. Somehow, I didn't meet a boy who wanted to marry me.

I'm not bad looking — not ugly, not plain. I was quite pretty as a girl with dark curly hair and deep blue eyes. Boys asked me out, but the dates petered out. They went on to someone else — someone livelier, I supposed, someone more confident, more sure of what she wanted. I didn't know what I wanted, and then, of course, I didn't know who I really was. And there was no one to ask.

You will have noticed that my mother hasn't been mentioned. I can't remember her. I remembered my father sometimes when I was growing up — or bits of him. I didn't remember his face until — well, I'll come to that in a while. I only remembered a tall, dark-haired man who hardly spoke to me. He would meet me in the hall or on the stairs where I might be playing, and he would start as if he had encountered a stranger in the house then he would look down, frown, and pass on up the stairs to his study.

I never asked about my mother, of course. Children, even very small ones, always know what is forbidden territory.

You don't want to know about my life before I came back to Foulstone. Why would you? It's of no significance. I gave up the bank and lived in the house in Kendal to look after my aunt when the cancer came, and then uncle in his old age. I was safe there. It is amazing how the years pass, sliding into each other so silently that you don't notice until you see a grey-haired stranger in the mirror, and you realise it's you.

There is one thing I have left out. It's another mystery. For no reason, I would sometimes feel a kind of swooping sick emptiness inside me and there'd be a smell and a taste in my mouth. The nearest thing I can describe it as is a taste of metal. It wouldn't last long but it frightened me.

When I was young, I didn't dare ask aunt or uncle. They'd think I was mad. I was frightened that I was mad, that I was like my father, somehow wrong. I might be on a bus or in a café, or in the kitchen in the Kendal house and I'd feel this sickness and then there'd be a sudden dark smell, sickening, of something rotten. Sometimes I'd turn faint, and Auntie Mary put it down to growing pains — I never knew what they were, but when my periods came, the smell was stronger, of blood, too, and iron. I think I mixed them up, but at least I had an excuse for the fainting and sickness. And sometimes on those few dates I had, I'd feel that lurch of emptiness and then the smell of something rotten. The young man would be embarrassed, and he wouldn't ask again.

I didn't know it was Foulstone until I came back.

Sometimes I'd ask my only neighbour, old Mrs Sykes, if she could smell something. I told her I thought I could smell drains, but she never could. Mind you, she wouldn't have admitted it. That would mean admitting her house was damp. She didn't want anyone poking about her home, she said. She managed all right, thank you very much. I agreed with her. I didn't want anyone poking about, either.

I never asked her about Foulstone, but she, the private old lady, didn't mind a gossip about the people who had lived up there all those years ago. Mr Revell's wife died in childbirth, she said — not that she'd known her really. Mrs Sykes's mother who had lived in my cottage talked to her sometimes when she walked down the lane. Mrs Revell often walked alone. She had a little girl with her occasionally, a little dark-haired girl who was adopted after her mother died. Blue eyes, she had, the child, pretty little thing, toddling down the lane. Mr Revell had lived alone up at Foulstone Manor — until he shot himself.

I didn't move a muscle at those words. I hadn't known that, but a memory stirred, a memory of Uncle William in a black suit, Auntie Mary mentioning a funeral, and the two of them whispering when he came back, but the memory was gone and Mrs Sykes was still talking. Bad business, Mrs Sykes said, but no one had anything much to do with Mr Revell. Recluse, they said, mad, they said.

I asked her who had adopted the little girl. A Mrs Goss, she told me, who'd been the housekeeper at Foulstone Manor all those years ago. Came from up Highdale to work at Foulstone. She never came back nor did the child. Mrs Sykes didn't know what had happened to them, or who owned Foulstone, but she knew that Mr Revell had inherited the house from a Mr Dearlove — he was a cousin or something, but that were fifty years ago. No one remembered now.

I've thought a lot about that pretty little child toddling down the lane, and I think, what has she to do with me? I can't remember her. She sounded innocent and happy, perhaps, alone with her mother, but it was as if Mrs Sykes was telling me about strangers.

Mrs Sykes's mother had told her about Mr Revell. She'd had a milk round so she knew all the goings-on, delivering the milk in cans in a pony and trap. Off-comer, she had said he were, a southerner. Never mixed. Always on his own, walking about the hills and woods. Miserable looking beggar, Mrs Sykes's mother had told her. The wife were from down south, as well — pretty lady. At least she gave you a smile, but she walked alone, too. Nowt so queer as folks, Mrs Sykes said, moving on to tell me about the girl who'd drowned herself up at Scandal Beck — a scandal, of course, as the girl had been pregnant and not married, a girl who'd been a cousin of her mother's. Everyone hereabouts is somebody's cousin — except me, of course.

I could get Mrs Sykes to talk about her mother when I shrank from knowing anymore about the Revells. Strong as an ox, she'd say, though she weren't above five feet. Lifted them milk churns as if they weighed naught. Mrs Sykes's father was one of thirteen. One of his brothers were lost in the first war. They never knew what happened to him. Fancy that, Mrs Sykes would say, never to know what had happened to your child.

Then I'd have to change the subject again and I mentioned the smell. Must be imagining it, I'd say to Mrs Sykes. I was just checking. But I wasn't imagining it.

I became used to my own company once I moved into the cottage belonging to Foulstone Manor. I didn't miss Mrs Sykes, though we had been friends of a kind. I felt safe down in the little valley where the cottages are side by side on the little lane which leads to the ruined mill. No one comes our way, I'm glad to say.

The cottage gardens are across the lane. Mrs Sykes's garden has run to seed now, her vegetable plots overgrown and her flower beds full of weeds. Mine has two apple trees, one with sour crab apples which I used to give to Mrs Sykes to make her chutney; the other sometimes gives sweet apples, and the plum tree fruits well in the late summer.

I make jam. Auntie Mary taught me that, and I grow some vegetables in my little greenhouse and herbs in pots and strawberries. There are snowdrops in February — great swathes of them spilling down the riverbank, daffodils in spring, then bluebells like drifts of smoke down the bank, and Canterbury bells, lavender, lupins, stocks, and white daisies in the summer. I like an old-fashioned garden. And roses — I love roses, the ones that Uncle William used to grow at the Kendal house. He taught me how and when to prune, what was the best soil. I've a lovely old velvet moss rose called William Lobb from the Kendal house. Uncle William grew that.

In the winter I do my knitting and sewing. Auntie Mary taught me to knit and to darn stockings and turn sheets sides to middle. Nothing was ever wasted. Mary made my clothes and then I learnt from her patterns. Good, serviceable clothes.

I read and listen to the wireless. I like the concerts on the Third Programme — it's Radio Three now. The Home Service is Radio Four. I don't know why they had to change it. The Home Service — that's what we always listened to in Kendal. Still, I like the plays on that. I haven't a television. I don't want too much of the world in my life.

I came here after Uncle William's death, and I brought some of the furniture from the house in Kendal. The cottage belongs to Foulstone and Foulstone belongs to me. I don't want it, but I didn't want anyone else to have it. It has its secrets and I thought it could keep them if I was there to watch. I have lived here for ten years, and Mrs Sykes's cottage is mine, too.

There is a box at the end of the lane where the post comes and any deliveries from the town. Of course, I go down to meet the butcher's man and the milkman to pay for meat and milk, and to leave my notes. I'm always cheerful, ready for a bit of idle chat — it wouldn't do to get a reputation for oddness, and I walk up to the village once a week and buy a paper to find out what's on the wireless and then I use it to light the fire. A man delivers logs and coal from time to time, and I chat to him, too. Mrs Gibson from the farm across the bridge brings me eggs, and I talk a bit to her about the weather. I'm not that keen on her — she has eyes everywhere, but I don't want her thinking that there's something wrong with me and gossiping in the town.

But then Sheila upset everything with her letter. Sheila had worked in the bank with me. I met her sometimes in Kendal for tea and a look about the shops. I was always Jo to Sheila, always the girl with the blue eyes. Sheila was tall and blonde, and there was a summer when the sun shone, and I went to stay at Sheila's farm, and we wore shorts with scarves tied round our waists and our legs were tanned. And Sheila's mother called me Jo, too.

There were two boys camping at the farm. Public school boys. They spoke like my father. I remembered that. Cut-glass, Sheila's mother said, but they weren't stand-offish. We went for walks with them. Sheila's mother made us picnics. We sat by the river and dangled our feet in. The boys swam, and Sheila went in wearing a shirt over her swimming costume. I didn't have a swimming costume. I'd never needed one.

They made a campfire on some nights, and we cooked sausages. And then we walked, Sheila and Richard together, laughing and joking, Sheila slapping him away with that easy confidence she had when he tried to put his arm round her. Simon and me, quieter, but under the trees he put his arm about me and kissed me. And that was the first time. There were a few other times as I have told you, but the emptiness came and the smell — the sensations that had frightened me as a child. Simon looked puzzled as I pulled away. We could hear Sheila and Richard laughing somewhere and I called out to her and we four went back to the farm.

The summer ended. The boys packed up their camp and went away. Sheila went to London to study nursing, and I went to the wedding. Sheila and Richard — Richard who became a doctor. Sheila always wrote, and they came back with baby Amanda who was christened in the church at Crook. I was asked to be her godmother.

Sometimes they came up to see Sheila's mother and I went over to see my godchild, but Sheila's parents died, the farm was sold, and they had no reason to come north. I went to London a couple of times, but I didn't keep it up. I felt awkward in someone else's house, but the letters still came. Sheila invited me to London again and again, but I never went, and she told me about Simon who had married and had two sons.

I used to think it might have been me in another life. I stopped thinking that when I came back to Foulstone. In any case, I was only Jo for a summer, blue-eyed, tanned Jo in her shorts. I was Joan again in the autumn.

Sheila wrote to ask if Amanda could come to stay with me. I hadn't the courage to say no.

2

Amanda

I didn't particularly want to visit Auntie Joan, but Mum thought I should, at least for an afternoon. I loved the place straightaway; Auntie Joan's cottage was really old-fashioned and cosy, with its open fire in the parlour and black kitchen range. She had some lovely old furniture, a gate-legged table, a dresser with copper pans on it, all polished and shiny, and old rugs on the flagged floors. There were still wooden shutters at the windows, and she still used oil lamps. It was like stepping back in time and I liked that. I peeped into the next-door cottage on my way out. That looked a bit run-down, but I liked the look of it, too. I wondered who had lived there. And I was fascinated by the old house which I could see through the winter trees. Mum had told me about it — she knew how to tempt me — how Joan had been left a lot of property including a derelict manor house which she was going to let just go to ruin. Of course, after hearing that, I was dead keen to see it, even if I didn't much want to see Auntie Joan.

She's a funny old stick, Auntie Joan. Not old, really, about my mother's age, fiftyish, but very set in her ways. She's very sharp, with a dry sense of humour sometimes. I kept saying Auntie Jo at first — it's what Mum called her when I was little. I couldn't help it. She insisted on Joan, but I got my way with calling her auntie.

I wasn't keen on her when I was a child. Not that we saw much of her, only when she came to London once or twice. She never seemed to enjoy it, though Mum always made her welcome, and when we came up north to the farm to see my grandma, Joan was awkward with me as if she felt she was an imposter godmother. She never brought a present — only money which she gave me in a brown envelope, like wages, I used to think when I was older — as if she felt she owed me something. Mum would tell me to say thank you and then I'd leave them to talk.

I needed a place to live while I was studying at Lancaster University. My dad had given me a car, a second-hand orange Beetle which I called Clementine, so if I stayed with Auntie Joan, it wouldn't be too far to travel, and I liked the empty cottage next door to her, and its ruined garden, the quiet and hills and woods to walk in.

I stayed at a bed and breakfast in the town which I thought was lovely and quaint — a town in Westmorland, but on the very edge of the Dales. The rounded hills were beautiful and the town full of interesting, old-fashioned shops. You could buy fresh bread from the baker and the greengrocer displayed his vegetables outside in wooden crates. There was a bookshop and stationer's and even a dress shop. You could get everything you needed, I thought, charmed by its busyness, its narrow main street, and yards tucked away off the street where there were little cottages and workshops, and by the woman driving a pony and trap along the street, followed by a flock of sheep and a dog, none of them at all concerned by the cars stopped behind them.

I went again to see Joan after that first awkward meeting — I didn't think she was all that pleased to see me, but she gave me tea and fruit cake and politely asked about my history studies. Nineteenth century rural industry, I told her. I'd discovered there was a ruined mill at the end of her lane. I'd like to research that, I said, and there were plenty of other mills,

Moorfield, Birkett's Mill, Margill Mill. She looked a bit wary about that, but I went again a few times until I plucked up the courage to ask about the next-door cottage. Would she consider letting it to me? She looked even more wary about that — it was damp, the furniture was old, there was no running water, an outside toilet at the back, no bed —

Of course, I dismissed all that. After all, I had stayed plenty of times at the farm up in Crook — no running water there, no electric light —

'There were beds, Amanda,' she said rather tartly, 'I slept in one, as did your mother.'

But then she laughed, and I did, too; somehow the ice was broken, and it was arranged — for at least until I had to start at the university. I had to go home to London, but she promised she would sort the place out, air it, and have a look at the furniture — old Mrs Sykes's and some she had in store in the barn by the old mill.

Mum was pretty surprised but glad, I think. She's a generous soul, my mum, loyal to Joan because of that summer when she met Dad.

I wonder what Joan's life would have been like if she'd married Uncle Simon. Joan isn't plain. She has good skin and lovely deep blue eyes. My mum has more lines, especially round her eyes. She says she's laughed too much. I don't think Joan had laughed very much at all. She has lines running from her mouth to her chin, dragging her face down.

She's not a smiler, but she laughed that time about the beds, and I saw what she might have been.

3

Joan

The cottage wasn't too bad, I thought. I'd had the windows open for a few days — it had been dry weather for a change and the wind had got in to freshen it up. I had the chimney sweep in — the soot of ages came down, but as I'd moved out a lot of the furniture, it didn't matter much. Mrs Sykes had an old-fashioned black kitchen range like mine with a bread oven where you can keep things warm and a stove top to cook on. I was used to them — we'd had one in Kendal, too. Auntie Mary gave me the job of cleaning it with black lead polish. I do my own regularly. It takes a bit of doing, I can tell you, and I set about Mrs Syke's range before I got it going. Hard work and dirty, but a satisfying job when the thing is all gleaming afterwards. I'd plenty of coal, wood, and oil lamps. I cleaned the windows and lit the fire in the parlour, too, so that the place would be warmed up when Amanda came back.

I thought she'd be all right for the time being. Mrs Sykes had been a houseproud woman. The cottage was basic, but it had not been in a filthy state when Mrs Sykes had died and some of the furniture was still usable. Granted, there was only a pump for water, but Amanda could boil kettles on the range for washing, and there was a tin bath and a pot in the bedside cupboard if she didn't want to brave the outside toilet at night. She'd manage the stairs all right. She's a strong young thing. I have running water and a bathroom, but I wanted to see how she'd manage. Maybe she would get fed up and not want to stay too long.

I had to laugh when she said she was used to making do. Not what I saw in Sheila's house in London — electricity, electric stove, fridge, proper bathroom and comfortable beds. I saw her bedroom there — very pretty. Nice and warm, too, with an electric fire with a log effect in the fireplace.

And so was Amanda — warm, I mean, and accepting. She seemed so natural with me that I couldn't help liking her. Anyway, she'd be in Lancaster a lot of the time. I thought she'd enough sense not to want to live in my pocket. She liked walking so she'd want to be out when it was fine. I decided not to charge her any rent even though she asked. I didn't want anything that suggested permanence. She'd not be here forever.

I took some towels in and some crockery and cutlery — stuff that came from Auntie Mary. Good things I never used — knives with bone handles and nickel silver forks and spoons, some crystal glasses, not matching, but I had a feeling that Amanda wouldn't mind. There were china cups rimmed with gold, painted with roses, blue and white Willow pattern plates, some pink plates I remember eating from. Men on horseback outside an old inn. I used to think of Foulstone when I looked at that old inn, but whether the plates came from there I didn't know, and I'd never asked.

And there was a vase — what they call blush porcelain. It had a scene painted on it in an oval, with shepherds and sheep in trees. I remembered Auntie Mary telling me it was a present. From her sister, she'd added. If there was a sister. I never knew if there had been a Margaret whose daughter I was supposed to be. I'd wondered if it was a present from my mother, and that was why she hesitated. I didn't ask, of course. I don't know why I brought it with me to keep in a cupboard. There was stuff in my spare bedroom — Mary's boxes. Things she'd kept for me. I'd thought of getting rid, but then I would have had to open them. There might be things I'd not want folk to see. I didn't want to know anything about them.

There was a pine cupboard by the fireplace into which I put the glasses and crockery. I looked at the pink plate. The back told me that it was Myott's country life — Amanda would like that. She seemed to like old things, although she looked a very modern girl in her jeans and her bright jumpers and her ponytail.

I stretched to put the plate away, but I had to sit down suddenly, faint and sick for a moment, and I could smell it — Foulstone. I hadn't felt like that since Amanda came.

I closed the cupboard door and went out. I felt miserable. I realised that I'd enjoyed doing up the cottage. I felt — I don't know. Happy, I suppose. Mopping and polishing. Liking that the cottage looked homely and clean, and fresh for Amanda. Now it felt spoilt. Even the autumn leaves in the copper jug on the table seemed a mockery.

I went back into my own cottage. I closed the shutters in the back bedroom and on the landing. I didn't want to see that house over there. I didn't want to think about it.

4

Amanda

'Honestly, I can't smell anything — except the fire and lavender polish. And those are lovely.'

'You don't think it's damp — I mean it is, and I thought —'

Auntie Joan looked really anxious. I could smell damp sometimes when I went in the cottage, but it went away when I built up the fire. I reassured her, 'No, it's fine, I sometimes smell it but it soon goes.'

'Nothing worse than damp?'

'No,' I told her, not knowing what she meant.

'And you are comfortable?'

'I am, I am, I'm thrilled.'

I was so delighted when I came back that I kissed her on impulse. She turned very pink, but I could tell she was pleased.

She'd done so much. The windows shining, and all the things in the cupboard, and two pewter candlesticks on the mantelpiece, linen napkins on the table, pans in the kitchen and the range lit, and a fire glowing. I slept on the sofa that night — well, I didn't sleep. I didn't tell Joan that. My bed hadn't yet come, but I wanted to be in my new home.

At dawn, which came magnificently red, then gold, then pale green and pink, I got up and made tea. The back kitchen window looks out onto a kind of grid because the cottage is lower than the path behind the house — a path that goes nowhere, except to the remains of a building where they used to dry the fleeces, so I went upstairs to look out of the landing window where there's a field with some sheep and then woods, and then Foulstone Manor.

The sky was turning to a slate blue and the sun touched the fells with copper. I had never seen a dawn like it, the copper turning gold and flooding down the slope which was turning to a deeper rose. To the north-east I could see the gold-tipped curves of more hills, and everything was still. I could see chimneys and the impression of the house through the leafless trees.

I couldn't help being fascinated. I was dying to ask Joan all about it — her Auntie Mary had been a servant there, but her mistress had died and the husband, a man called Gerard Revell, had died not long afterwards. And Joan inherited the house. That's all Mum knew. Joan never talked about it, she said. She had not known the people and Mary had not told her anything. I'd have wanted to know. I did want to know.

But I knew I shouldn't rush in. Auntie Joan left me to myself for a few days after I'd moved in. The bed came in pieces fortunately — just a single bed which the delivery men managed to get up the stairs. There was a little chest of drawers, a chair, and a single wardrobe. The back bedroom which looked over the field towards Foulstone Manor I turned into a sort of study — well, just an old pine table and a chair. My books had to stay on the floor, but I hadn't many and I'd be using the library at Lancaster University — if I stayed here, of course. That was another thing I'd have to wait to talk about. Joan might not want me here when I started at Lancaster.

At the end of that first week, I went to Kendal and after buying some notebooks and a rag rug from a junk shop, I purchased a three-legged table, and a bamboo cabinet for beside my bed. Six pounds the pair — extravagant, really, but I couldn't resist. I thought about the rocking chair, but at ten pounds it was going too far.

It was dark by the time I got back so I lit the fire and the oil lamps and put two candles in the pewter candlesticks. The little parlour looked very cosy. I was pleased — home, I thought.

I invited Auntie Joan for a cup of tea so that I could show her the table and the rug and the lamplight. She didn't say anything when she looked down at the rug, but she turned very pale. I didn't think she looked at all well — a headache she said and left immediately. I wondered if I'd offended her by buying furniture — did it look as if I was presuming too much?

The morning after Joan's sudden departure, I felt uncomfortable and restless. I wanted to go and ask how she was, but her front door was closed. Sometimes a closed front door has a look — you seem to know that it doesn't want you to knock, that you're not welcome. Silly, I suppose, but that's how I felt. Joan's face had that look sometimes as if a door had closed. Her lips would fold into a line and turn down. I knew I'd intruded into her life, but I had thought she had accepted me. Her sprucing up of the cottage seemed to tell me that. Now, I wasn't sure. I wondered if she had changed her mind, so as the day was fine, I thought I would go for a walk and try to see her later. Maybe she would be feeling better, and we could have a cup of tea. Perhaps I'd be able to tell if she didn't want me.

I stood on the bridge and looked down into the river which flowed very fast and glittered in the sunlight. There was shingle which formed a kind of beach. A man was standing there throwing a stick for his dog which plunged in and out and barked at his master for more. I thought what a lovely place for a picnic in the summer and wondered if I would still be there, or if Joan would suggest that I should be looking for somewhere permanent for January. I crossed to the other side from where I could see down our lane. There was smoke curling from Joan's chimney, so she wasn't ill. At least that was a comfort.

I took a narrow stony path up towards the fell, passing the farm where Joan had told me she got her eggs and then at the top, I looked down again. I could see the ruined mill, the outhouses, and the barn, and Joan's front door still firmly shut. I could see the roof and chimneys of Foulstone Manor. I wished I had binoculars so I could see more closely. I walked on, eventually coming down to the Dent Road which I crossed to find a footpath which I hoped would lead me back.

Eventually I found myself in the woods and I could see the river glittering down below a steep bank and at last I came to a gate and some broken down fencing. I knew the gate led into the field behind the cottages. Therefore, the fencing must mark the boundary of Foulstone Manor. It was tempting.

I wormed my way in to find myself at the back of the house. There were stables, and ruined glasshouses. It was so overgrown with bramble and ivy that I had to pick my way very carefully to reach the terrace where steps led up to boarded-up French doors. Some stone urns remained, very cracked and thick with creeper. There was a cast-iron bench fallen over, its wooden slats rotten and its metalwork rusty. The windows were boarded up, so it was no use trying to look in. What struck me was the silence and the stillness yet there had been enough wind as I had walked to make me feel fresh and alive.

It was as though time had stopped here — which it had, but I also felt in that stillness something inimical. This wasn't a fairy-tale place, a place that you thought a magic wand would bring back to life. It wasn't a place where you imagined a family strolling on the terrace on summer nights. It wasn't a place where you might have heard music drifting from an open window and voices and laughter.

I worked my way along the terrace, trying to avoid the broken glass. Rounding a corner, I almost tripped and looked down to see a rusty iron ring all tangled with ivy. I'd stumbled on what looked like a wooden hatch. Coal chute, perhaps. I picked my way very carefully after that. What would I say to Joan if I returned with a twisted ankle? Or worse if I fell and couldn't get up? No one knew I was here.

Creeper grew up the boarded windows, but, eventually, I came across a window from which one of boards had fallen away and I looked in through a cracked pane. I couldn't see anything much except what seemed to be shapes crowded together — furniture, perhaps, draped in dust sheets. I could smell damp and something else, something rotten as though something had died in there. I couldn't help but think of mice or rats, or some other creature that had perished in there. It was a smell that caught the back of your throat, sort of gaseous and sickly.

I turned away to take a gulp of fresh air and went back the way I came in. I couldn't resist one last look at the house. The sun had gone in. That was the way of the weather here. The light changed so swiftly, brilliant and glittering one moment, dark and louring another. This was a house for threatening weather, I thought, a house weighed down by the dark sky.

5

Joan

Amanda had looked hurt, and I was sorry. It was the rug. It's hard to describe what I felt. When Amanda pointed to it, it was as if the room lurched for a few seconds. It was the colours, red, blue, green like a kaleidoscope, and the smell, of course. And then I saw — just in those few seconds — a high brass fender with holes through which spots of firelight danced; a child's cradle; and I heard — just a snatch — a voice singing. Then they were gone, and I just wanted to get home.

It was a memory — I knew that, and it shook me to the very core because when I came into my own cottage and sat down, it came again. I knew it wasn't the Kendal house. Auntie Mary wouldn't have a rag rug. Rubbishy things, she said, fit for the poor house.

A rag rug on a wooden floor painted white but chipped near the skirting boards. A cupboard with two sets of doors — toys in the lower part, a spinning top, and books. A little bed with a white counterpane. And that cradle — I didn't know if there was a baby in it. I didn't know whose voice was singing, but it was a woman. I couldn't see her.

These were things I'd never thought about before, I couldn't understand why I should think about them then. The change, I supposed. Amanda's coming, blowing in like the wind to stir up layers of dust and reveal what's beneath. Remembering Sheila and that summer, and somehow knowing I'd wasted a life. Seeing Amanda full of life and hope, making plans, looking forward. Something lifting in my heart that day when I cleaned out the cottage.

Change, though. I didn't much want too much change, even though I liked Amanda. Her stay would only be temporary, and I could get back to normal. Thinking about what I'd done or hadn't done with my life was a bit too — well, upsetting. And at my time of life, what was the point of getting all worked up about what couldn't be helped?

But what if I couldn't stop remembering? I couldn't tell Amanda to go now, or even to get rid of the rug. I couldn't say I didn't like it. She'd think I was daft. She'd looked hurt enough when I left so suddenly. And she was so good-natured, and innocent, I thought. She had no secrets behind those clear, blue, honest eyes.

I was afraid. Afraid of remembering and afraid of finding things out. There were secrets which had been kept from me. Mrs Sykes had told me that Gerard Revell had killed himself. They said — whoever they were — he was mad and that worried me. And I had remembered Uncle William's black suit, and now I remembered a black tie and arm band, and the two of them whispering.

Why had Gerard Revell killed himself? I thought of him as Gerard Revell, but he was my father — a man who was pretty much a stranger to me. And my mother? Was it my mother whose voice I heard in that room with the fireguard and the white-painted floor with its rag rug?

When Amanda appeared at my door, I caught the whiff of Foulstone as she stood at the door asking how I felt. She asked me to come for supper the next night — a surprise, she said. If I was well enough. How could I refuse? I couldn't have her thinking I was ill — or worse.

Her smile when I said yes told me that she had been afraid that she had offended me by buying her rug and her furniture.

But I had thought all morning about what I was going to do, how I was going to deal with those memories and those questions. I suppose when a memory is awakened you can't unwake it, just as you can't unsay a word or unread a sentence.

I tried to keep myself busy that morning, but I'd find myself standing in the middle of the kitchen or the parlour just doing nothing, forgetting what I had come into the room for, and then I just sat down by the fire, and I saw that fireguard again and through the flames I saw a staircase going down into a large hall with a flag-stoned floor.

I was seeing a child on the stairs looking down at the shadows. She's afraid to go down and she clutches one of the thick, twisted rails of the banister. I know how that feels. The wood is warm, and I can feel the carving and I know that when the child looks up to where the rail joins the banister, she will see leaves and a little carved face staring back at her and she doesn't like that.

Someone comes down behind her. There's the sound of silk rustling and there's scent, a sweet light scent like flowers. And the child looks up and a hand comes down to take hers, a woman's hand...

The log shifted on the fire, the flames died down and the child was gone. Of course, I knew who it was. The little girl that Mrs Sykes had spoken about. But whether the reaching hand belonged to the child's mother, I didn't know. Even if I had seen a face in those flames, in that memory, I wouldn't have known if it was my mother. I had no memory of my mother's face.

I thought of the little girl as the child. It seemed easier, but I couldn't stop the image that came next. A door — a big oak door studded with nails. And I heard it slam. A door from forgotten dreams. I remembered now, though, a childhood dream in which I went down a dark staircase to that door. I went out into the gloomy morning and always the door slammed shut.

And now, I remembered his face, the face of Gerard Revell, the stranger who had been my father. A thin, dark face with dark brows and a broad forehead from where the dark hair swept back. A stern, unbending face. Unsmiling. Blue eyes, I remembered, dark blue. Like mine, I supposed. Never seeing me, though.

The smell of pipe smoke as he passed and the smell of damp and rottenness — in my memory the two were mingled, but I didn't know if the rotten smell was to do with him, or even if I had smelt it as that child, or only when I had left Foulstone.

And I had no idea if I would speak to Amanda about any of it, but I would ask her if she had been up to Foulstone and if she said she had, I'd decide then.

6

Amanda

I'd made a chicken casserole from a packet of sauce. Mum had given me some tins and packets for my pantry — a little room off the kitchen which I liked very much. Of course, we had a fridge at home, but the pantry with its stone shelves was very cool. There were pots of jam from years back — probably belonging to Mrs Sykes who had lived here before. I thought perhaps I'd better not risk them, but I dusted them off and arranged my few things on the shelves — playing house, I suppose, but I enjoyed preparing the casserole which was bubbling on the range, and there was home-made bread which Joan had given me, and some cheese and fruit.

The table looked lovely with a candle in a china candlestick which I'd found in the cupboard, the kind with which you'd light yourself upstairs, with its own saucer and a little china snuffer — chipped, but you wouldn't notice that. I put some berries and leaves in the blush vase. The glasses and the cutlery all shone.

Joan smiled when she came in and saw what I'd done. She looked better and I hoped she would stay this time. I offered her a sherry. I knew she'd refuse, so I told her that my father had sent it back with me and that I was to share it. I didn't laugh when she sniffed it suspiciously, but she conceded that it was nice enough, and she didn't object when I topped up her glass before I went into the kitchen to get the food.

She praised that, too, though I noticed that she hadn't much of an appetite. She did eat some cheese and when I offered to make some coffee, she stopped me and said she wanted to ask me something. I sat down again. I knew what it was.

'You went up to the house.'

'I didn't mean to, honestly. I came back through the woods, and I saw the break in the fence. It was an impulse.'

'What did your mother tell you?'

'Only that you inherited it from people your aunt worked for, but that you didn't want to live in it. She wondered why you didn't sell it.'

Joan didn't answer that. 'What did you think of it?'

I moved the breadcrumbs round my plate. I didn't want to offend her, but I knew I couldn't just say that I'd found it interesting. I looked up. She was looking back at me. I thought she looked afraid and suddenly vulnerable. And young. The truth then.

'Strange,' I said, 'so quiet and still. I couldn't imagine…'

'What?'

'A happy family living there.'

'I don't think one did. I think it might have been a very unhappy family.'

And then she told me about Gerard Revell and how she had been taken away by Mary and William Goss when she was about three. She had known that Gerard Revell was her father, but the idea had meant nothing to her. She had not known what a father should be. She was told he was dead, and it was Mrs Sykes, her former neighbour, who said that he had shot himself. She remembered nothing about her mother.

'I suppose you could say that I don't know who I am really. I don't even know if Joan is my name — it's what Mary Goss called me.'

'But you must have a birth certificate.'

'I've never seen one. I haven't done anything that required one — I've never been in hospital or applied for a passport or anything.'

'But why did you never want to know?'

'Because what I remember was always horrible — well, not horrible. Disturbing —'

'Because you found out that Gerard Revell shot himself?'

'Yes, I suppose that did shock me, but I've remembered things from when I was a child there — a nursery, a fire, a rag rug —'

'So that's why you felt ill.'

'Before that — when I looked at the rug, there was a smell — you'll think I'm out of my mind.'

'No, I won't. It was there when I looked in through a cracked window. I smelt it — rotten, as if something had died in there. Something sickening, anyway. Hard to describe — I don't know — just really unpleasant.'

'It is. I've smelt it before — I've always associated it with Foulstone. Something I remembered, but it's not a thing you can explain to anyone. People would think you were mad.'

'But smell — it's very powerful. We do remember smells — but yours is a horrible smell because you connect the house with your parents' deaths.'

'Maybe, but that rug, it — well, it's just that I've never remembered anything before, and it shook me. It's as if I can't stop remembering now, and I don't know how to cope with it. What if there's something terrible up there? Why did Gerard Revell commit suicide? And why can't I remember my mother?'

'If you found out, do you think it would be better? I mean there might be papers or something at Foulstone. We could—'

'I don't know. Don't ask me anymore. It's enough for one night.'

'You'll be all right?'

'I will — after that sherry. It was very nice, I must say. The things I've missed.'

'Dad will send us more.'

Joan smiled at that, but she looked serious again when she said, 'I won't be able to unknow what I might get to know. And when you've gone…'

I let Joan go. She looked tired and strained, and I felt anxious, so I washed up and put away the cutlery and dishes. Then I went to sit by the fire. I thought of what Joan had said about unknowing. I wanted to know the story of Foulstone Manor, but Foulstone wasn't romantic like Thornfield Hall. There had been secrets there, terrible secrets, but after all, there had been a happy ending for Jane Eyre. "Reader, I married him." I loved that. But this story was real. I knew one of the main characters and I also knew that not all stories have happy endings.

A marriage never talked of. A mother whom a daughter had never known. A father who had shot himself. Suppose the secrets that Joan found out were too terrible to get over. And I'd be responsible if I pressed her to find out more. It occurred to me then, that for the first time in my life I was responsible for someone else. I had always been looked after, made much of, loved. Now I was beginning to realise that it was not just my feelings that were important.

I'd always had someone to turn to, and I thought of Joan's lonely life. And Foulstone louring over her. She might never escape it if a door was opened on those secrets.

Suppose, though, that the memories did keep coming back to her like pieces of a puzzle she couldn't finish, the missing pieces never to be found. I imagined her never at peace, always haunted by fragments of her past. That would be terrible, too.

I intended to go to the library in Kendal to begin my research into the woollen mills. I thought maybe I could find out something about the history of Foulstone Manor. I might find out something about Gerard Revell. There'd be newspaper reports about the suicide, surely. I did not have to tell Joan. That would be for me to decide — no one else could advise me.

I suddenly thought that being an adult out on my own was more difficult than I had realised. I'd started something out of curiosity, but Joan's strained face showed me that I'd started something really serious.

The oil lamps had gone out, so I took my chamber stick with a fresh candle and went upstairs. Moonlight shone very bright through the landing window, and I looked out. The trees were black against the lighter sky and the chimneys of Foulstone Manor were black, too, and rather forbidding.

It wanted to keep its secrets.

7

Joan

It was the strangest thing. I felt suddenly that I wanted to escape. That question as to whether it would be better to know had shaken me. Amanda meant well, I could see, but she thought it was easy to decide. She, who had had a happy childhood, could never understand the terror of knowing and never again unknowing.

I got to my own door. *No*, I told myself, it wouldn't be better. Let sleeping dogs and all that. *You're Joan Goss*, I told myself. *You'll still be Joan Goss even if you once had another name. Nothing will change.* Anyway, what good will knowing do? Mary Goss didn't want me to know anything. Best forget, she'd said. The past is the past and you've your own life to lead. Not that I had, of course. I'd not done anything with my life. Too late now.

I fumbled with my keys and in that moment in front of the locked door, my thoughts changed again. I couldn't get in and I wanted to. That's what I mean by strange — all these feelings, swooping up and down like birds. No wonder I felt dizzy. I felt a great sense of loss after Mary and William died, but I trained myself to put one foot in front of the other and I arrived —

Where? I asked myself then, standing in the cold with the keys in my hand. Nowhere came the answer, or to a place where nothing could be felt too deeply, nothing could be thought about too closely, a place where life plodded on, safely packaged in routine. Safe, yes, but without purpose or meaning. Never looking forward or backward, but the price of looking forward was to be paid by looking back. I didn't think I could do that.

And then I thought, as the locked door opened, *Just do it. Do something. You can't undo that conversation with Amanda. You won't stop remembering now. It's not Amanda's responsibility to uncover the secrets. It's yours.*

Mary's boxes. That's what I thought of. I'd never looked at them. I lit a lamp and took it upstairs. I paused at the landing window and looked across to Foulstone. The moon was very bright and the trees very dark, but I could see the chimneys, black against the midnight sky. It wasn't going away.

I thought of my mother looking out of a window over there, looking down on the cottages, turning away to look at the cradle — the cradle that was ready for an unborn child. I don't know how I knew that, but I did. I knew that cradle wasn't for me. Perhaps that was a memory, another long buried one. And as I looked, clouds covered the moon, and I saw a face — the face of a young woman. I saw it as clearly as I had just seen Amanda's. A delicate pale face with such a sad expression. She looked — I don't know — as if she was lost. So lonely. Then the face was gone.

I didn't even know her name. I remembered telling Sheila that my mother was dead and when Sheila had asked what her name was, I had said Margaret and I had come to believe it, I think. It was easier than thinking about the mother I couldn't remember. I couldn't remember Margaret, either. I don't even know whether she existed. Mary Goss might have made her up, but she made her real. My mother had been real, though — she'd lived over there at Foulstone Manor. I wanted to know who she was. She deserved that, surely. She deserved to be known.

I dragged Mary's boxes from under the bed. They weren't even locked. The first contained linen, tablecloths and napkins, guest towels, all neatly folded and smelling faintly of lavender. Kind Auntie Mary maybe thinking I might have them when I married — not that such an event was ever referred to. Keeping things for your bottom drawer they called it, the assumption being that a girl was bound to get married sometime. Or, more likely, Mary realising that it wasn't going to happen and packing it all away in the box.

There was a little box, too, which rattled when I picked it up. Inside, on a ring were three keys. I recognised the largest one because I had one exactly the same — the key to the front door of Foulstone Manor. I'd never used it. I put them in my pocket — one for the back door, perhaps. What the other one was, I'd no idea.

In the second box were gloves — kid gloves for small hands. Not my hands, nor Mary's. A lady's hands. I couldn't help looking down at my own hands, weathered and red with clipped nails — I never noticed them. They were just there to scrub, to dig and to prune and to be shoved into woollen gloves in the winter. A shawl — the kind they call an Indian shawl of the finest and lightest wool with a paisley pattern. A nightgown of fine lawn with pintucks and ribbons. A soft leather pouch which contained a double string of pearls. They looked very beautiful in the lamplight.

These were my mother's things, I was sure. Mary Goss would not have owned such things. They fitted that pale delicate young woman in the shadows. I wanted to weep for her and for me. For her, because she had died so young, and for me, because I could not remember, and because these things which were mine now might have been mine in a different life, if she had not died, and if I'd grown up at

Foulstone Manor in a happy family. Pearls were no use to me. Pearls for tears, Auntie Mary used to say. Another old saw. Perhaps it was true in my mother's case.

I didn't weep, but there was a lump in my throat. I rummaged further into the box to find a leather folder and the papers inside. The birth certificate which told me that I was born on March 10th, 1922, to Helena and Gerard Revell at Foulstone Manor, near Rawthdale in the county of Westmorland.

Helena Revell. A lovely name. A name with music in it. Who was Helena Revell? I wanted to know, whatever the cost. It was time to show some courage.

There was another name, of course, the name of the child. *Joanna Revell.* An unfamiliar name on my tongue, whispered into the silent room — where was she now? That pretty little blue-eyed child.

Someone else I didn't know.

8

Amanda

Suicide of a Recluse. That was what *The Westmorland Gazette* told me.

The smiling librarian had accepted my explanation that I was researching the woollen industry and wanted to look at old newspapers from the 1920s, and she showed me into the archive room. She explained that there was a collection of newspapers from the First World War and some years after, but most of the newspapers were now on microfiche which she would demonstrate if I wished. I told her I would look through the old papers first.

I'd worked out the possible dates. Joan was about the same age as my mother, who had been born in 1922. Joan thought she might have been six when she was told her father had died, so I was looking for articles in 1928. It took ages, but I found the report of the coroner's inquest into the death of Gerard Revell of Foulstone Manor on September 28th, 1928.

Recollection of the horrors of war, was said, at a Kendal inquest today, to have caused the suicide of Captain Gerard Revell, who shot himself on Monday, at his home, Foulstone Manor, near the town of Rawthdale. The deceased had been found in the cellar of his home. There was a service revolver at his side.

Further details told that Gerard Revell had been a serving officer in World War One. He had attained the rank of captain in the London Irish Rifles and had been awarded the Military

Cross for gallantry. After the war, he had inherited Foulstone Manor from a Mr Arthur Dearlove, whose son, Nowell, had served with Captain Revell. Nowell Dearlove had been killed at Ypres in 1918.

The coroner referred to the evidence given by Mr Arthur Dearlove's solicitor, Mr Lamb of Kendal, who spoke of the friendship between Mr Nowell Dearlove and Captain Revell who had been injured in the action in which his friend had perished. Mr Lamb gave his opinion that Captain Revell had suffered greatly at the death of his friend, and at the loss of his wife. Mr Lamb had told the court that Captain Revell had been a distinguished poet just after the war, with his poems appearing in a periodical, *The London Mercury*. However, he had not published anything in his latter years.

The coroner mentioned the suffering endured by "the gallant men who had served at the Front." He went on to say that the effects of the war were only now being understood and that he had very great sympathy for Captain Revell.

The verdict was suicide during temporary insanity.

Gerard Revell, a war hero. Well, I hadn't expected that. His suicide seemed a tragedy to me — he had mourned his dead friend and his dead wife and had killed himself, unable to bear his grief. Perhaps he had not been able to look after his daughter. And the war itself. We'd read about it at school — the poems of Wilfred Owen. The one about the gas attack. I remembered that one. The bit about the gassed man's face like a devil's sick of sin, and the way in which he had choked on his own blood. It had made more impression on us than all the facts in the history books.

Perhaps Gerard Revell had come to believe that none of it had been worthwhile, that as Owen had said, it was not sweet and fitting to die for your country. And he had been a poet, too. I wondered whether it would be possible to find the poems in *The London Mercury* — maybe the English Department at Lancaster University would be able to help. I made a note of the title.

Gerard Revell had obviously been a lonely man — there was no mention of any friends or relatives. No mention of a daughter. "Recluse", the headline said. Had he given his child away because he could not bear to think of his dead wife? Did Joan look like her mother?

There was some mystery about Foulstone Manor. Why was the death not spoken of? Gerard Revell had been a hero. Maybe because suicide was shameful then, and the idea of insanity, even if it was temporary. And why was Joan so afraid? Unless she had seen something terrifying — some mad act of her father's, something she was not meant to see, and which was so frightening that it had been locked away in her unconscious mind. Dad said that it sometimes happened, especially in children. And in Joan's case, she had been taken away as a little child, possibly given a new name, certainly given a new mother, albeit a dead one. It wasn't surprising that she had forgotten everything.

The word insanity did give me the shivers as I stared down at the newspaper. Perhaps I could find out about Nowell Dearlove and how he had died. If Gerard Revell had witnessed that, it might explain his state of mind. Joan would then know why he had shot himself. The inquest report gave the date of Nowell's death as 1918 — near the end of the war, perhaps, which made it even more poignant.

I wondered if there was any announcement of Joan's birth. It would be usual, especially for people who lived in a manor house. My parents had announced my birth in the newspaper — I could not imagine why, but people did that. It would be interesting to see if there was anything about Foulstone Manor in the papers, or about the Dearlove family.

The Westmorland Gazette for the year 1922 was available. I had to start at the beginning, but I supposed that in scanning the articles my eye might light on the names I was looking for. By the time I got to August, I was beginning to tire of rooms to let, agricultural shows, prize days, sports days and rugby matches at Rawthdale School — that was a thought — had Nowell Dearlove attended the school? The death of a headmaster, Mr Hart, made the news in January, so did the engagement of Mr John Herbert Upton of Ingmire Hall. I scanned to the end of 1922, but there were no births of interest, certainly not the birth of a daughter to Mr Gerard Revell of Foulstone Manor, nor had I come across the name Dearlove.

It was a great pity I didn't know the date of Joan's birthday — I had not thought to ask, of course. I had assumed that she was the same age as my mother, but maybe she was older. She certainly looked it.

1920, perhaps. I found Dearlove first in September 1920. Mr Dearlove, it seemed, had died from a fall at his home, Foulstone Manor, near Rawthdale. He had suffered from heart disease, and it was thought that a dizzy spell had caused him to fall down the stairs. His housekeeper, Mrs Mary Goss, had found him at six o'clock in the morning at the foot of the staircase. She had not heard anything in the night and she had no idea why Mr Dearlove should be up before her. Joan's Aunt Mary — who had stayed on to housekeep for the Revells. What secrets had she never told?

The report repeated the story about Nowell Dearlove. The verdict on Arthur Dearlove's death was accident. So that was straightforward enough. He had not been shot, stabbed, or poisoned by Gerard Revell, though he could hardly have murdered Mr Dearlove under Mrs Goss's nose, so to speak. Not pushed down the stairs. Letting my imagination run away. The madman as a murderer and then a guilty suicide. Ridiculous, I told myself.

I ploughed on until the end of 1920, but there was nothing about Joan, and I thought I was wasting my time. Joan had been born — it didn't matter exactly when. I returned the paper to the pile, being very careful to keep them in order. Someone else hadn't been so careful. The 1923 paper caught my eye. There was a headline at the bottom of the page:

MISSING SOLDIER

Considerable mystery surrounds the disappearance of an ex-service man from London. Mr Samuel Bate, aged thirty years, has not been seen since he left home in August last. His wife had asked assistance from the magistrate at Bow Street. Mrs Bate reported that her husband had told her he was going up north in search of employment. He had been much depressed by the lack of work available. He said that he had a connection in a town called Kendal in Westmorland. Mrs Bate had not heard him mention the place before and did not know of any connection her husband might have.

The last sighting of Mr Bate was at the Oxenholme railway station where he alighted from the London train. He asked the porter if it was possible to get transport to the town of Rawthdale. The porter told him that there might be a carrier going that way and the missing man left the station. Enquiries proved that the missing man had not been taken to the town by a carrier.

Mr Bate is 5 feet 7inches and slim; has a thin pale face with sharp features; very light brown eyes. He was wearing a dark grey suit, a dark brown trilby hat and lace-up boots. His wife reported that he was carrying a dark-coloured mackintosh and brown suitcase.

I couldn't help wondering if this other soldier had ever been found, whether he had ever reached Rawthdale. I thought of his wife perhaps left waiting for years for news, but Mr Samuel Bate's sad story was not my business just then. I wanted to find out about Nowell Dearlove who had been killed in action in 1918. I went back to the stack of newspapers and found the papers for that year.

I had felt a cold shiver when I'd read about Gerard Revell's insanity. Now I felt something more — as if I was frozen from the inside. The archive room had a dusty warmth about it, but I really felt suddenly very cold. It wasn't the young man's death, though that was horrible enough. It was the date. Nowell Dearlove had been killed on September 24th, 1918, the same day on which Gerard Revell had taken his own life. Ten years to the day.

It seemed to bring to vivid realisation the grief from which Gerard Revell had suffered all those years. They had been friends, had fought together, and Gerard had been there when Nowell was killed. A line from Owen's poem came back to me: "In all my dreams, before my helpless sight…"

The newspaper report gave the barest details:

Mr Arthur Dearlove of Foulstone Manor in Rawthdale has received news that his son, Lieutenant Nowell Dearlove of the London Irish Rifles, was shot and died of his wounds at Ypres on September 24th. The Adjutant, in communicating the news, said that Lieutenant Dearlove had received from his company the recognition of being a brave officer whose cheerful courage was maintained to the end.

Ypres. I had heard of that, the site of famous World War One battles, and I knew it was in Flanders, but nothing more than that. That could be remedied by the university library at Lancaster. There'd be memoirs, surely.

I stopped myself. I'd have to hear what Joan would say. She might not want to go any further.

When I got home Joan's door was closed. I didn't knock. I knew I should think first about what I had found out. I took my notebook upstairs. I paused on the landing to look out of the window, and I saw her coming across the field. Something about her hunched shoulders and bent head suggested misery. In her grey coat with her grey scarf tied over her head, she looked almost like a ghost in the fading light of the raw afternoon.

9

Joan

I saw Amanda at her landing window. I felt the cold iron of the keys in my pocket — the keys which I had never used before. Even when I went to look at Foulstone, I never took mine with me. I'd hidden it in a drawer in my dressing table in a box I used to keep my pencils in when I was at school, a lacquer box with a picture of Venice on it. I don't know where that came from. Auntie Mary had never been to Venice — as far as I knew. Now I had Mary's keys — three keys to unlock the mystery.

I had not used Mary's keys or mine this afternoon, either. I had taken Mary's out of the drawer because it was another small step. The first step had been to talk to Amanda, the second to open Auntie Mary's boxes. The third had been to take the keys, the keys which opened that heavy, iron-studded door I remembered from my dreams, the door up to which I had walked this afternoon. But I had stayed on the path and just looked at the house with its boarded-up windows, its ivy and creeper. I thought of the child coming down those steps and a car waiting. Mary in a brown coat and green hat, carrying a suitcase, and William opening the back door of the car. I couldn't go any further.

But I kept Mary's keys in my pocket when I knocked on Amanda's door. If I didn't knock immediately, I knew I wouldn't be able to ask what she had found out at the library. I put the pearls on the table when she went out to make the tea.

'Helena Revell,' I said when she came back, 'my mother's name. She had been Helena Lovelace.' I couldn't bring myself to say that other name. I still wanted to be plain Joan Goss. It felt safer. It was much too soon to say that I was really someone else. A lovely name, too, but it didn't suit me, I thought, looking at the pearls.

'Helena, it's a lovely name,' Amanda said.

'I thought so, too. These must have been hers. I opened Mary's boxes.'

Amanda picked up the pearls which glowed in the lamplight. I was tempted to ask her to put them on so that I could see them round a slender neck, but I only said, 'I want to know who she was.'

'I've found out a bit about him,' Amanda said, and she told me what she had discovered at the library.

'A poet?'

'Published in *The London Mercury*, some sort of literary magazine, I imagine, or a newspaper. I thought I could find out at the university — that is, if you want...'

I couldn't answer for a moment. It seemed unreal. Gerard Revell, a published poet. 'A war hero?' I asked. I couldn't believe that, either. Not that grim-faced man who passed me on the stairs.

'Awarded the Military Cross for gallantry, the newspaper report said.'

'And mad.'

'Temporary insanity, the inquest found — it doesn't mean—'

'It's hereditary,' I said, thinking my usual thoughts, thinking how peculiar Gerard Revell had been as a father.

'It was the war, obviously, and the death of his friend, and the death of your mother. It's understandable. It's nothing to do with you, Auntie Joan.'

'Except for the smell.'

'I've thought about that,' Amanda said, her face full of sympathy. 'It could be a memory of something that happened to you, as a child. Something frightened you, maybe. It could have been anything. You could have been locked in the cellar by accident — the smell of damp, or rot, or both, could be what you remember, and if nobody talked about it, then it stayed with you.'

A memory came to me then. I remembered another door somewhere off the kitchen. I saw the little girl, that tiny girl, trying to reach the door latch, jumping up. Then Gerard Revell's face, white and furious, his hand on the child's arm, gripping too tightly. I remembered then the child's terror, the smell of something hideous in the child's nose, the dark stubble on the white face, the burning eyes, and the child screaming. And the sickness afterwards. And I remembered that my mother wasn't there. And I remembered what Mary had said.

'Something the madman did,' I said. I didn't want to tell her that memory. 'Mary called him a madman — I heard her once. She didn't like him. I didn't realise that then, but I do now. War hero, poet, whatever, that doesn't make him a nice man, or a good husband or father. I was frightened of him.'

Amanda looked a bit crestfallen at that. She'd been carried away with the romance of it all, I supposed. She'd found a hero. Even the suicide made him an object of pity. But I thought of that sad, delicate face I'd seen and those little gloves. What about my mother?

'Did he have a temper?' Amanda asked. 'I mean, suppose he was haunted by what he had seen. We read some poems by Wilfred Owen at school, and they show how terrible the effects of war were. So, he might not have been able to help himself.'

'It was a silent house — it was as if everyone went on tiptoe and whispered for fear of disturbing something. I remember that. Mary taking me into the kitchen. Out of the way, I suppose. Mrs Sykes once told me that her mother used to see my mother walking alone. She never saw her with him, but sometimes I was with her, toddling along beside her. I don't remember that.'

'You were happy together, outside.'

'Outside Foulstone.'

'You didn't go in this afternoon?'

'No.' I put the keys on the table. 'I thought I'd wait for you.'

Amanda looked pleased. 'Tomorrow then?'

'When it's light. We're not going in the dark.'

Amanda laughed and said, 'Sherry time. We deserve a drink.'

I didn't say no. There was something very companiable about sitting in the cosy parlour, sipping our sherry, and feeling the warmth slip down the throat. I could get a taste for this, I thought.

'What are you smiling at?' Amanda asked.

'This — I thought I might buy a bottle, or you could get me some. I don't want people thinking —'

Amanda laughed at that. 'That you're a secret drinker. Who cares?'

And I thought, who indeed? Why should I care what people think all the time? Because I'd been taught to. 'How much is it?'

'About seven and six a bottle, I think — I'll go up to town tomorrow. We might need a couple of glasses when we get back from the house. Oh, I've just thought. Town. Where are they buried?'

I had never given a thought to this. I know it's hard to believe, but I don't suppose I wanted to know. Auntie Mary certainly hadn't wanted to tell me. Amanda looked stunned when I said, 'I have no idea. It was never mentioned. At the cemetery here?'

'Tomorrow, should we?'

'You can get to it through the woods, there's a path above the river, but I don't know if…'

'Shall I look when I go for the sherry?'

I thought of Helena Revell, my mother, whose grave I had never heard of, a grave unvisited. No one to put flowers there or to stand with bowed head in mourning. I still go on the bus from time to time to the church where Mary and William are buried — they were all the parents I had known. I take roses. I always thought how good they had been to me, but now I thought that Auntie Mary had kept too many secrets.

'I'll come.'

10

Amanda

We went along the path by the river until we reached a little cluster of houses and a farm from where a narrow road took us to the cemetery gate. It looked very peaceful under the pale winter sky. The nearer graves were newer ones, so we walked up the sloping path to look for the graves from the 1920s. We came across the grave of a soldier: *662301, D.B. Spicer, Royal Field Artillery*. He had died, aged nineteen, on the 30th of November 1918. The inscription read *"Ubique Quo Fas et Gloria Ducunt"*.

'What does it mean?' Joan asked.

I had to think about that. 'It's to do with right and glory — something like where right and glory lead.'

'To the grave,' Joan said. 'It is terrible — the war was over. Poor boy.'

'I wonder if Nowell Dearlove's name is on the War Memorial in the churchyard. His grave will be in Belgium.'

Joan didn't answer; she was walking among the other graves, peering at the inscriptions. I left her and went across the path to another part of the cemetery. I passed all the melancholy stories set in stone, the beloved wives lost, the husbands sorely missed, the daughters asleep in the arms of Jesus, the treasured children died too soon, Edward Brownlee who had died at two weeks old, following a brother who had died aged eight in 1916. Little Peggy Greenwood, aged six, had died in 1918, now all alone in the deep shade of a yew tree. Too dark. Too cold, I thought.

Many of the graves were too time and weather worn to make out the dates; some obscured by lichen, some buried by ivy and weeds, or the crosses had fallen over. I stopped by the grave of Hannah Fishwick who had died on the 24th of September 1928. Thomas Birkitt, who had been killed in France on the 28th of November 1918, was remembered on his parents' gravestone. There was no grave for Gerard Revell in 1928, and no Helena Revell.

I went over to Joan who was standing quite still, looking at a headstone which read,

"Shall see Him face to face, and tell the history saved by grace."

'Their history isn't told here,' she said. 'There are no graves for the Revells.'

'I wonder where they came from.'

We walked back to the gate in silence until Joan said, 'Down south, Mrs Sykes's mother told her, but there's only one way to find out if that was true.'

'The house?'

'I have the keys in my pocket.'

Joan took the keys out and handed them to me. I felt the weight of them, the weight of responsibility.

'If I keep them, I might change my mind,' Joan said with a half-smile.

'The article in the newspaper said that Nowell Dearlove served in the London Irish Rifles. A London Regiment. He was twenty-one when he was killed. I wondered if he lived in London, at the university, perhaps, and he joined up in London.'

'Where he met Gerard Revell. They might have been from London. Gerard Revell didn't have a northern accent. I remember that.'

'Didn't Mary ever say?'

'Least said, soonest mended, that was Auntie Mary's way. Ask no questions and you'll be told no lies. Silence can be a lie — that's what I think now. Mary told no lies, but she wouldn't tell the truth, either.'

'Wanting to protect you, perhaps, or hadn't the words to tell you.'

Joan thought about that. 'I daresay you're right. When I think about it, she never really talked about anything but the weather, the price of meat or veg. Safe, I suppose. There were a lot of things you weren't supposed to talk about or ask back then. Death, madness, illness, the war. Even the second war. You just have to get on with it — that was Mary's attitude. Make the best of a bad job … a bad job and people being killed all over the place. And me — I just accepted it. Kept my thoughts and feelings to myself.'

'You must have been lonely, Auntie Joan, wondering and not being able to talk about anything.'

Joan stopped on the path. Her expression was sad. I wished I hadn't said about her being lonely, but she looked straight at me and said, 'I think I knew that I wasn't right somehow, but I got too scared to want to know anything. I sometimes felt a horrible emptiness, a kind of sickness. I can't really describe it. And the smell — I was scared of these peculiar feelings. I thought it was just me. Yet I knew there were secrets, and I couldn't fathom them. I remembered the other night that Uncle William went to a funeral. I remember now that he was away all day. And nothing was said when he came back — just a lot of whispering. It was later, of course, when Auntie Mary told me that my father was dead. Mr Revell, she called him. I didn't know who she meant by then and I was too young to ask.'

'William went to Gerard Revell's funeral? To London, perhaps?'

'Mrs Sykes's mother called them off-comers. It means they didn't belong here, though given what I know about Mrs Sykes, if they came from Kendal, they'd be off-comers. Not a patch on the Dearloves, her mother used to tell her.'

'Did Mary ever speak of the Dearloves?'

'I've no idea. Nothing was ever said about Foulstone. Not until Uncle William said I'd inherited it from Gerard Revell. Uncle William told me to leave it to rot.'

'Did he say the word "rot"?'

'Yes, why?'

'It just seems a harsh word — as if he hated the place.'

'He never said a bad word about anyone. Not even Gerard Revell. I don't think he ever spoke about him except to say that the house was mine and that I should stay in Kendal. I can't remember what he sounded like when he said it. Perhaps it's the way I said it.'

'But you did it, you left it untouched.'

'I was frightened of it, yet I wanted to be near it so that no questions could be asked.' She paused there as if she were thinking it all out. I kept quiet. That feeling she described of sickness and emptiness seemed awful to me. She was only a child and had no one to tell. I couldn't imagine that. My mum had always been there when I was frightened — not that I was often frightened. I'd had a happy childhood.

By then we'd reached the gate into the fields behind the cottages and the boundary of Foulstone Manor. We stopped there and looked through the trees. We had a choice to make. We could go home and have a sherry — the bottle was in the deep pocket of my sheepskin coat — or we could go through the break in the fence.

11

Joan

'Are you sure?' Amanda asked.

'No, I'm not, but this is for Helena Revell, my mother. I know Gerard was the hero, the poet, the one who suffered so much that he shot himself, but what about her? She's important, too. Where is she? She lost a child. That's what Mrs Sykes said, and I remembered a cradle. Why was she forgotten? She vanished, except for that brief mention.'

'But he grieved for her.'

'So your newspaper article said, but we don't know that. I'm sure he suffered from his experience in the war, but he never looked at me — three years old, I was, and I don't remember him ever talking to me. He gave me away. He made me suffer. Perhaps, he made her suffer, too. And he sent her away. If he'd wanted her, she'd be buried here where he could see her grave. He didn't want us.'

I could tell Amanda was shocked at my angry words. I was shocked at myself. I hardly knew myself these days what with all these memories tumbling about, but I knew I was right. I'd seen my mother's face. 'I remembered her face — just for a moment — a delicate face, fragile and very young and very sad. As young as you are, and her life over before she could live it.'

That brought it home to her. I could tell and I was sorry, but she was young. She had a future. I wasn't old, but I felt it then, thinking of Helena's young face. She couldn't have been more than twenty-one. I was forty-eight, but I had never felt young, except during that summer at the farm. And I wasn't having

Gerard take all the pity. What happened to Helena? I wanted to cry out, but I waited, looking through the break in the fence Amanda had spoken of when she said she couldn't imagine a happy family living here. I was aware of the silence, too, the sense that in this ruined house, there were secrets — that ought to remain secrets, I wondered, feeling the chill in the frozen air.

The sky had darkened over this brooding place. I felt like turning back, back to the warmth of my kitchen, my safe parlour, but it wouldn't be safe because the past had spoken, and it would again. It would catch me out, whisper in my ear when I was cooking, or listening to the radio, or the wind in the woods, or the rain on the window. I might never sleep again.

Amanda spoke. Her young brow was furrowed as she sorted out her feelings. 'It's complicated,' she said, 'more complicated that I thought. When I remembered what I'd read at school, I just thought what terrible things Gerard must have seen. I don't know, Auntie Joan, I honestly don't know what I think about him — I mean, if it excuses what he did to you…'

'I don't know either, now you say that, but Mary and William knew something that they never wanted to tell. Let it rot, he said. I think it means something terrible. I mean why did I have to pretend to be Margaret's daughter, unless they were hiding something?'

'It is odd. Why didn't they just adopt you legally?'

'I don't know, and I don't know if I want to know, but it's no good our standing here getting frozen. Let's get through that fence and see if I've the courage to go in. You won't know till you try — so Mary was always telling me.'

Amanda grinned at me. 'Grandma Hill up at the farm always said that, too — when she wanted me to try her black pudding. I did know — without trying. It looked horrible.'

'Good for your blood, they said. I thought that meant you could have bad blood. I suppose I'm going to find out.'

We went round to the front of the house, picking our way over the stones and tangled bramble and the crumbling steps of the terrace.

The oak door resisted. Of course it did. Foulstone didn't want me there. That thought made me more determined. Amanda needed both hands to turn the key and we both had to do a good deal of pushing and shoving before we were in the hall, breathless and with dirty hands.

A silence and a stillness held there, a silence so thick that it seemed almost as if you could touch it, as if the house was holding its breath — a breath held for nearly fifty years. Waiting, I thought. To tell its secrets? Or to send me packing — to watch me scuttle away in fright? Breathing out its foul smell after me.

The light was greenish from the ivy-covered windows like being underwater. Not the sea, I thought, something more like the water of a stagnant pond, and the smell, of course, though, oddly, it wasn't as strong as I had known it down in the cottage. Perhaps it *was* just damp and decay, which I'd made into something worse just by imagining or remembering — whatever it was I half-remembered from childhood.

It was that cold I could feel the chill of the flagstones through my boots. I remembered the stone floors and the panelled oak walls. There was the iron lantern above us, an oak chest by the wall above which hung a green-tinged mirror, tarnished at the edges. I didn't want to look into that. See myself — no thanks.

The doors that led off the hall were closed and there was a passage by the stairs which led to the kitchen where I used to sit with Mary. And that locked door was where Gerard Revell had — I felt even colder suddenly. An icy wind seemed to sneak from down the corridor. Amanda had mentioned the cracked windows at the back of the house. I'd have to get them fixed. Suppose someone got in —

We both started at the sound of something falling. I looked down into the gloom of the passage. Of course, there was no one there. Just darkness and shadow. The wind moving.

'I'd better look,' Amanda said. She held up her torch and stepped forward. How I stopped myself from clutching at her to hold her back, I don't know. I heard her footsteps and saw the shadows moving as the beam of her torch shone along the floor and up to the ceiling.

'Some plaster must have fallen,' she said when she came back, 'there's a big lump of it on the floor by a door. Cellar door, it looks like.'

'Yes,' I said, finding my voice, 'I remember that door. It was always locked. We'd better keep away from there. We don't want to have our heads knocked off.'

'Where to start?' Amanda whispered, as we moved towards the stairs.

I couldn't answer. I felt as if I was holding on for dear life, looking up those stairs into the darkness above. Poised between the sudden rush of fear which would send me to slam the door in memory's face and the longing to find out.

The beam of Amanda's torch pointed upstairs, moving up and down as if her hand was shaking. That noise had given us both a fright. Then the light steadied, and I heard her breathe out, but she waited. It was for me to decide. I looked at the carved newel posts and banisters and the first few steps, thinking it was a long way up, imagining Mary Goss looking up as I ascended, shaking her head, telling me least said, soonest mended. *Not in this case, Auntie Mary*, I thought. *You meant well. Best that I forget, but you should have spoken about my mother. No, Mary, no, I'm not listening this time. And I'm not being frightened off by Foulstone.*

'Upstairs,' I said. 'There was a nursery. I think I remember that.'

The rag rug was there, the fire guard, the little iron bed without its mattress, the chipped skirting board, the cupboard, its door closed. Not that I wanted to see if the toys were there. And the old-fashioned cradle made of dark wood. That was there. I couldn't imagine a baby sleeping in that, even back in the nineteen-twenties.

'Yours?' asked Amanda.

'I don't remember. For the child that was coming — Mrs Sykes said she died in childbirth, but why is she not buried in the graveyard here?'

'Unless she was in hospital — in Kendal, and they — maybe Gerard Revell's buried there, too, that they are together. We could go and see.'

'We could,' I said. I didn't want to hurt her feelings again. She wanted to believe that my parents were lying together, a romantic end to their sufferings, but I knew that wasn't true. I felt it in that nursery, and I knew it because of that glimpse of Helena Revell looking from her window. I knew there were secrets. If they had been together at their ends, Mary would have told me where they were. She wouldn't have invented Margaret.

There was no answer in here, though. The cradle, the cupboard, the rag rug told me nothing except that it was a forlorn place, a room in which a woman had felt afraid and alone. It certainly didn't belong to me. I didn't look round fondly at a place where I'd played and sat on someone's knee by the fire. I remembered the things but none of the feelings that might have been attached to a person who remembered a happy home, only this sadness and emptiness.

12

Amanda

At the bottom of the nursery stairs, Joan stopped before a closed door. She stood quite still and stared at it.

'I can't remember,' she said. 'I don't know where these doors lead.'

The door she stared at was just in the right-hand part of the corridor. I directed my torch, and we could see other doors off the corridor, and then we looked to the left where we could see three more doors. Beyond the doors on both sides was darkness and such a deep silence, as if something was waiting down there. More empty rooms, I thought, dreading the idea that we might have to explore them all.

Joan turned the handle. The door opened onto a bedroom. In the torchlight we could see a four-poster bed on which a ragged counterpane still lay and some yellowed pillows in a heap. There was a dressing table thick with dust, its mirror tarnished like the one in the hall, and a huge wardrobe.

'I remember this room. It was my mother's. I remember the child sitting on the bed. She had to be quiet. There was someone else — a stranger in white. A woman in an apron that crackled. A nurse, I imagine. My mother must have been ill — the baby, I suppose. I don't think I saw her again. Perhaps she died soon after. And me, not knowing anything about — anything...'

We were silent then, thinking of forgotten Helena Revell, of the delicate, fragile face that Joan had seen in the night. She had been sick and then she had gone from Joan's life — just gone. I couldn't imagine that, imagine being two years old and never having my mother. It seemed unbearable to me. I thought Joan looked haunted as she gazed round the room, remembering things so long buried. I wondered if this had been a good idea.

I shivered. It was terribly cold, and I could see how the wallpaper hung loose in parts and there were scatterings of plaster on the carpet which had once been blue but was now frayed and worn and dark with neglect and damp. There was the smell of something bitter, something that caught in your throat. And dust, and sadness, I thought. Joan was right. Someone had suffered here.

'You look,' she said, pointing to the large wardrobe.

It looked very forbidding. I was suddenly frightened of what we might find, of where all this might lead. Joan was, too. I could tell by her stillness. She was holding her breath.

I opened the wardrobe door. There were empty wooden hangers which rattled as I looked inside and just one box which I felt as I groped down into the darkness. A cardboard box which felt damp to the touch, but there was something inside.

We took it with us and some papers from Gerard Revell's desk in his study. We were able to open the door to that room, but Joan didn't come in and I didn't want to stay. It was too cold and smelt of damp and rot and that something which caught at the back of your throat. Something that made me frightened, though I didn't say so to Joan.

I opened the box we had discovered, and inside it we found Helena Revell's diary.

PART TWO: 1921–1924

13

Summer 1921

'It's perfectly straightforward — there are many variations, 'fowl' with a 'w' for example, or "Fullstone", or "Fulstone" with one "l" — that's found in Yorkshire. Round here, some people say, 'Fulstun'.' Now, if we were living in Fowlstone with a "w", you'd think of hens, wouldn't you? Foul comes from the Old English "fugol" which just means bird.'

There was a kind of irritated precision in Gerard's words that Helena had heard before. Sometimes she thought that she did not know him really, but she had committed herself and it was up to her to accept his occasional impatience. He would learn more about her, too, and perhaps he wouldn't like all of it. She just nodded. She had only wondered what it meant.

'There's a Foulsyke up the valley — a farm with a barn by a stream. It simply means a dirty stream.'

'Oh, I see, I was just curious about where I am to live. It sounded an odd name to me.'

'Nothing sinister about it, I assure you. You'll like it here. I'm sick of London. I need space and air if I'm to work. It's a good house. I am — we are lucky to have it.'

Helena hadn't thought the name sinister, just unusual. 'I know we are, and I am lucky to be coming to live here with you. We will be happy here, I'm sure of it.'

On the train she had felt light-headed, joyful, as the landscape unrolled in all its different varieties. Flat fields coming into green, woods tenderly light with their new leaves, towns at a distance, villages with cottages and meadows, toy cows in fields, washing on a line, a child waving.

Gerard had held her hand and smiled when she waved back with her free hand. And the sky had been a great bowl of translucent blue like the one in the hall at home — but that had a crack in it, a hairline crack so fine you could hardly detect it. Her mother hadn't cared. She would hold it up to the light and it was like looking into the sky. And now the bowl was gone. It had smashed into tiny fragile splinters when her mother had fallen and not got up again. Helena's joy dissolved when she thought of that, but she felt the warmth of Gerard's hand. Mother would have wanted her to be happy, and she was.

But, as they travelled further north, the sky seemed to darken, as if the bowl of sky started to crack and splinter. By the time they reached Kendal, it was pouring down and it didn't stop. A long black car met them at the station. Gerard called the driver Goss. She and Gerard got in the back of the car — a big, old one from before the war, she imagined. She hadn't much experience of travelling in cars, but it was comfortable with the hood up and a rug about their knees. They rolled up hills shrouded in mist and down again through a little town with a very narrow street where people walked along the narrow pavement, hunched against the rain.

And then they were at Foulstone Manor. Helena's breath was almost taken away as she gazed at the house with the woods behind and the hills beyond, rounded shapes in the mist. A grey stone house on a slight rise. Seventeenth century, Gerard had told her. There was a stone porch inside which she could see a round-headed doorway and a heavy oak door. There were mullioned windows on the ground floor and bigger windows above.

Just for a moment, she saw a movement at one of the upper windows. The housekeeper, perhaps, watching out for them. It was not, as she had feared, such a grand house. It was big, bigger than any house she had ever lived in, but it looked as if you might live in it and feel at home.

A woman came out to meet them, a woman in her forties, Helena judged, with curly brown hair and a kind smile. A friendly face to greet them. She called Gerard 'Sir'. And he smiled at that.

'Very good, Mrs Goss,' he said, 'meet Mrs Helena Revell, my wife.'

'You're welcome, I'm sure, Mrs Revell. Everything is ready, sir, tea in the parlour, and all the rooms cleaned and aired for you — and Mrs Revell. I'll show you round after your tea — if Mr Revell is agreeable. You'll like it, Madam.'

Helena saw that the rain was clearing and there were patches of blue and a lightening of the sky. The hall was welcoming with its friendly-faced tall clock, its dark oak panelling and beams, its quarter-turn staircase with turned balusters and flagstone floor warmed by old Persian rugs. There was a fire in the wainscoted parlour, not a very big room, but a charming one with its old furniture and well-worn sofa and chairs, its midnight blue curtains and faded yellow wallpaper. It looked lived-in, as though people had been content there. The little gate-legged table by the fire was old, but shiny with wax polish. Mrs Goss had done her work well. There was the scent of lavender and smoke. Helena could hardly believe this room was hers — that she could sit here and look out on the fields and the fells and that great blue bowl of sky. Her mother would have loved it, but she didn't want to think about her now, or the broken bowl.

They ate ham sandwiches and fruit cake, and cheese, and drank their tea from old china cups with gold rims. Helena lifted the silver tea pot carefully. She felt nervous. After all, these were not her things, though Gerard had told her that the house and everything in it belonged to them now. He seemed to be comfortable enough, but then he had stayed there before.

Mrs Goss took them round the house and talked of Mr Arthur Dearlove, the previous owner from whom Gerard had inherited the house. 'As kind a gentleman, Madam, as you'd ever wish to meet, and a generous one to me and Goss, and young Mr Nowell — well, Mr Gerard will have told you all about him, I'm sure. This was his room if you want to —' She opened a door.

'No, thank you, Mrs Goss, I'd rather —'

Helena caught a whiff of something damp, a smell of mould, and a brief glimpse of a made-up bed and bookshelves, but Mrs Goss closed the door quickly. She looked flustered. Helena saw the closed look on Gerard's face. She had seen it before. Nowell Dearlove was not to be talked of. She knew a little about Gerard's closest friend who had been killed in the war and whose father, Mr Arthur Dearlove, had left all he had to the friend who had come to tell him what had happened to his only boy. Nowell Dearlove had been shot, and Gerard had gone out under heavy fire to rescue him. That was all she knew.

Mrs Goss was apologising. 'I'm that sorry, sir, I should have thought. It's only that Mr Dearlove went into the room so often, and he talked of Nowell all the time, but we're not all the same. It's different for you — being there, I mean...'

Gerard turned away. Helena felt sorry but shut out. She could not know fully what Gerard had experienced. She could not share that. She had talked to her father about it, and he had told her that she must not ask. Gerard would want to leave it behind — not that he would be able to. His friend had been killed, but many young men began again, fell in love, married, had children. If you love him, her father had said, then you will make him happy, and you will accept that there are some things that will take time to heal — your love will help him. He told her that Gerard had asked him for her hand. She was torn — how could she leave her father? He would come to Westmorland, he said, to stay in her lovely old house.

But that promise could not be kept. Her father knew he was dying. He would live to see her marriage arranged. But no longer.

She came as a bride to the lovely old house after their quiet wedding in Chertsey. Only Aunt Maud and her husband were present and a friend of Gerard's from his office — a friend who could not stay for the wedding breakfast. A friend who was also the photographer and who went away with his camera and the photographs she never saw. It seemed that there had been an accident with the camera. She had been terribly disappointed, but Gerard had declared that he needed no photographs. He could see her every day. That was enough for him.

Gerard Revell had no one else. And, neither did she, really. Her father's death had almost broken her, but Aunt Maud had got her through it, and Uncle Hubert, who was good at saying nice things, pressing her hand, and telling her how beautiful she looked and how pleased he was that she would be looked after, and how proud her mother and father would have been, and how happy to see her settled.

She had wondered at the absence of anyone from Gerard's life. No one, Gerard had said, whom he cared to invite to their wedding. A new start was what he wanted — what he wanted for them. He had given her the pearls that had belonged to his mother who had died long ago. He could not remember his parents. He had been brought up by an aunt, but she was dead, too. In any case, the past was gone — he would prefer to forget. It was the future that mattered, he had told her, the future at Foulstone Manor.

'I only have you,' he had said, and something had shifted in her for he had looked so forlorn. Gerard Revell deserved to be loved.

She believed that. Sometimes, he was distant, but once before they were married, she had seen him in the park. He had been talking to a man in a shabby coat and dark hat and she had waited until the man went away. She had seen the man put something in his pocket and Gerard had watched him slouch away with his head down.

'Just a poor old soldier down on his luck,' Gerard had said when she had asked who the man was. 'He needed money. What could I do but give him a helping hand?'

She loved him for that. For his kindness to a stranger.

Helena and Gerard had been happy in those first months; the summer was hot nearly all the time, and Gerard showed Helena the garden and the woods, and took her up to the fells, and along the footpaths by the river where there was honeysuckle in the hedges and wild roses, and buttercups in the grass. They took tea under the trees and in the evenings, still remarkably warm, they sat on the terrace playing cards and listening to the music on the gramophone coming through the open windows, and hearing the owls hooting in the twilight, but as autumn came on, he spent more time upstairs in his study, or walking alone. He needed to think, he told her.

But one night when Helena was looking at the starlit sky from her bedroom, she felt a sudden piercing loneliness for her mother and father, so piercing that the tears started to her eyes. It was the beauty of the night, she thought, looking up at the great showers of stars falling down a sky like the spangled dark blue silk chiffon scarf that her mother had worn. A still night, the sort of night they had used to walk in their garden, Helena between them, a very loved daughter. Oh, she missed them.

She almost felt that Gerard thought he had done enough for her, as if he had measured the time, and she had received her portion. The honeymoon was over. A traitorous thought which she tried to push away. Gerard was a writer. What did she expect? she chided herself. She had been pleased enough with the idea when she had met him. And her marriage could not be like that of her parents. She knew that. Not all couples were as happy as they had been and with such an unspoken understanding between them.

Mrs Goss was very kind. Sometimes they sat in the kitchen when Gerard was out walking. Never when he was in the house. Somehow, she knew that he did not approve of her making friends with the servant. Not that Helena thought of the older woman as a servant to be ordered about. Gerard could be peremptory at times which Helena found uncomfortable to witness.

She wondered if he felt that he must assert his authority because he was not the true heir. Perhaps he felt guilty that he had inherited what ought to have been his friend's house and money.

Mrs Goss talked a little to her about Mr Dearlove and Nowell and what a happy house it had been when Mr Nowell was a boy. Oh, yes, she remembered Mr Gerard coming. They was close friends those two. Mr Nowell looked up to him, she could tell that. And then the news came… She'd sigh then and start some job in the kitchen or say she must get on. She never said anything more about Gerard; she only asked whether the master would be wanting tea when he came in.

The nicest times were when she and Gerard sat by the fire in the drawing room — not parlour, Gerard told Mary Goss who from then on avoided naming the room at all. Perhaps Mr Dearlove had used the word "parlour". Helena liked the homely word, but she used "drawing room" to please Gerard; however, she could not bring herself to address kindly William Goss as merely "Goss", even if Gerard were present. She always called him Mr Goss. At least in this room, Gerard seemed to relax. He would tell her about the walk he had taken, about the plans he had discussed with Mr Goss about the garden, and about a future when they might have children. A son, he hoped, who would inherit Foulstone Manor. Then he would take her hand and kiss it and call her his beautiful bride and she knew he would come to her that night.

She had been surprised when Mrs Goss had opened the door to the bedroom which was to be hers. She didn't say anything in front of Mrs Goss — perhaps this was the way in which Mr and Mrs Dearlove had lived. However, Gerard must have seen something in her face. He needed a bedroom of his own, he had explained — just dreams, he said, but I don't want you to be disturbed. Some things I can't forget. As you must understand. She thought she understood.

He would not talk much about his work. She had read the poems he had published about the war and had praised them. The one called 'The Ghost', she thought must be about Nowell. She had found it very moving, but disquieting, too. It began with the line 'Seeking my dead' and spoke of someone yearning for another so he could speak to him of 'that monstrous hell', the other who was 'the one, the truest and best' and whose hair was golden. Mrs Goss had said that Nowell Dearlove had been fair-haired.

Gerard thanked Helena for her compliments, but that was all. She dared not ask any more about Nowell. She remembered what her father had told her. She had to accept that there were some things that Gerard must keep to himself. His dreams and his poems were not to be shared. He told her that he was working on a new set of poems. But he did not show them to her or ask her opinion. Yes, they were about the war, he told her, but the work was devilishly tricky. When they were ready, he would send them to a friend whose opinion he valued, a friend who worked at *The London Mercury*, the literary magazine in which his first poems were published.

What was Helena to do with the long hours when Gerard left her? She wondered about that, too. Mrs Goss ran the house which was always shining with polish and scented with lavender. She'd been shown the larder where Mrs Goss's jams and chutneys gleamed like jewels in their jars: damson, strawberry, gooseberry, apple, and tomato chutneys all lined up with their paper lids tied with string. Bottles of elderberry and blackberry wine filled one shelf. Of course, Gerard didn't drink those. There was old port and good claret in Arthur Dearlove's wine cellar which Gerard fetched for himself — Mr Goss had no idea about wine, it seemed.

The laundry room smelt of starch and soap, and upstairs there was a linen cupboard stacked with white sheets and towels and table napkins. There was a back porch where old boots and coats were hung, and next to that, down some steps, the place where the coal was stored. And a little room next to the larder where Mr Goss polished the silver which gleamed on their shining dining room table in the evenings. Gerard enjoyed living as a gentleman of property and means. Helena liked the kitchen with Mrs Goss in it and the warm, bright copper, the warm pink plates with their old-fashioned country scenes, and the smell of new bread, or a rabbit stew. She felt at home there.

Her own home was sold, her father's money in the bank. She had brought nothing from it, except the photographs of her mother and father. Not that they looked anything like the vibrant living realities they had been in a house where laughter had prevailed and supper had been taken in the kitchen, the formal dining room used only for visitors.

She kept the photographs of her childhood in her dressing table with the one taken when she had been eighteen — so young and eager, and innocent. She didn't want to look at it now. She'd salvaged some pictures, too, one of the remains of the abbey at Chertsey which she'd been given by a friend, and an engraving of the Wey Bridge where cattle browsed under trees and a lovely woodcut of a kingfisher diving into a stream — a favourite of her mother's. Scenes of her childhood. Gerard had said she must sell everything else. They had no need of it. They had Foulstone.

She did like the house, but she could never feel it was hers. A cuckoo in the nest, she thought. Nothing was hers. Somehow Gerard seemed to have taken it all to himself. She watched him sometimes staring at a silver fork or spoon and smiling. Then he would rub at the monogram — the monogram of the

Dearloves. She wondered if he were trying to polish it away so that it should be his entirely.

Perhaps she could ask for a room of her own — a sewing room? Somewhere that she could make her own — write letters, write her diary, read, sew. She could make curtains for her room, just be herself rather than that woman who perched on the sofa in the drawing room, who sat bolt upright at the dining room table, holding someone else's silver, and eating from someone else's china plates and dishes.

Gerard had his study and his bedroom, side by side at the end of the left-hand corridor at the top of the stairs where her bedroom was first in the right-hand corridor. Next to Gerard's room was Nowell's own room. She had been down there once, thinking she had heard someone whistling. Gerard never whistled. But there was no one there. All three doors were locked.

'Master has the keys,' Mrs Goss told her when she met her bringing up sheets and towels to fold into the linen cupboard. She sounded uncharacteristically offended.

Helena stopped to help her. 'Tell me more about Nowell, Mrs Goss,' she asked, thinking about the poem and the locked room.

'Oh, he was a lovely boy, always so cheerful and busy, and he loved his dad. Devoted to each other, they was. Always together those two up on the fells, playing croquet in the garden, fishing. He was at the school here. Boarded, but he came home when he was allowed. An exeat, they called it, and the boys would come from the school — oh, Mr Nowell had tons of friends. He was that popular, and they'd play cricket and swim in the river down there by the bridge and fish. Then there was the holidays. Long summer holidays — I'm talking about before the war. Picnics they had — my pork pies,

Wensleydale cheese, William's tomatoes. Lemonade in stone bottles. Tied 'em with string an' dropped 'em in the river to cool. Hot days they was then, long summer days… That dratted war — Mr Nowell wasn't never the same. And not to know where he is. That nearly broke Mr —'

They heard footsteps in the hall. Mrs Goss shut the cupboard door and went downstairs. Helena went to her bedroom. She didn't want Gerard to know that she had been talking to Mrs Goss. She would go out in a minute or two when she heard him come up the stairs.

The little room next to her bedroom became hers. Mr Goss put up her pictures. Mrs Goss found a washstand with a marble top which she could use as a desk on which she put the photograph of her parents. There was a table with a sewing machine — a brand new one. Gerard had sent for that. He seemed pleased that she wanted to be busy. She couldn't help thinking that he was glad not to have to come out of his study to entertain her — as if she were an inconvenient guest who stayed too long. So that's how it became — she in her small corner and he in his.

Helena often thought about those locked rooms, and of Nowell Dearlove, the blonde-haired boy diving into the river with his friends. She had not had the chance to ask Mrs Goss more about him, but he haunted her sometimes. She imagined him calling to his father along the corridor, his voice merry with laughter. She thought she glimpsed him occasionally — just a shadow in the passage, a flash of gold, a sound of feet, whistling. She wasn't frightened. She just wished she'd known him, had known Foulstone Manor then when it had been a happy home where she knew from what Mrs Goss had said that there had been love, openness and trust. But Nowell whom she imagined she might have loved had been killed in the war, and all that golden promise snuffed out like a candle flame. That war which had changed everything.

She had been at school when the war started. By the end, nothing was the same. She, and others she knew, had felt that they were poised at a moment between the past and the future. The past, before the war, had been safety, certainty, schooldays, tennis and tea, and Tennyson, the park in that long summer of 1914, picnics, lunch in the garden, fog in the winter, crumpets at the fireside.

When the war had ended, leaving the world in ruins, there was the future and what you were to do in it. It had seemed wrong to think of one's own life when so many millions had lost theirs. A distant cousin had been killed. She had met him when they were children, when he was a skinny little boy with one front tooth and a black eye. He had been an accident-prone child, always falling out of trees. How had he fared out there in the mud and the trenches?

They hadn't known the truth at the beginning. They'd seen the tents and recruiting rallies in the parks, the flags flying above the children's kites, heard the drums and the trumpets as the battalions went by in marching order, the cheering crowds lining the streets, the dragoons engaged in sword-drill by Knightsbridge barracks, the hawkers selling penny Union Jacks. They'd seen the exhibition trenches in Kensington Gardens, all neatly laid out, well-furnished and dry for the comfort of the gallant men. The papers had reported the cheers that greeted Princess Louise's farewell speech to the Kensington Territorial Regiment. "I hope you will come back, brave fine fellows." A thousand men from one London borough.

It had all seemed so hopeful, but news came of trenches knee-deep in water, of fresh troops marching to Ypres, of retreats and battles lost. Mons, Marne, Ypres, Loos. Her father had frowned over his newspaper. Her cousin had joined up — still small and skinny, his mother wrote, but a man had only to be five foot three to get in by November 1914. He had been gassed at Loos in 1915, one of sixty thousand casualties. First Ypres, Second Ypres, Third Ypres, Passchendaele, the Somme. She remembered the names and the casualty lists. No Man's Land. The great explosion at Messines, the shock of which it was said had been heard by Lloyd George in Downing Street.

And the aftermath. Helena had seen the men on crutches, men with a jacket sleeve neatly folded up. Once in the park, she had given two shillings to a man with one eye and had steeled herself not to flinch when she saw his face, the skin crudely sewn and burnt red and shiny. He had not spoken, just held out his hand.

She had known something, had felt fear and shock, apprehension, and tremendous pity, but clearly not enough for Gerard to talk to her. Her father had talked, but then he had not been there.

That first Armistice Day — Helena remembered that. Standing in Whitehall with her father, their hands clasped, hearing the deep boom of the first maroon, the rasping of brakes, the clatter of horses' hooves as they were pulled up. The traffic stopped on land and river, people turned to stone, and a great stillness and a silence so profound that she felt she could have touched it. Then the eleven strokes of the great clock. The future seemed a blank in those two minutes.

Her schoolfriend, Lily Mountjoy-Smythe was more sanguine, more determined to live the fullest life she could. Her sights were set on a secretarial course and a flat in Bloomsbury. She wanted to meet artists and writers and to work on a fashion magazine. A thoroughly modern girl was Lily with wealthy parents who owned a white stuccoed house in Kensington and a country house, with a trust fund, and a fund of self-confidence. Beautiful, too, with thick chestnut hair, bobbed of course by 1920. Helena kept her long, pale hair. When she met him in the summer of 1920, Gerard said he liked it that way.

Helena was invited to share a flat in Bloomsbury Place, three rooms on the top floor with painted furniture and bright cushions, bamboo tables and bookshelves. It suited Lily with her amber cigarette holder, her scarlet lips, and her tunics and shorter skirts — no changing two or three times a day. Just once — a chiffon theatre dress from Derry and Toms, or a beaded silver slip of a dress with silver shoes for an evening party, and Lily went to plenty of those. Helena's dresses were shorter now, but always plain and dark in colour. Lily would look at her critically, peering through her cigarette smoke, holding her cocktail glass. Black, she'd say, not navy — too respectable, and why those long sleeves? It's not winter in here nor at Jack's.

It was at Jack Fournier's that she met Gerard Revell. Jack was Lily's cousin. Gerard was a writer, Lily had said, published poet, Captain in the war. Did something heroic but won't talk about it. Strong, silent type. He'll suit you, and you can see him whenever you want if you come to live here. Time you spread your wings, my chick.

Helena remembered standing in Bloomsbury Square looking up at an aeroplane, its smoke trailing behind, like writing on the sky. A message for her, she wondered. It was still an extraordinary sight to see that fragile thing so far above and imagine a man at the controls, a man who had become a bird. You could fly to Paris, Lily had said, her green eyes gleaming, two and a half hours and lunch at Maxim's. Home by midnight. Lily had been to Paris, of course.

Helena watched the aeroplane disappear, watched the smoke dissolve into cloud, turned up her collar against the rain, and walked to the bus stop. She had made up her mind.

She could not leave her father on his own. Of course, she could go down by train at the weekends, but he would miss her, and he was not always well. She saw sometimes how he rubbed his hand about his heart. Of course he would miss her. Her mother was dead, and he missed her, too. In any case, she could come up to Bloomsbury and stay with Lily and see Gerard Revell with whom she'd had tea after the party, and who seemed to like her. He wasn't much keen on parties, he told her, too noisy, too crowded, too many people wanting to ask questions all the time about one's work, or one's war service. Those were private matters. He liked to be out in the open air.

And that's what they did during the summer, walked in the parks, on Hampstead Heath, along the Embankment, though sometimes when the weather was cool, they went to an art gallery. He avoided modern art, especially the war artists whom Lily had invited to her parties. Paul Nash had lived in Gower Street, his painting, *The Menin Road*, was much talked about. He and his brother, John, had served in the Artists' Rifles, but Gerard had no wish to revisit those scenes.

Helena had liked his quietness, the way he was so courteous to her father with whom he talked books and politics, whether there would ever be a Labour Government, and whether they would build all the houses they promised, whether the recently founded Communist Party had a future, all matters to which she listened, and which made her think of the tension in her own mind between the uncertain future and the safety of the past. To which should she turn?

Her father persuaded her. A country house, he had said when she told him of Gerard's inheritance, and a fine, upstanding young man whom you love and who obviously loves you. Her father must have known then that he did not have long to live. He wanted to see her settled, and safe. Lily Mountjoy-Smythe had asked her if she were sure. Of course she was sure. But Lily had looked sceptical and said, 'You hardly know him.'

Helena chose safety. She accepted Gerard's proposal in October 1920.

14

Autumn-Winter 1921

As the summer turned into autumn, Gerard seemed to be increasingly distant, yet the weather was beautiful, still warm, and there was a golden light everywhere, the plums ripening and the apples turning red, Michaelmas daisies beginning to purple the flower beds, the buttery sun seeming to be a blessing on the wounded world. The roses still glowed, pink and white foxgloves spiked against the grey stone walls, and scarlet nasturtiums still blazed in the vegetable plots. Helena raised her eyes to the hills as if she might glimpse Nowell striding down towards her, his face flushed and smiling. Mr Goss's face was nut-brown as he worked in the flower beds and the kitchen garden. Such an abundant harvest, Mrs Goss gloated, taking out her preserve pans and jars for pickles and jam.

Helena walked in the woods where the trees were turning to copper and bronze, and by the river which glittered in the light until it was time for tea under the trees. Gerard came to join her, but often his dark face in the dappled light looked set into a misery she could not fathom.

On September 23rd, Gerard suddenly announced that he must go to London to see his publisher. He'd had a letter from London which he had opened at breakfast time and at which he had frowned. He had frowned at Helena, too, when she asked if it were bad news. She was surprised when he said it was from his publisher — such a cheap looking envelope and the paper looked creased. She imagined a publisher's letter would come in a thick envelope and be written on thick, creamy paper. Gerard had crumpled it into his pocket.

'Aren't you excited?' she asked. 'It might mean —'

He looked at her as if he did not understand what she was saying. 'Oh, yes, of course. But I like it here — with you. This is all I want.'

They had come out onto the terrace to take advantage of the sun. As Gerard spoke and looked over the garden and woods towards the fell, Helena did not know if he meant her or his house and land.

He did not come to her room that night, and in the morning, he was gone before Helena got up. Mrs Goss said that her husband had taken him for an early train. Helena did not want to ask when he would be back. It seemed humiliating that he had not told her.

'Back tomorrow, William said, late.'

'Yes, I —'

Mrs Goss turned away without comment. Helena thought she probably knew that he hadn't told her but was too kind to say anything. At the door Mrs Goss turned round and held something out. 'I forgot to give you this.'

Lily's writing was on the envelope. Helena hadn't heard from her since she had come to Foulstone Manor. Lily had been in Paris when the wedding took place. Her wedding gift had been the beautiful engraving of the ruins of Chertsey Abbey with the square tower of church in the background, a scene Helena knew very well, a scene that sometimes made her heart ache.

But Helena hadn't written to Lily, either. She didn't know what to tell her. She was afraid that something would slip out, something that might suggest that she wasn't altogether happy. She'd tried to write, but the words were stilted as if she were writing to a stranger. She tried to describe Foulstone Manor.

She wanted to tell her how comfortable it was, how old, how beautiful. She sounded like someone who was a guest at a country house, someone who did not belong. She wanted to say something amusing about the empty rooms, about the old retainers, about the chimneys that smoked sometimes, about the wind which rattled the windows, about the rain and the damp in the cellar, so that Lily would know that it was all tremendous fun and that she was at home there.

But Lily would know. She might live for the moment, but she saw through people. She always saw through Helena who remembered her words, "Are you sure? You hardly know him." What had Lily seen in Gerard that she had not seen?

Gerard did not like Lily. He disapproved of her rackety life. Once, not long after they had come to Foulstone Manor, Helena had wondered how Lily was getting on and Gerard had said, 'I couldn't care less. She won't be coming here. She's the sort of woman I can't stand. Too confident of her charms, which at best are superficial, at worst, cheap.'

Helena had been stunned. "Cheap" seemed so unfair. She should have defended Lily, said what a good friend she had been. Lily was loyal and she loved her parents and her little brother, Peter. Poor infant, she would say, imprisoned in that ghastly boarding school. What it is to be free. Lily just wanted to live; she had a capacity for joy.

She didn't say any of these things because Gerard had told her then that she was his ideal. Surely, she did not need anyone else. And that night he came to her bedroom.

Helena looked at the letter. It was postmarked Paris. Mrs Goss had not given it to her at breakfast. Helena thought she knew why.

Tears started to her eyes. It was as if Lily were there before her, drinking champagne, tossing her chestnut bob, earrings dangling, red beads rattling, scoffing, 'Wear this red dress, give the hero a fright.' Lily did not much like Gerard. Helena did not wear the red dress.

Lily's breathless writing told her she was getting married — a Christmas wedding. Lily would wear fur and white velvet. All Souls, Langham Place. The rector, Arthur Buxton, friend of her family, had served in the war. Helena was to come. She must telephone — as if she could, thought Helena. Though how lovely it would be to hear that carefree, laughing voice. Helena should bring Gerard — he could talk to Arthur Buxton — wedding breakfast at Claridge's. Dancing. Jazz. Oh, and her fiancé was French — divine — they'd live in Paris —

Christmas in London. A society wedding, Helena thought. All Souls — dozens of people, unlike her own wedding in Chertsey, a cold day in April and only three people there. Claridge's and jazz. She knew she would not be going. At least she thought she had an excuse. She hoped. She hadn't told Gerard yet. She hadn't told anyone. It wouldn't matter if she told Lily. Lily wouldn't be writing to Gerard to congratulate him.

Helena had her letter in her hand when she told Mrs Goss that she was walking up to town. Mrs Goss didn't say anything. If Lily wrote back, the letter would find its way into Mrs Goss's apron pocket.

Helena liked the little country town with its busy shops. You could get everything you wanted and Mrs Goss did. She went up on a Wednesday, market day, to buy silver sand for sharpening the knives, or fresh fish or a chicken. Helena liked the forge where the blacksmith in his leather apron wielded his bellows and the flame became a red glow, and she could feel the warmth coming through the open door. She liked the look of the blacksmith's strong, intent face as he hammered the horseshoe on the anvil. Mrs Goss had told her that he had fought in the war in one of the horse battalions. She could imagine him caring for the horses with that same intentness. He looked like a good man, but she was too shy to do more than smile at him.

She liked the clog maker's window, the ironmongery shop, the shoe shop outside which a man in a white apron nodded to her, and the little sweet shop, and the smell of leather from the saddler's. There was even a hat shop and a gentleman's outfitters. People acknowledged her; she would have liked to make friends, but Gerard had no wish to socialise. She imagined that Arthur and Nowell Dearlove would have known all the people who only nodded to her. A stranger who lived in a house belonging to someone else.

She had walked in the churchyard, too, to look at the graves and had paused by that of Arthur Dearlove. She wished she had known him. Mrs Goss spoke so fondly of him and Nowell.

There was no grave for Nowell. He was lost out there in the fields of Flanders where the poppies grew, so the poem said. Helena had looked at his name on the War Memorial and read the words, "Their bodies are buried in peace: but their name liveth for evermore." Yet, Gerard never spoke that name.

Gerard came back from London a day later than was expected, but he had nothing to say about his trip, except that he was thinking of changing his publisher, from which Helena divined that his visit had been unsuccessful in some way. She told him about the baby and for the first time, she saw his face light up with the smile she had scarcely seen.

October sent the gift of glorious sunshine, quite exceptional weather for autumn. The days were warm and lazy; they sat in the garden or walked by the river where Gerard skimmed stones. He looked happy, as if some cloud had lifted from him. Hope, she thought, a hope for the future in our baby. They could put the past behind them. Not forget. Never that. She could not forget her mother or her father, but her child would have what she had had. Of course, Gerard would not forget the war. There would be other children and he would live a new life through them. A boy called Nowell, she thought, or a girl called Joanna.

Helena went to stand by him. Gerard laughed as he skimmed another stone. 'Five!' he cried. 'I'll be teaching my son to do this.' There was a sudden chill in the air.

'It might be a daughter.' *A little girl for me.*

The Indian Summer was over. They woke up to frost on November the first.

There were a few frosty mornings when the world glittered, but thereafter November settled into dreary greyness with fog shrouding the hills and mist in the woods, hanging motionless about the leafless trees, and rain on some days pouring ramrod straight onto the lawn, filling the house with the smell of damp and smoke, and a smell of something rotten. Mrs Goss opened windows to disperse the smell. Mr Goss examined the drains and went down into the cellar, but it must be the dratted weather, he reported to a sullen Gerard.

When the rains stopped, Helena looked out at a waterlogged lawn in which a single figure stood looking at the sky from where a weak sun made pewter of the water, and as she looked to the misty woods beyond, a memory flashed into her mind of a picture she had seen in a gallery where she had been with Lily, a Paul Nash landscape of mud and dying trees — the Western Front. She opened her mouth then closed it again. She didn't look at Gerard, but she heard the door close a few moments later. Gone without a word as always. No Man's Land — the territory between them.

Remembrance Day had passed. Gerard had gone for a long walk. Helena was not invited to accompany him. Seeing his set face — the familiar door shut against her — she hadn't dared ask why he was not going to the Armistice ceremony at the church though Mary told her that William was going. 'For Mr Dearlove, for Mr Nowell,' she had said. Helena had seen the tears in her eyes and pressed her hand. Mary did not ask why Mr Revell was not going for Nowell Dearlove.

At least it wasn't raining. Mr Goss still stood in his dark waterproof cape eyeing the clouds. Helena went down to the kitchen to tell Mrs Goss that she fancied a walk — just through the woods. The kitchen was sweet with jam scents, cider, bay leaves, thyme, and the range was warm, but she wanted to be outside in the air, however damp and cold.

Mrs Goss stopped in the act of chopping her red cabbage. 'It'll be that muddy. Take care. Don't stay out too long.'

Helena put on a pair of stout boots and an old waterproof cape that hung in the back porch. It was very long and rather heavy, but she didn't care. She didn't want to go back through the house for her own mackintosh and hat. There was a shabby woollen cap hanging there which she pulled on to cover most of her hair. A few fair strands escaped but it didn't matter.

For a second or two, Mr Goss didn't seem to know her. 'Eh, lass — I thought for a moment —' He looked at her boots. ''Appen it'll not rain but watch your step on those muddy paths.'

Helena walked across the field, aware of the smell of rubber and stale pipe smoke. Perhaps the waterproof had been Arthur Dearlove's — or Nowell's. That gave her comfort in her loneliness, but she was surprised that the cap and coat had not been got rid of. Mrs Goss had told her how Mr Revell had put away everything that belonged to Mr Dearlove and Nowell. Boxes and boxes in the attics. And Mr Dearlove's papers up there, too. Gerard had taken over Mr Dearlove's study. She wondered about Nowell's room and that glimpse she had when she first came of the made-up bed and books on the shelves. Perhaps that, too, was empty now. If so, why keep it locked? Locked rooms, including Gerard's study and his bedroom. She was not invited into those rooms.

The woodland path was dreadfully muddy; Helena kept her head down for fear of slipping. She ought to be careful. It would be horrible if she lost the baby. Gerard would not be furious, or at least he wouldn't show it. He would be silent. It would be her fault.

A crow flew up from a tree, cawing irritably. Her heart gave a little lurch. What was it about today? The woods were always lovely, she had thought, but the silence after the bird seemed too thick and she was aware of the mist trapped down here in the trees, giving everything a ghostly air. So still. As if the wood were holding its breath, waiting.

She should go back, but in a minute or two she would reach a tree stump and be able to sit down. She walked on, and then she was there.

And so was he. A figure standing in the mist, a gleam of water before him, the dead trees behind, and all the mud churned up about his feet. Shocked, she stood still and stared.

A man in a long dark coat and a dark hat, standing as still as she, a white face staring back. A ghost in the mist — her head was full of images. That painting. Only a few seconds and she turned away, an intruder into something she could not understand. She half ran, slipping and sliding in the mud, but she had to stop to get her breath. She couldn't help looking back. He had advanced to the edge of the clearing and was still staring after her. He seemed to give her a half wave, then he was gone.

She made herself stroll back to Foulstone Manor. Mr Goss had gone. She looked up to Gerard's window. He was there staring out at her, standing completely still. She pulled off the cap and waved it at him — perhaps he had not recognised her. He waved back and disappeared.

She met him in the hall, having disposed of the cap and cape. She told him about the stranger, saying nothing of ghosts or mud-caked terrain and dead trees. Gerard looked very strained and questioned her closely about the man's appearance.

'A long coat? What colour?'

'Just dark and a dark hat. I only saw him for a moment or two.'

'Did he speak?'

Ghosts don't speak, she thought, but she only said, 'No — he just stared at me. Got a fright perhaps, at me appearing out of the mist.'

'He wasn't a labourer — someone from a farm. Poacher?'

'He could have been, I suppose. I didn't see a gun.'

'He didn't threaten you?'

'No, he just looked. I wouldn't have been worried, except —'

'What?'

'He stared so intently.'

'I'll go out and have a look about the woods. He's probably made off now — poacher, I'll bet. Or a tramp making for the workhouse. Still, we don't want that sort coming onto our land.'

'Tell Mr Goss, just in case.'

And that was it. Gerard returned to say he had not seen anyone. The man did not come back. Helena wondered very often what he had been, or who, but she did not speak of him to Gerard. Mrs Goss had told her that there had been a lot of tramps during and after the war. Many of them were ex-soldiers looking for work. Mrs Gibson up at the farm had often let them sleep in one of the barns.

'You had to do something,' Mrs Goss said, 'poor souls without a roof over their heads, even them as ran away. Deserters they was, but no one told. They gave 'em food. Somebody's son or husband. Neighbour, even. And them as had been fighting for us all — no work, no home. The world's a terrible place sometimes.'

The man had been an ex-soldier perhaps, and so a ghost of sorts.

15

1922

The new year brought heavy snow and biting winds. It was too cold to go out and the blizzards covered the fields; drifts came up to the windowsills. A heavy fall of snow up Dentdale caused an avalanche which destroyed trees and some outbuildings. Dent village was cut off for weeks and it was near impossible for them to get up the hill to Rawthdale.

Mrs Bents came to Foulstone with the milk when she could and the farmer who butchered his own meat sent a boy floundering through the snow with meat and eggs. They had everything else they needed; Mrs Goss's hams and pickles and cheese. And there was plenty of wood for the fires and coal for the kitchen range. Gerard sometimes went out between the snowfalls. Just for some air, he said.

There was no more talk of his publisher or a new one, no further reference to any new work, but he still stayed in his study for hours. Helena had to stay in bed for most of the time. After her encounter with the man in the woods, she had not felt well. Morning sickness, certainly, for which Mrs Goss supplied ginger tea or chamomile which helped, and soup which did not, though Mrs Goss insisted that she eat something, and she did for the sake of the baby. Not that she could taste much, just something faintly metallic.

But none of these helped with the smell — she'd wake up and the first sensation was always the smell of something damp and rotten. She felt breathless and panicky; her dreams were disturbing, too — the man in the woods, being lost in the fog, drowning in mud. They had come after a peculiarly restless night after a few days when the weather had changed to storm and rain.

One night, a snapping wind made the windows rattle so that Helena couldn't sleep. She got out of bed to see if the catch was fastened. There was a fitful moon which momentarily illuminated the garden before the tossing clouds covered its face again. In those seconds she saw something move on the lawn. She waited and when the moon showed again, there was a figure, a figure in a cape, its face covered with something white like a bandage or a scarf. He waved his arm. She didn't see it again, though she waited for the next gleam of moonlight. Was it Nowell come in his cape? Come to tell her he was dead?

She woke next morning with the fragments of the dream in her head — for surely, she had dreamt the figure on the lawn. She couldn't tell, she only knew that he had been in her dream at waking. The taste of metal was on her lips and the smell in her mouth, so strong she thought it might choke her. Mrs Goss couldn't smell anything in Helena's room, but she thought that it must be them cellars. Mr Goss had discovered a leaking tap down there, but he'd made sure it was turned off, but still she supposed damp got about.

'We never had damp in the old days. Mark my words, it's the war. It's sent the weather all turnabout. But warm days'll come, bound to, you'll see, and you'll feel better. 'Tis only a passin' thing because of your condition. Now let's tidy you up for the doctor.'

Doctor Graham came on his sturdy Dales Galloway pony when the road was passable. A good-tempered middle-aged man with reassuring blue eyes in a red face, scoured by the wind, a cheerful smile, strong but gentle hands, and a no-

nonsense attitude. He agreed with Mrs Goss about the smell and the dizziness of which Helena complained. She would be particularly sensitive just now.

'Nothing to worry about,' he said, 'but rest as much as you can. Stay in bed. Sleep is the best medicine, especially for the headaches. It'll all pass. And drink warm milk at night to help you sleep. With a pinch of ginger, Mrs Goss. You've a good nurse there, Mrs Revell. Trust her. And your baby is fine — he or she will be blooming by the time the March hares come.'

Doctor Graham must have spoken to Gerard because he came to hold her hand and to repeat the instructions about plenty of rest.

'Doctor Graham says your symptoms are all very common — nothing to worry about. Our son is going to be a fine, healthy boy — providing you do as you are told.'

He was unusually attentive and read Jane Austen aloud to Helena until her eyes closed and she'd hear him cross the room and close the door. She felt too ill to care what mood he was in. She only wanted her child to be healthy — boy or girl.

Joanna came in March, with the north-west winds, the scattering, sleety showers, but with the daffodils, too, and two boxing hares on the lawn as Doctor Graham had foretold. 'A peewit's pinch,' Mr Goss called the weather when he brought Helena a posy of the first daffodils and looked in the cradle to say, 'She'll do very nicely. Pretty little thing. Pretty name, too.'

'It was my mother's,' Helena said.

Mrs Goss was thrilled. She became Helena's and Joanna's nurse, feeding Helena up with spring lamb and the choicest young vegetables, apple puddings, teacakes, and gingerbread — for the sickness, she said, for occasionally Helena would feel the nausea and the smell would assail her sometimes in the mornings.

Only Gerard was not pleased. She had not given him a son. She knew he thought that. She had asked him if he liked the name Joanna, and would he like to give her a second name? His own mother's, perhaps? His face had that familiar closed look. Joanna was enough, he said. Enough for a daughter, she thought, though, of course, she didn't say anything. She was bitterly disappointed, and, for the first time really, very angry. It wasn't as if Gerard was Lord of the Manor and had inherited from his ancestors — a boy to carry on some ancient line. Who was Gerard Revell? She realised that she had no idea. And there was no one to ask — not even Lily. She remembered his words, "She won't be coming here." No one came.

It was a relief when he went to London early in May. He had business, he said, with his solicitor and the bank. Not a customer of the Yorkshire Penny Bank in the town, of course. Nothing to concern her, he said.

The warm days came as Mrs Goss had foretold. There was a heatwave in May, and it was lovely to sit out under the trees with Joanna in her perambulator. Smoke from Mr Goss's beehives drifted from the kitchen garden to mingle with the scent of lilac and apple blossom.

Helena began to feel well again and even Gerard's spirits lifted. They played croquet on the lawn and had tea. Gerard went for walks, of course, but he came back in a cheerful mood. Helena hoped that the clouds had lifted, that Joanna, a pretty and good-natured baby, was bringing out something in him that would endure. She even thought about another child — but not yet, she thought. In time — when she felt really better, and when she could trust him to accept that the next child might be a girl.

Gerard stayed with her in the evenings when by August the weather turned cold and wet. They played cards, listened to the new wireless — a programme was broadcast for half an hour on Tuesday evenings. They had the gramophone, and he read to her from some of the poems of Robert Frost, a poet he admired.

Helena read about the war poet, Wilfred Owen in the newspaper that Gerard left on the breakfast table. The reviewer had stated that "Amongst the young poets fallen in the war, Wilfred Owen must always stand as one of the bitterest losses." The reviewer had quoted the whole of the poem 'Futility', about the sun warming the body of a dead soldier and the poet asking why had the sun shone at all to make the earth when it could not wake the boy? Helena thought of Nowell Dearlove. Out there in the fields of Flanders, forgotten with all the other fallen soldiers. She had wanted to ask Gerard where Nowell was buried, but she had never dared. Nowell was a closed book between them.

She had folded the newspaper and left it for Mrs Goss to give to Gerard. She never mentioned Wilfred Owen to him, and they stuck to Robert Frost.

No second child came, even though Gerard wooed her again. He was patient when she refused him. She told him she had not quite recovered from the birth of Joanna, but deep down she was afraid that his warmth to her was solely borne out of his desire for a son.

He did not pay enough attention to his daughter, but Joanna thrived, becoming rosy and plump. The blue of her eyes deepened, and her dark hair began to curl.

On a golden afternoon in early September when they sat on the terrace, Helena pointed out to Gerard how like their daughter was to him. He wondered if they might soon have a son who would look like his sister. He took her hand, but it was all she could do not to flinch.

There were some of Arthur Dearlove's books in the revolving bookcase in the drawing room. Helena picked up a copy of Walter de la Mare's poems and Nowell's name was written inside. The date was August 1914. Nowell, still a schoolboy, had known nothing of what was to come. The poem 'The Listeners' she knew. A traveller and a promise, and no one in the moonlit empty house, but the listeners there heard his voice and the sound of the horse's hooves retreating. Ghosts. She slipped the book into her pocket.

Nowell, she thought sometimes, was closer to her than Gerard, Nowell whom she glimpsed coming out of his room, wearing a cricket sweater, tanned, and smiling to himself. Nowell before the war.

She dreamt of him often, too, but they were confused dreams in which he appeared as the stranger in the woods, though with golden hair plastered with rain, caked in mud, as though he had lain down in it, looking at her as if he wanted to tell her something, and when she turned back, as she had in reality that day, the farewell wave turned into a beckoning. When she stepped towards him, as she had not on that day, he vanished. And on waking, she felt a terrible sense of loss, emptiness, and a sickness which came with the smell of mud, decay, and something like the smell of gas.

Suddenly September changed to autumn with gales, plummeting temperatures, and rain. Gerard's mood darkened and he retreated to his study. Helena could not submit to his requests that he should come to her. She told him she was not ready. She did not tell him that she was frightened of the even worse sickness that might come with a pregnancy and that she was frightened of the smell, and still of Gerard's insistence on a son.

The summer interlude had deceived her, she thought, when he rose abruptly on a wet morning towards the end of the month and announced that he was going to London. She did not ask why, and he did not tell her. Something in the unopened letter he had stuffed into his pocket. She wondered whether there were any money troubles. She had no idea how much money Gerard had inherited from Arthur Dearlove.

In truth, she was relieved to be rid of his brooding presence. Even Joanna had not been well. She had had croup — her barking cough wrung Helena's heart. The cot was in her room so that she could sit up with her at night when the cough was worse, rubbing her back and giving her teaspoons of water. Mrs Goss boiled kettles and they held the baby over the steam rising from a bowl. Then they wrapped her up and took her outside on the terrace to breathe cool air. It seemed to help calm the cough. On the day that Gerard left for London, Joanna's temperature went down and apart from a runny nose and snuffling cough she was much better. Helena wondered about that.

The weather improved for a day or two. Mrs Goss minded Joanna while Helena went for a walk in the woods. She was drawn to the clearing, but there was no one there on this fine afternoon so she sat on the fallen tree and took out Nowell's book.

Strange, unearthly poems giving a sense that there was always something unseen, hovering close by, some other world peopled by shadows; a grave haunted by a lover; a mother reading to two children yet a third was there, unseen but listening; another invisible third silently stooping over two quiet speakers — benign presences, she thought. And in another poem, the "time worn windows" of a house called "Alas". Foulstone. Not a happy home. It had been once, she knew, remembering Mary Goss's talk of the old days when the merry boys had come. Poor Nowell. Poor boys. How many of them had been lost in the war?

She turned the pages. There were words underlined in pencil: "And thou must come/ hating thy journey, homeless, home."

This from the poem entitled 'Haunted'. Had Nowell made those marks when he was home on leave, foreseeing that he would die out there?

It was very still in the clearing as she sat quiet, thinking of Nowell, of her dreams, and of the grey figure she had seen in the woods and on the lawn. She did not know now if she had imagined it all, her nerves strung tight as wires, her loneliness, her unhappiness, her fear. Was it that she conjured Nowell out of her own head because she missed him? How could you miss someone you had never known?

He was there in the laughter she imagined in the dark corridor, in the glimpses of a tanned face and golden hair, in Mrs Goss's words, in his poetry book. She felt she knew him. The true heir of Foulstone Manor who should be sitting in the sunlit parlour with his father. In Gerard's poem, also, "the truest and the best". Gerard missed him, too. Perhaps, that was it. No one could replace Nowell, not even Gerard's wife and child.

Helena felt helpless. She understood loss and grief, but she had believed that, though changed, one had a duty to life. Her father had said so. He had not shut his daughter out because his beloved wife was dead; indeed, he had taken more care of her than ever before. They had grieved together, but he had wanted his daughter to live her life. Her mother would have wanted that, and it was his duty to see that she did.

There was nothing to be done, but to endure, and to hope that in time Gerard would find a way out of the grief that locked him away and look up one day to find a loving wife and daughter waiting for him. Not that she knew if she loved him at all. Perhaps it was her duty to school her heart into acceptance of what she had chosen. For Joanna's sake. Lovely little Joanna. There was joy in her laughter and her funny, endearing nonsense songs.

She heard a blackbird singing. Nowell whistling through the woods, his hair wet from his swim. Devoted to his father, loved by his friends. Nowell had been Gerard's friend. It was up to her to find that quality in her husband that Nowell Dearlove had so admired, and to try to love him again. To make Foulstone the happy house it had once been with laughter in the corridors and all the rooms unlocked to let in a cleansing wind from the high fells.

The blackbird stopped singing and in the quiet, she heard the bubbling river and the wind in the trees. She lifted her face to the sun and closed her eyes. Did someone touch her or was it a leaf falling on her coat? She didn't move, but she felt Nowell there.

16

1923

Gerard had become acquainted with Sir Anthony Gresham, a local landowner and magistrate whose large house was on the outskirts of Rawthdale. They had met first on the train from London and then by chance in the bookshop in town. Sir Anthony invited them for dinner, and they had met other neighbours of note — people who lived in large houses in the Lune Valley, people who hunted and went to Scotland for the grouse shooting in August, to London to watch cricket and go to the opera and ballet. Helena was glad to see Gerard enjoying himself.

Naturally, he had cachet as a decorated soldier and as a poet. War poetry was very much in vogue among the younger people to whom Helena talked, though the older generation still clung to the idea of a glorious victory. Still, they obviously approved of Gerard's MC, and even if they preferred the new Tarzan adventure, they didn't seem to mind his being a poet. And he was a gentleman. His wife a lady, too. Helena heard that comment from Lady Gresham and smiled to herself. They seemed to believe that Gerard was a cousin of the Dearlove family, come into his inheritance when Nowell was killed. Gerard would like that. Not that it mattered to her. It would be local gossip. Mrs Goss had told her how people talked. She even heard Gerard talking to someone about finding a new publisher for his new collection. Perhaps it was true, she thought. Perhaps Gerard was leaving his sorrow behind him.

They had been to a Christmas party at a house called Thornstead. There was a superb dinner and dancing and at midnight they drove home. Helena thought later that it had been one of the happiest nights of their marriage. 'Good sorts,' Gerard said. 'It's nice to get out and about. We should have done this before.' It was not the life she thought she had chosen, but if Gerard enjoyed himself then she was willing to play her part.

He took up hunting with the Lunesdale hunt. The season lasted from October to late April, and he was out all day on a Saturday and often stayed the night at Thornstead or at the house of the Master of the Hunt, who held the lordship of the manor of Rawthdale and lived in a grand house near the village of Melling. There were point to point races near Kirkby Lonsdale and shooting parties for pheasant and partridge.

The outdoor life suited Gerard — the owner of Foulstone Manor was relishing his role as a country gentleman. There was no more talk of going to London to see his banker, though he went to London occasionally to buy his tailored hunting coats, shooting jackets and plus fours from Lock and Company, boots from John Lobb, and shotguns from William Evans in St. James's Street.

Helena began to feel quite dowdy next to her splendid husband. Lily would have fitted into this new life with more aplomb, she thought, not that she ever mentioned her to Gerard.

They were invited to the Hunt Ball and Gerard insisted that she send for a new frock, though Mrs Goss had offered to make one. Gerard did not snap Mary's head off; he only pointed out that he wished to give his wife a treat. Helena had no wish to go to London and be scrutinized by a court dressmaker in Mayfair. Nor did she wish to leave Joanna, even for a few days. In the end she went to Musgrove's in Kendal to choose the style and fabric and to be measured. The seamstress showed her a Worth's pattern and said she would be able to copy it. The colour would be ideal for madam's fair hair.

When it came, the dress fitted perfectly, dark blue shot silk — she still liked her navy blue — and very striking with long dark blue silk gloves and her pearls, navy kid shoes and the sheerest of silk stockings and her mother's silk chiffon scarf with its fall of stars. She wore that without the piercing ache of loss. Mrs Goss put up her hair and pronounced her a picture, and Gerard's eyes had gleamed appreciatively. 'My word,' he said, 'won't the Greshams admire you?'

And they did. It was wonderful; Helena felt as Lily might have felt. It was the music and the dancing, and the feeling of freedom from the shadows of Foulstone. She felt for one night that she belonged in her own right. She could be the confident and elegant Mrs Helena Revell on the arm of her handsome husband. She danced with Sir Anthony and the Hunt Master and with various young men to whom she could lift her blonde head and smile, even laugh with the bashful young man who trod on her toes. She caught sight of Gerard dancing with various partners who gazed at him admiringly. The supper was marvellous, fresh salmon, chicken in aspic, caviar and ices, and the champagne intoxicating.

A beautiful dawn streaked the sky with pink and copper when they arrived home to the perfectly quiet house. They stood looking up at the brilliant sky. Gerard held her hand, but they did not speak as they went in and tiptoed upstairs like two secret lovers.

She had no choice, and when she woke alone in her bed, her beautiful dress was on the floor with her slip and one shoe and the torn chiffon scarf — there were sequins scattered on the carpet. Fallen stars, she thought, the tears springing to her eyes, and her gloves were by the door. She must tidy up before Mrs Goss came with the tea.

When she bent down to pick up her things, the smell was in her mouth and the taste of metal on her lips.

It was as Helena had feared; she felt ill throughout the first months of her pregnancy. Doctor Graham came. It was the same story. She must rest and take her ginger tea and as much of Mrs Goss's chicken soup as she could manage. The sickness would pass, Doctor Graham said, and when it did, she must take gentle exercise — just a walk in the woods.

It did pass. By the end of August, she was able to take the toddling Joanna down to the bridge to look at the water and to throw sticks and wait on the other side for them to float under the bridge.

On a hot day, Helena walked on her own down to the riverbank where she sat on a rock with her swollen feet in the cool water and watched a fisherman on the opposite bank. She thought about the child that was coming. Joanna was such a lovely, easy child, but Gerard still wanted a son to inherit Foulstone Manor. Why couldn't Joanna inherit, she thought, why not a daughter? She had inherited her father's money and she would have lived in the old house had she not married. Did she wish she had not? Then she would not have had Joanna. Too silly to keep going round in circles.

Perhaps, the child would be a boy, and all would be well. She would have two wonderful children to love and to nurture. To watch them grow. That was a future worth having. And there would be no war to take her son away. He would be a golden child, even though he was conceived in… She had schooled herself not to think about that morning when they had come home from the ball. They had both had too much to drink. The memory of it frightened her. The violence of it. The ache of it which she felt now, the echo of what he had done. What he had done to her.

She shivered, feeling the sun on her head and the beginnings of a headache. She should go back. It was foolish to have come alone.

She was aware of the smell of cigarette smoke. As she bent down to slip on her canvas shoes, she glanced under the bridge where in the shadow of the arch, she could see a motionless figure in a long dark coat like the figure from her dreams. Then she saw a hand stretch out to toss something in the water and a plume of smoke breathed out. Something about the stillness of the figure disturbed her. But she knew it wasn't Nowell. She was not afraid of Nowell. She loved Nowell. This person was real — she'd seen the smoke.

She stood up, dizzy with the heat and the effort. Sick with the taste of rot on her tongue. The taste of death.

The figure was gone.

The baby came too soon. He would have been a son. Not that Helena felt any more anguish than if it had been a daughter. She stayed in the nursing home in Grange-over-Sands for two weeks. She was to have rest and plenty of sea air in her lungs.

They were kind to her, but of course, a miscarriage was not uncommon. She must not grieve too much. There would be more children. She was young and healthy. Nature made mistakes, but time would put them right.

It was all true, as was the implied suggestion that she should pull herself together. Her husband needed her, the sister advised her — the sister, kindly, of course, but not married. She spoke wistfully of a wife's place at her husband's side.

Helena wondered if, like so many women, she had lost her fiancé in the war. Her husband must be a very busy man, sister said.

Too busy, Helena thought, to come to see her. But that was not it. She remembered his face when after her luncheon at which she just picked, she had risen from the table and had almost fallen, and the blood had gushed onto the carpet.

Mrs Goss had remarked on her pallor when she had come back from the riverside. 'You shouldn't have been out in all that sun. You should have a lie down.'

Gerard had heard that. Helena said she was perfectly fine, though she wasn't. She had a headache, felt sick, and that smell of something rotten was still in her nose and throat. She should have gone to lie down, but she did not want to admit she had been foolish. And she had — she had sat too long dreaming, and that figure under the arch — she could hardly tell him that another stranger had frightened her. Just because the man was there and had stood so still. Had not even looked her way. He had done nothing. It was her fault that she had made a bad situation worse.

Mrs Goss had put her to bed and Mr Goss had gone for Doctor Graham. But it was too late. When it was over, and she had been given a mild sedative, and they were waiting for the car, she had said, in her drowsy state, 'Poor Nowell.' She had meant her lost son. Not that she had mentioned the choice of name to Gerard.

His face had turned to stone. 'Nowell is nothing to do with you.'

Mr and Mrs Goss had come in then to help her downstairs and to take her to the nursing home. Gerard was to stay behind — for Joanna's sake, of course.

That had been the end, that moment when he had said the words about Nowell. There would be no son named Nowell. Helena returned from the nursing home, more than ever an exile at Foulstone Manor. When she thought of her parents, she felt crippled by loss.

This aching loneliness. How was she to bear it? Homeless, home. Nowell did not return to the woods or to the corridor. There was no glimpse of a golden head or the sound of whistling and laughter.

The winter was long and hard. November was the coldest that Mrs Goss could remember. There was ice inside the windows, the taps froze, the ground was hard as iron and then in early December came the rain, the smoking fires, the damp wood, and the house damp, too, the kitchen floor forever muddy, and Mrs Goss wearing her clogs, clattering about the kitchen, the cellar door swollen so that it was impossible to open. There seemed to be a permanent smell of something rotten down there which puzzled Mr Goss.

Gerard went down himself — there was nothing to see. Yes, a bit of damp by the old sink and round the window frame, but otherwise perfectly dry. He thought that water was coming up under the floor and instructed Mr Goss to take up the stone flags by the cellar door and re-align them and put fresh mortar down. Gerard would see to the damp in the cellar — Goss had enough to do. In any case, the stairs were a bit rickety for Goss to manage. William Goss didn't say anything to that. He just got on with lifting the heavy flags.

On the dry days in the later part of December, Gerard continued as before — hunting and shooting, staying away as often as he could. No doubt the story was that his wife was still convalescing or was too delicate to be seen at parties. There was only Joanna to keep Helena company and to take on her toddling walks, but she was happy with her daughter and content enough with Gerard's presence when he occasionally sat with her of an evening to listen to music or read. Reading was easier than talking and talking was easier when they discussed what they had read. Like guests in an unfamiliar house where the hosts had deserted them.

She thought she might like a bicycle. It was too hilly around here for one, of course. Oh, but the freedom. There was the car, the 1914 Wolseley, as she now knew it to be. Mr Goss had sometimes taken her out in it when Gerard was away, but she never felt at ease in case Gerard asked what she had been doing. Not that he often did. She didn't want to get Mr Goss into trouble. And when Mr Goss offered to teach her to drive, she knew it was out of the question. There was no point in suggesting it to Gerard.

Instead, she took her solitary walks to the woods, hoping for comfort, for some sign that Nowell had not deserted her, but he was not there. Gerard had repossessed him. And at Foulstone Manor, despite the beauty of the snow at Christmas and the joyful face of Joanna opening her presents, Helena could not feel at home. Nowell was gone, and kind Mr Dearlove of whom Mrs Goss still spoke so fondly. Something about Gerard cast a blight on the house, though neither she nor Mrs Goss spoke of it.

17

1924

When Helena returned to Foulstone from a solitary walk in the spring, Mrs Goss told her that they had a visitor — a lady from London. Lily, thought Helena, Lily who had written to say she was back in London. Lily come to forgive her for not answering, to bring champagne and laughter. And, praise be, Gerard wasn't here.

But it wasn't Lily. Helena's heart sank. The woman on the sofa was as unlike her brightly polished Lily as it was possible to be. Not a lady but a thin, nervous looking woman with a gaunt face under a shapeless black hat, the dark smudges under eyes suggesting exhaustion and the sheen of her skin suggesting that she was under-nourished. You saw women like that in the war, Helena thought, poor people who hadn't enough to eat. She wasn't old, just worn-looking in her shabby black coat with its rubbed velvet at the collar and cuffs. She wore thick lisle stockings and ugly brown lace-up shoes. She stood when Helena came in and a pair of thick woollen gloves fell to the floor.

Helena darted across the room to pick them up and begged the woman to sit down by the fire. Mrs Goss was sent to bring the tea which Helena knew would have been ready for her.

'I'm Mrs Bate, ma'am,' the woman began, 'I'm sorry to disturb you but I didn't know what else to do. It's the letter, see, what I found — I found out an' I thought — there was an address in some papers —'

Mrs Goss came in with the tea, sandwiches, and cake which she put on a small table, giving Helena an inquiring look as she turned. Helena gave a slight shake of her head — the message was that she didn't know the woman.

'Take something first, Mrs Bate, please, and then you can tell us what we can do for you.'

Helena motioned Mrs Goss to sit. Her practical good sense and kind heart would be very useful. She could not think what the garbled introduction meant, but they would have to wait. She made sure that Mrs Goss ate something as well, for Mrs Bate, who, though she looked hungrily at the table, seemed too nervous to eat. Mrs Goss persuaded her to take something.

'Get something inside you, my dear. It'll make it easier to tell your tale when you've warmed up a bit. It's good ham, from up the farm, and that bread's mine. Made this morning.'

Mrs Bate obeyed but kept her head down. They could hear the spoon tremble against her cup and the clink of the cup in the saucer. She put down her cup and saucer. There were crumbs on the black coat which she tried to brush off with the folded napkin she had forgotten to use.

'Now, Mrs Bate,' Helena said, feeling very sorry for her, 'do tell us how we can help you.'

The story came out — a rather muddled tale, told in a backwards and forwards way, but they managed to piece it together. Mrs Bate came from London — from Battersea. Her husband had left home at the end of August in 1923 and had not been heard of since, though she had been to the police who had investigated at the railway station at Oxenholme. Mrs Bate had been to the police in London, but Samuel — that was Mr Bate — had told her he was going to Kendal and the police found out that he'd asked a porter if it was possible to get a lift to a place called Rawthdale. The porter said it was a long way.

He didn't know how long it would take but Samuel thanked the porter, and went off. Samuel had said he knew a man in Kendal what would give him work. He hadn't mentioned Rawthdale.

Mrs Bate thought he'd run off — he'd done that plenty of times before. But after a few weeks she'd gone to the police and when he wasn't found she thought he'd gone for good. She just had to accept it. But then — she was moving her lodgings — cheaper ones — and didn't know what to do with his stuff. She found an address in his papers and she looked on the map. There was the bit of a letter what started with the words "dear" and "love" — a woman, she'd thought. He'd gone off with his fancy woman. She offered Helena the scrap of paper.

Samuel Bate had not used capital letters, and there was a little space between the two words. Helena saw how the mistake had been made. 'No, Mrs Bate, he must have meant Mr Dearlove, who once owned this house. Was your husband in the war? He might have known Mr Dearlove's son, Nowell, who was killed in 1918.'

'He never said that name, but he never said nothin' about the war, 'cept it was hell on earth, but he wasn't the same man when he came back. I couldn't manage him — he'd get into such rages. No job, you see. It wasn't fair, he said, some folk had all the luck — folk what didn't deserve it —' She twisted the napkin in her hands — 'He was that bitter. He'd not speak to me for days.'

'I understand, Mrs Bate, my husband is like that sometimes. It is the effect of the war. My husband is Mr Gerard Revell. Did Mr Bate ever mention him?'

'No. Mebbe he wanted to see Mr Dearlove — thought he'd give him some money — if he knew Nowell Dearlove. See,

Samuel allus said he was owed — the war had done him in. He mighta asked for somethin'.'

'Mr Dearlove is dead, and my husband isn't here, I'm afraid, so I don't know if your husband ever came.'

'He'd go off all the time for days at a time. I couldn't deal with it. He was angry cos we had nothin'. But the last time I'd had enough of his ways. There was a row. I thought it was a fancy woman. See, sometimes he had money — said he'd been labourin' an' it wasn't fit for a dog an' a man what'd fought for his country deserved a drink, an' I said what kind of coward would hit his wife —'

'He hit you?'

'An' more than once, I'd had enough an' he'd to tell me where he was goin' this time. That's when he said Kendal an' I told him he needn't come back an' he didn't. He took every bit o' money we had and that wasn't much — I couldn't even pay my rent. Had to borrow from a neighbour. I think I knew when I saw it'd all gone. I don't know why I came. I suppose I wanted to know about the woman an' if he was livin' prosperous an' me in the fish shop an' not a decent rag to my name. But now, I don't know. It don't seem to matter anymore. What's the use of knowin'?'

She looked such a terribly lost and bewildered creature. Helena thought of the man in the woods and the one under the bridge last autumn before... Could it be? But then would it help to tell her? And it was months ago. Samuel Bate could have moved on. Mrs Bate would be no better off. Still, she asked, 'Your husband — what was he wearing? Mrs Goss could ask in the town if anyone remembers.'

'I was at work — at the shop. It's a fish shop so I start early an' I just left him. His grey suit was gone and his raincoat — a dark one. Just what any working man would wear.'

Helena did not know. The man in the woods was so confused in her mind with her dreams, with Nowell, with the man on the lawn in his cape and scarf, the man under the bridge. She might have dreamed him in the heat. He had simply vanished. It was better not to say.

'I don't remember anyone coming, Mrs Bate,' Mrs Goss said. 'We don't have many visitors. I'm sure I'd have remembered. I'll go and ask my husband. He works in the garden here.'

'I suppose your husband was an officer,' Mrs Bate said when Mrs Goss had gone. 'Only, you havin' servants an' that.'

'A captain, yes.'

'Did he get a medal?'

'Yes, the Military Cross.'

'Brave, then.'

'They were all brave, I think, the officers and their men.'

'Samuel said most of the officers was all right, but some was hopeless, cowards, he said. It wasn't fair — they got all the glory for doin' nothin' cos they was toffs. An' he was owed. Not fair, he was always sayin' that. But life ain't fair, is it?'

'No, I don't think it is. Was Mr Bate wounded?'

'In the head, I think, more than anythin' else. He never wanted to go. Conscripted in 1916 an' then he deserted.'

'What happened to him?'

'Prison. He served half his time. Got let out cos he said he'd go back. He was knocked out in 1918 — blown up, but they sent him back, though it was near the end by then. Suppose they didn't know that. They said his wound wasn't serious. An' it wasn't I don't think — on the outside anyway, but who knows what was goin' on inside? Needed all the men they could get, though Samuel said he wasn't fit.'

Mrs Goss came back to tell them that William did not remember any strangers calling at the house back in the summer, but they would both ask about.

Mrs Bate wrote down her address and Helena said that Mr Goss would drive her back to the railway station. She gave her ten shillings. It was all she could do.

'A poor-looking creature,' Mrs Goss said, as she stacked the tea tray. 'Makes you wonder what happened to him. Probably changed his mind and just took another train to anywhere — it didn't sound like they got on very well. She's probably better without him. I did wonder, though…'

'What?'

'William said there was a man hanging about. I remember last summer when you — you know — William asked James Gibson up at the farm who told him they'd had someone stayin', but he'd moved on.'

'Did he mention him to Gerard?'

'That I don't know. Might have done — just a warning, you know, about a tramp about.'

'Did he look like a tramp?'

'Shabby looking, William said, nothin' to remark on. William never saw him again. That was when you was in the nursing home, I think, or before, maybe. It was all such a bustle when you went. I can't rightly remember. Then me and William took Joanna up to the farm — you know, my brother's farm up at Highdale. We stayed for a weekend because Mr Revell said he would be stayin' at Sir Anthony's.'

'I don't remember. You took Joanna away?'

'Yes, good as gold she was an' me an' William was glad to get out of the house for a day or two. Mr Revell was that — well, never mind all that. An' you wouldn't remember — you wasn't so good at the time. Anyway, whoever that man was, he didn't come to the house. We told Mrs Bate the truth.'

'I hope —'

'What?'

Helena took a deep breath. 'I hope Gerard is not at the station, coming back from London.'

'I'll not say anything. Least said, soonest mended. We don't have to tell him about her.'

Mrs Goss took the tray away. Helena sat and looked at the fire. She could not say why she would not tell Gerard about Mrs Bate — the war, perhaps. Mrs Goss knew, though. It was as if they were both hiding something.

Gerard came in, and Helena could tell by his face that he knew. She could tell, too, that he was displeased. Mrs Goss was looking anxious as she came in behind him.

'Giving tea to a perfect stranger — came here for money, no doubt. Some old-soldier story. I suppose her husband put her up to it.'

'She said that he was missing and that —' Helena began.

'She had come here to see Arthur Dearlove. Trading on his son's death, I'll bet. Some story about her husband knowing him in the war. And you two fell for it. How much did you give her?'

His sneering tone prompted a flash of defiance from Helena. 'Ten shillings. I thought her story was true. If you had been here —'

'I saw enough at the station. I saw what she was. You know nothing about the kind of men I had to deal with. You think they were all heroes. They were not. Some were crooks and cowards, as they were before the war, and, no doubt, still are, like that wretched woman's husband.'

He went out of the room, and they heard him go upstairs and unlock his door.

When they heard it close, Mrs Goss said stoutly, 'I believed her.'

'So did I.'

Helena crept up to her sewing room. She had no wish to meet Gerard again. She took up a little dress of Joanna's that needed repair. But instead of taking up her needle, she stared out of the window.

Mrs Bate had called her husband a coward. He had probably been a crook — he got money from somewhere. And he had been a deserter. Gerard had used the words "crook" and "coward" — he sounded as if he hated the man, as if he had known him.

An image flashed into her head — of Gerard and a shabby man in the park, walking away with his head down. Right at the beginning when he had said he had given the ex-soldier something. She had loved him for that. Suppose it was all a lie and Gerard had sent the man away because he'd known he was a coward and a crook. Had known him?

They heard no more of Mrs Bate. Helena tucked the address in the back pocket of her diary. She did not know why, except that she still believed Gerard had been wrong about her. Perhaps she had taken up her new lodgings, thrown away Samuel Bate's papers and belongings, and accepted the idea that she would never see him again, or maybe he had returned home, and they had reached some sort of compromise, and were living together in the best way they could.

As she and Gerard did. He had apologised for his harshness — so unlike him. It was just the idea of some crooked ex-soldier exploiting some invented relationship with a man who was dead, a man who had been a hero in the war, and who had given his life for such as Mrs Bate — surely, she saw what kind of woman she was?

Helena did not, though she did not say so, but she noted that Gerard did not mention Nowell by name. That was clearly still forbidden territory, but she said that she accepted that he had been upset. What else could she do? Her heart shrank from him, though he took her hand and kissed her.

By the summer, it was clear that Gerard wished to get rid of Mr and Mrs Goss. He didn't use those words, though. He suggested they needed a nursemaid for Joanna and the new baby now that Helena was pregnant again.

Mrs Goss was too old to look after two children, he said. In any case they needed a more educated young woman. A local woman with a local accent was hardly the proper person as a companion for Joanna who was talking now at two years old. Helena would not be able to take care of Joanna. She must rest — after the last time. Her foolish walking alone had brought about that catastrophe. Gerard had no desire for another premature child. As if Helena had.

As for Mr Goss — it was time to hire a younger man for the gardens and the odd jobs. A younger man would not need to live in. And a good cook could be hired. A cottage could be found for her. The empty cottage at the mill would be eminently suitable. A char woman could come in for the heavy work and the laundry could be collected. The nursemaid would live in. It was time that a nursery was set up. Joanna could not sleep in her mother's room indefinitely. Helena needed to be quiet and to rest. There were three good rooms on the top floor, room for two children and a nursemaid. A schoolroom, too, when the time came. The rooms used by Mr and Mrs

Goss could be converted to a schoolroom and other bedrooms when the time came.

He had thought it all out, Helena thought, every detail. But why? What he had said about Mr and Mrs Goss was just false. Mrs Goss was in her forties and never a day's illness. Mr Goss was a little older, but a strong and wiry Dalesman. And all the big houses employed local people — the Greshams included. She could only think that it was because they had worked for the Dearloves. The land-owning neighbours thought he was a cousin — the rightful heir to Foulstone Manor. He wanted to forget the Dearloves, too — even Nowell, she thought, even Nowell, 'the truest and the best', whose name was never uttered. Nowell who was exiled, too, whose golden head she never glimpsed now, and whose laughter was stilled.

Yet, the smell of metal was still on her lips when she woke, and the taste of death was still on her tongue. That's how she thought of it now — death in her mouth like the time at the bridge. She was filled with a nameless dread. And she dreamed of the man in the woods with mud up to his knees, and the man on the lawn with his bandaged head and dark cape. Nowell, longing to come home? And who was that other who haunted her dreams, that silent, inimical figure by the bridge who had brought death with him?

And what, she thought, was her role to be when the nursemaid arrived? Was she to be separated from her children, to see them, perhaps once or twice a day? A prisoner in her bedroom for the rest of her pregnancy, and a prisoner thereafter, for if a son came, she would be of no use to Gerard again.

It was fear she felt, but it was anger that made her fight back, and the thought of losing dear Mrs Goss whose silent understanding gave her comfort, and who loved Joanna. And

Mr Goss, stolid, taciturn, but with so kind a look in his eyes when he took Joanna round the garden and when he looked at her. She could not bear to be without them. She told Gerard that she would pay the wages of Mr and Mrs Goss. She reminded him that she had her father's money. She wanted to keep them. They were devoted to Joanna. Joanna to be exiled to the upper rooms in the keeping of a stranger who would not care about her? No, she said. She nearly said, "Over my dead body". But fear stilled her tongue. She only repeated, "No." She could not, would not manage without Mrs Goss.

Gerard's face took on that familiar closed look. He was a stranger to her. He left her bedroom, but he did not say anything more about the Gosses.

The nursery was set up; Helena went up to see it. It was not what she would have chosen. It looked like a nursery from a Victorian novel with a little iron bedstead with bars at the side — like an orphan's bed. Helena shivered when she thought that. Little, chuckling Joanna orphaned up here in the care of a stranger. The floor was painted white with a rag rug in front of the fireplace with its big brass guard — even the fire was to be jailed in. And there was a cradle ready for the baby, an intricately carved dark oak contraption which looked as though it ought to be in a museum. She thought of the white one which had been ordered for Joanna and which was still in her bedroom. Not suitable for the heir, presumably.

However, Joanna had to sleep in the new nursery, but Mrs Goss promised to sleep in the room prepared for the new nursemaid when she came, and she would keep that connecting door open and there'd be a nightlight. Helena was not to fret — Mrs Goss would keep Joanna safe and cosy.

Doctor Graham did not come. A doctor from Manchester came and a nurse who was to stay until the baby came. The nurse ruled Helena's bedroom which was now officially a sick room for the Manchester doctor had decreed complete bed rest and quiet.

'You must be tranquil, dear lady, at all times. Nothing must upset your nerves.'

Nerves, Helena thought, who had talked of nerves?

At least Mrs Goss had charge of Joanna. The nurse was pleasant enough — her role was simply to make sure that Helena rested, yet she always had the feeling that she was being watched and assessed, and that reports were being made to the master. Sometimes Mrs Goss came in for an hour or so when the nurse was off duty and Mr Goss could look after Joanna. Sometimes she would sneak Joanna in to sit on the bed and be caressed. She was very good and quiet and seemed to sense that Helena needed to be treated gently.

When Mrs Goss came alone, Helena was soothed by her presence. She liked to listen to the soft country voice telling her about Highdale and the farm where she grew up, the long winters, looking for the black-faced sheep in the snowdrifts; and the famous Swaledale sheep that were worth thousands, and which were hefted on the fells; her brother on a sledge in the snow; the hams and flitches hanging from iron hooks, the sheep's head broth that lasted for days, black peat for the fires; and the tea parties at the Methodist Church.

'Where I met William — stockman on a farm he was, an' me in service up Hawes way. Mr Dearlove knew them folks, an' when they was givin' up the house, Mr Dearlove he offered me a job. We snatched at it. We'd only a little cottage. Not much of a place, and we was very glad to come here and work for Mr Dearlove.'

'A kind man.'

'That he was. A good man. Never treated you as a servant, always thanked us for what we did. It's a queer thing, Mrs Revell, in the olden days, centuries back I'm talkin', they'd say in my family that an ancestor of ours lived at Foulstone. He'd have been a tenant, I suppose, but he lived here. There was a Lund that owned the house, and we had cousins Lund in Hawes.'

And then she would be off again about Miles Lund, the grocer in Hawes, his wife, Jennet whose name was a very old one, their daughters, Ann and Agnes, and the farm called Fee Fow up on the fells, and how the children thought a giant lived there. Sometimes Helena fell asleep, but Mrs Goss never left her to wake up alone. It was only when she woke to the sound of the door opening and the starched busyness of the nurse coming in that Mrs Goss stood up. She was always carefully polite with the nurse, adopting the role of servant to a superior being, asking the nurse if she had rested, if she would care for tea, or fancy a nice bit of Yorkshire ham for her supper.

Of Gerard, Helena saw very little. He came in when the nurse was there, always kindly asking if she were rested and if she had eaten — as if he were a visitor to a hospital ward, a visitor for some distant relative. Was she tranquil in her mind? he asked very often. The nurse would answer for her, saying that Mrs Revell had slept well or had been restless in the night, but that nurse was keeping her quiet.

Helena had to dissemble, to smile at Gerard and the nurse, to keep her hands under the counterpane so that they should not see them tremble because of the rage she felt. She trusted neither of them. This constant asking if she were calm, if she had had a quiet night, and the exchange of looks between them as if there were a message within a message that she was not supposed to understand.

She dared not mention the smell to the nurse. Morning sickness, the nurse diagnosed — as if Mrs Goss couldn't have dealt with that. But it was worse than that, she knew. She dared not mention her dreams, either; the man in the woods, the man on the lawn, the man under the bridge, Mrs Bate's husband, all haunted her dreams. She could say nothing of that for the nurse would be sure to tell Gerard.

One night, Helena woke screaming. Her dream had been of the man under the bridge who was dead there by the bridge, his bandage soaked in blood, blood on his hands, blood in the river which turned crimson as she looked. Had she killed him because he had killed her baby son?

The nurse who slept in the adjoining dressing room came to soothe her — she was given something to calm her down. The nurse sat by her bed. Helena thought she was writing things down, but Helena did not know if she were speaking aloud. Had she cried out the name of Mr Bate in her dream? Was the nurse writing it down for Gerard?

When she woke in the late morning, she asked for Mrs Goss. The nurse hesitated, but when Helena said she would fetch Mrs Goss herself and made to get out of bed, she went to get her.

'And stay upstairs with my daughter until I send for you.'

The nurse scuttled out. Scared by her tone, Helena thought. For once she had got the upper hand, and she was going to keep it. Gerard would find a very different wife when she asked to see him — Mrs Goss could go and get him, not the spy. It was time to assert herself. The nurse must go.

'Where is my husband?' she asked when Mrs Goss came.

Mrs Goss looked uneasy. 'I don't know, my dear. He went off this morning with William to the station — he didn't say when he'd be back. I asked if you was all right. He said I was to mind my own business —'

'What's worrying you, Mary. I can see there's something. Tell me. I've had enough of obeying orders, and that nurse's so-called sedatives. Keep calm, she says. Well, I won't.'

'Oh, Mrs Revell, don't take on. I'll tell you. It's that nurse. She went in to see the master at breakfast. Said she was worried about you — you'd had nightmares, been screaming about Mr Bate an' then when she gave you the sedative you was sayin' Bate was dead an' goin' on about the smell.'

'What did he say?'

'That the specialist would have to come. You'd have to go away if you was not — if — you was unfit —'

'Unfit for what?'

'To look after — Joanna and the baby.'

'Lock that door, Mary. I don't want her coming in. I'm sure that she reports everything to Gerard, everything I say — he wants to prove I'm mad, to take the children away from me —'

'But he can't — the baby's not born yet.'

'He can afterwards. He can bring that doctor and the nurse will swear that I am not in my right mind.'

'He can't. Me an' William will tell the truth. If anyone knows you, it's me. I'll tell that doctor.'

'Mary, think about it. A doctor, a nurse, Mr Gerard Revell of Foulstone Manor.'

Mrs Goss's mouth tightened. 'You mean servants. Just servants — with no education. Country folk that don't know anythin', compared with a fancy nurse from Manchester. Just servants an' he who don't belong here. Why, me an' William belong at Foulstone more than him.'

'I don't belong here either, Mary. I never have.'

'Mr Dearlove would have thought so — Mr Dearlove would have seen that you're a lady, an' Mr Nowell he'd have — oh, the pity of it. All lost. Good people. I never minded bein' a servant. Mr Dearlove's father was here way back. They belonged, but him, he never should have —'

'It's too late, Mary, he's here and he owns it, whether we like it or not, and he wants rid of me. The nurse — my dreams — the smell. It sounds mad — I'll bet it sounded mad to her.'

'I thought you'd got past that. You've not said.'

'I haven't dared. You can't smell it. I know there's damp, but what I can smell is worse. I can't describe it — it's like death in my mouth. Rank and foul decay.' Mrs Goss just stared at her. 'I'm not mad, Mary, I beg you, don't believe them. If you desert me...'

'I won't, I won't. But, if the baby comes, surely —'

'And if it's not a boy? And, even if it is, he doesn't want me here. He wanted to get rid of you and William.'

'You never said.'

'I said I'd pay your wages and I wouldn't let you go, but if I'm not here —'

'What about Joanna?'

'Oh, he has it all worked out. There is to be a nursemaid, and a jobbing gardener, a cook to live in one of the mill cottages, and a char woman to do the heavy work. He wants rid of us all.'

'But why, what have we done?'

'I don't know.'

'He's a madman.'

'I sometimes think he is. I have to go, Mary; I have to go before he comes back. He might bring that doctor. You have to find a way to get rid of the nurse. You must send her out on some pretext — you have to — it's my only chance.'

'I will help. William will, but what about Joanna? You can't manage —'

'You'll bring her — you and William to where I am — I've worked it all out, and you must tell Joanna that I haven't —'

'Don't fret none, don't fret, I'll look after her.'

PART THREE: 1970

18

Amanda

We were frozen. I could feel the damp in my bones, and what was worse, and very disturbing, was the way in which, at certain times as we read through the diary, I could smell that rotting, acrid smell — as Helena smelt it all those years ago. I knew Joan could smell it, too, when she paused in the reading and looked at me.

I could tell Joan had had enough. Her face was drawn and white and her lips almost blue with the cold. I should have thought. What fools we had been to stand in that upstairs corridor reading by torchlight, but once we'd found the diary in the box, we had to look and one page led inexorably to another. I picked up the other papers we had found, and we made our way downstairs. I had trouble shutting the front door which I tried to close by opening it wider so that I could slam it. I dropped my torch which went with such a clatter that we both jumped. I went back over the threshold to retrieve it. As I looked across the hall, I thought I saw something move in the corridor where the plaster had fallen — just a shadow, an impression of a figure. It was a second or two only. Then it was gone. A trick of the light — that changing light, a cloud shifting across the window.

I didn't say anything to Joan. I could tell she was not ready to speak of what we had discovered. That had been gruelling enough without my sharing that sudden moment of terror.

I lit the fire and made Joan sit by it before I went to make tea and scrambled eggs and toast. We needed something simple, homely — and hot.

When we had finished, I poured two sherries and sat down opposite her by the fire. She looked better, but I busied myself with logs until she was ready to talk.

'What happened to the rest?' she asked. 'Who tore the pages out? Him?'

We'd noticed that the diary ended with Mary Goss's promise, and there were pages missing. 'Mary Goss, I should think. She'd want to hide Helena's whereabouts if the missing pages told more about Helena's plans. Maybe in the rush of her going, Helena left her diary behind.'

'But why didn't Mary destroy it?'

'Perhaps she thought it would be a good thing if he read it. He'd know what he had done. But I'll bet he never went into Helena's room.'

'But where did Helena go?'

'She mentioned a friend — Lily Mountjoy-Smythe. Lily might still be alive. And remember, she had a younger brother. Mountjoy-Smythe is not a common name. Perhaps we could find him. He might be in London.'

'Or in Australia, or dead, or —'

'It's worth a try, surely.'

'You mean go to London?'

It might have been the moon the way Joan said it. I thought for a moment. 'We could stay with my parents. I want to know what happened to Helena. You were right, Gerard Revell was a cruel man.'

'Oh, I don't know, Amanda. I can't think about such a step now, it's so — I need to think. I'd better go. We'll decide tomorrow.'

At the door I stopped her with my hand on her arm. 'She loved you, Auntie Joan, that was clear in her diary.'

'I am not that little girl anymore. It's too late.'

She went out into the dark. I thought of Helena Revell and the terrible story we had read. She seemed such a tragic figure, so alone and frightened. And I thought of little Joanna, full of laughter, and of Joan now, and her lonely life. It should have been different.

19

Joan

I didn't sleep at all. I sat in that back bedroom and stared out at Foulstone, its black chimneys starkly outlined under the extraordinary moonlight. We sometimes get that, a night on which the moon is so bright that it might be day. You could walk about any of the dark lanes, and you'd see your way as if you had a torch in your hands. And the stars, great showers of them spilling down the sky. I remembered Joanna's scarf — Joanna, my grandmother. She sounded like a loving mother. Helena had compared the sky to that sequined scarf — not that I had much experience of chiffon anything, except in shop windows, not that I looked in that kind of window very much. I don't know anything about the stars, but Helena noticed them and had felt that awful loneliness. I never looked up. Never up, always down. Never forward. Never back.

But I had to look back now — that was hard enough, but forward was even harder, I thought again, looking at the dark trees as if it was there that I had to go, and risk being lost in a maze of narrow paths leading to where I didn't know.

Well, I knew something. Gerard Revell was a monster. The way he had treated her. Those private details — I could hardly bear to think of those. He was a cruel man — no war excused that. And he had wanted to get rid of Helena, my mother, to prove that she was mad.

But why? I hadn't wanted to talk anymore to Amanda. There was too much to take in. It was kind of her, that last remark. My mother had loved little Joanna and it did mean something, but that little, laughing Joanna was not me. She had been lost along the way. I'd seen the tears in Amanda's eyes when we read about Helena. I was frightened of it all — frightened of all these rushing feelings. I didn't want to find out that Helena was the mad one. That he had driven her mad.

Of course, I understood that sick, empty feeling she had written about. I'd felt it often enough. Loneliness and fear. I knew about them, but all those queer dreams, seeing ghosts, reading poetry in the woods all on her own, the smell of death. Yes, Amanda and I had smelt it. It was real all right, and I'd been haunted by it, but that might mean I was — well, tainted somehow.

Had Auntie Mary secretly thought Helena was mad? And protected me with her robust common sense? She had never talked about my mother. Least said and all that. Perhaps she was right. Look what all this ferreting about in the past had done. Turned me inside out so that I couldn't think straight. The woman I had glimpsed at the window and who I'd felt so sorry for. Maybe it wasn't like that. Perhaps it had been a mad woman looking at me. Maybe she had been taken away — maybe Gerard had come back with the doctor, and she'd been taken to an asylum and never been heard of again. William and Mary standing watching an ambulance taking Helena away and powerless to do anything. Mary, feeling too guilty ever to mention her again, or, like people did then, feeling the shame of it, worrying that I'd turn mad if I knew.

Maybe Helena was still there, locked up for nearly fifty years, forgotten, an old woman in her seventies. A mad old woman who remembered snatches of her former life, mumbling into her porridge about her lost daughter, Joanna, and no one believing her, no one knowing that she had been lovely Helena

Revell with pale hair and pearls and a blue chiffon scarf with sequins falling like stars.

Dear Lord, what was the matter with me? Such mad ideas. That house, the plaster falling, that rush of wind from the passage — no wonder. It was enough to drive anyone — get a grip, I told myself, shifting in my chair, aware suddenly of how cold I was. Make some hot milk, get to bed. But I was wide awake and couldn't tear myself away from the window.

Gerard Revell, though. Mary had called *him* the madman. The Mary Goss of that story would not have helped Helena escape — supposing she had for now — if she had thought Helena was mad. And William wouldn't have thought she was mad. He would not have taken a pregnant madwoman to the railway station. And he must have taken her if she had escaped. I hoped to God she had.

What did they tell Gerard Revell? Did he look for his wife, put notices in the papers, write to Lily Mountjoy-Smythe? And another thing I wanted an answer to — why was I taken away from Foulstone when I was three?

The moon was gone, yet I could see Foulstone as clearly as if I was standing by the broken fence and looking out at me through a cracked window was a face, the face I remembered blazing at me by that locked door. Then I knew I was stiff with cold and that my neck ached. I must have fallen asleep. I'd been dreaming — of course. I remembered thinking of Gerard Revell and that he was mad, and he had come into my dream — to warn me off. Rubbish, I told myself as I stood up feeling as if I was about a hundred years old. Nonsense.

It was dawn already, one of those frosty, deep red dawns that light up the fells and chase away the moon. Not quite. I could still see the fading disc in the sky, hanging on, but the sun rose higher, and light began to slip down the slopes.

I went down and made tea. The fire was still glimmering in the range, so I put on more wood and made myself a piece of toast. At eight o'clock I would go and knock on Amanda's door. I'd made my decision.

20

Amanda

In the event, I booked us into a quiet hotel in Bloomsbury. I felt a bit guilty not telling mum and dad that I was in London, but Joan didn't want to stay with my parents. I understood that. It was all so new to her, and it was private. My parents wouldn't ask questions — at least not in front of Joan, but I knew Mum would be curious and I didn't want to lie to her, either.

Bloomsbury was where Lily Mountjoy-Smythe had lived. Not that she would be Mountjoy-Smythe anymore, of course, but we didn't know the French husband's name. And that had all been half a century ago, as Joan kept reminding me.

I brought up the subject of Samuel Bate. 'Another mystery,' I said, 'I read about him in one of those old newspapers. It's strange that he disappeared, and it seems he did go to Foulstone Manor to see Mr Dearlove.'

'And Helena thought that Gerard might have known him. Someone else who vanished — like my mother.'

There was a P. Mountjoy-Smythe in the telephone book which the helpful hotel receptionist supplied. We wondered if it might be Lily's brother. Helena's diary had mentioned that he was younger than Lily and his name was Peter.

We didn't want to use the hotel telephone, so we found a telephone booth round the corner in which we stood looking at the black telephone, me holding the two pennies. It seemed such a cheek, but I had my story ready.

A rather clipped, upper-class voice answered, and I explained that I was a student of Art History researching the work of Paul Nash and his brother, John. The name Lily Mountjoy-Smythe had come up in a letter which seemed to suggest she was a neighbour who had known them quite well. Could Mr Mountjoy-Smythe tell me anything about her?

I was astonished at my ingenuity — and duplicity. So was Joan.

'Art History,' she said, 'sounds all right to me. You should write a detective story.'

It sounded all right to Mr Peter Mountjoy-Smythe, too, who told me that his sister lived in Bloomsbury still. He was sure she would be delighted to talk about her friendship with the Nash brothers. Lily liked nothing better than to talk about the old days. Peter Mountjoy-Smythe wasn't keen on the old days, but then Lily was living her Bohemian life in Bloomsbury, and he was at his ghastly boarding school in Sussex, eating gruel and freezing half to death on a rugby pitch.

I laughed in all the right places. He sounded nice. If Lily were as loquacious as her brother, she'd tell us all about Helena — except we'd have to tell her the truth about why we wanted to see her. I wrote down the address, thanked him profusely, and turned triumphantly to Joan.

'Number 12, Bedford Mansions, Adeline Place — about five minutes away. I have the phone number. Should we ring her?'

'What'll we tell her?'

'The truth, I think. I don't think we should tell her the Art History story — I mean if she does say she'll see us, it'll be awkward.'

'Right. You do it. Tell her Joanna Revell wants to see her.' Joan saw my astonished expression. 'Well, it's true.'

There was a silence at the other end of the line when I told the voice what I wanted. Another rather upper-class voice had announced itself as Lilian Mountjoy-Smythe. No French husband anymore then, I thought.

The voice came again. 'Do you mean Joanna Revell, the daughter of Helena Revell?'

'I do.'

'And you are she?'

'No, she is my godmother. She is looking for information about her mother.'

'I see. Very well, you had better come. Where are you?'

'In Southampton Street. We have come down from Westmorland.'

'In about ten minutes then. Ask for me. The porter will show you the way.'

It was an imposing place. A large red brick building of expensive flats with a grand entrance and half glass oak doors through which we went to seek out the porter, an equally imposing person in his braided uniform. I said we were expected, and he took us to the lift to go up to the third floor.

It didn't occur to me that Joan had never been in a lift. Even in shops, she'd take the stairs. She would not like to be so close to strangers in a lift. I realised that too late. She looked horrified when the porter slid closed the grated iron gate. It did go with a clunk. She watched him turn the brass handle to the number three and off we went with a lurch and a creak. Joan's knuckles were white.

'You look like him,' was Lily's opening gambit, after we had been shown into a large sitting room by her housekeeper. It was very bright with startling green curtains and cushions in green and red, and abstract paintings on the walls. I spotted a black lacquer cabinet in a Chinese style and in a corner a bamboo table on top of which stood a peculiar looking vase, all black and shiny, with peacock feathers in it. There was a large paper fan screening the fire grate with red dragons painted on it. The room looked very modern and old-fashioned at the same time, as did the woman sitting on the green velvet sofa. At first glance she looked like Helena's 1920's Lily, with her amber cigarette holder and scarlet lips, but her hair was an improbable red, she was very thin, and her face rather gaunt. I noticed the two sticks propped up against the arm of the sofa.

'I can't help that,' Joan replied tartly.

An inauspicious start, I thought, as Lily raised her thin, carefully painted eyebrows.

'Your eyes are lovely, Miss Revell, like his —'

Miss Revell. I glanced at Joan. She looked as if she might speak, but Lily Mountjoy-Smythe didn't notice, and the moment passed.

'He was a handsome man,' Lily continued, 'but — well, you ought to sit down. I'll send for some tea.'

She rang a silver bell on the lacquer table beside her where there was a pair of spectacles on a mother-of-pearl stick. A lorgnette, I knew that. She was certainly a character.

Joan took the direct route. 'My mother, Helena. I don't remember her at all. We have just found her diary and it led us to you. Did she come here after she left Gerard?'

The housekeeper came in with a silver tray on which were a sliver teapot and some very fragile looking cups and saucers in a Japanese style. No milk or sugar. I didn't look at Joan. The housekeeper poured the tea and handed us our cups. I could smell the scent of it as the steam rose. Joan sipped hers with a perfectly straight face. She wasn't going to be intimidated. I wanted to rush in and ask our questions, but Joan, of course, was patient. After all, she had waited almost fifty years already.

Lily was holding her cup without tasting. 'Helena came in the summer of '24. She told me that she couldn't live with Gerard anymore. He had become so distant and cold. He only wanted a son from her, and he was going to get a nursemaid for the children and sack the old servants —'

'They weren't old,' Joan interrupted.

'No, but, well they'd worked at Foulstone Manor for a long time. Helena was fond of them, and she didn't want a stranger looking after her children. She found Gerard impossible to live with. I have to say, I never liked him.'

'He didn't like you, either.'

Lily laughed. 'Touché, Miss Revell. I thought he'd suffocate her, that she'd be buried up there, the meek little wife of the hero and poet. Not that Helena was meek, but he was a type — the crushing type. And he'd want a son, of course. These country landowners always do. That's the mystery, though.'

'What mystery?'

'He didn't add up, Miss Revell. I mean you could understand the war stuff. I knew, we all knew, what they'd been through — and it was terrible. Don't think I don't remember. Of course, they didn't talk about it — those who came back, but with Gerard Revell — I don't know — it was as if he were acting the part. Lost his best friend, but fought on bravely, awarded the MC. But there were many in the same boat, just getting on the best way they could, but with him it was all *noli me tangere* — until Helena came along.' Lily sipped her tea. 'I'll tell you what it was — his eyes. Lovely colour, of course, unusual, but cold at times when he thought you weren't looking. Where, really, was the suffering — the genuine pain?'

Lily looked as though she'd shocked herself.

'You didn't believe in him?' Joan asked.

'No, I don't think I did, unconsciously, but I suppose he was different with Helena — when he wanted her, of course. Then he inherits a country house and they're off. Helena told me how he'd got in with the gentry — hunting, shooting, fishing and all that. Suddenly he was playing the country squire in need of a son to inherit the dear old pile that wasn't even really his.'

'What about my mother, what happened?'

Lily offered more tea. 'She wasn't well at all when she came to me. She was very strung up, waiting for news from Mrs Goss, who was looking after you. I said she should wait until the baby came, and then we could decide where she would live and what to do about a divorce. I'll confess I was anxious, too. I was worried he would demand her unborn child.'

'He couldn't do that, surely,' I said.

'Not in law, but —'

'If he proved her mad,' Joan said grimly.

'She had an old family solicitor in Chertsey. She wrote to him for advice. She had her father's money, so she knew she'd be all right financially. Then —' Lily turned to Joan. 'I am sorry, I really am.'

'What happened?'

'The baby started too soon. I got my doctor. An ambulance came, but she died, and the baby, too.'

'Where is she buried?'

'At the church in a place called Middlestone, near Chertsey, with her father and mother. Not far from where they lived. The Lantern House, it was called. The solicitor arranged it all. The funeral — like the wedding, I suppose. Bit short on guests. I couldn't go to the wedding – not that he'd have wanted me there. Three people at the funeral. Me, my cousin,

Jack, and the solicitor. I wrote to Gerard. He didn't reply, of course. He got her money, I imagine. He never contacted me.'

'He really did try to prove her mad,' Joan said.

'She was afraid he'd make trouble if the baby was a boy.'

'There are some things in her diary … well, strange things. She was haunted by Nowell Dearlove, Gerard's friend who was killed, and by — a smell.'

Joan's composure astonished me. She looked straight at Lily, daring her to raise those eyebrows.

'A smell?' Lily's tone was even.

'She was always very ill during her pregnancies. Morning sickness, but worse. She said she could smell and taste death in her mouth. We don't know what Helena meant, but it was to do with the house, I'm sure. Something rotten about it.'

Lily's green eyes glittered. 'Gerard Revell, I'd say. But Helena was not mad. She was perfectly sane when she was here. Not well, yes; anxious, yes, but she wrote to the solicitor, she was making plans — logical plans, too. As to the hauntings, that'd be his fault. He gave me the creeps.'

Joan laughed at that. I could see why. It sounded so schoolgirlish. Something eased in the room.

'Helena had a sense of humour,' Lily continued. 'She could laugh at herself. I used to tease her about her dark clothes, always wanting her to be more daring, but she just laughed and carried on as she was. She held me back a few times at school — I always wanted to go too far.'

'Tell me about him,' Joan said.

'Sherry first — it's time. I'll need a drink before I talk about him again. Bottle and glasses in the Chinese cabinet, darling,' she said, looking at me.

Joan took her glass from me. I'd trained her up in sherry, of course. It was very dry, but she didn't flinch. 'Where did he come from?'

Lily turned her astonished green stare on Joan. 'Do you know, I haven't the first idea. I met him at my cousin Jack's place. Still going strong, having parties, drinking cocktails, driving his sports car. Thinks he's twenty-five not seventy-five. He's only round the corner in Bedford Street. I'll ask him to come round.'

Lily made a startling figure on her bright green velvet sofa with her black-clad legs crossed and her red sweater and beads — great lumps of turquoise and some red, Chinese looking ones. They rattled when she bent to lift the telephone receiver. She wore black velvet beaded slippers, but I could see how her bare, mottled feet swelled out of them.

We heard her saying, 'Yes, darling, Gerard Revell ... no, not here. His daughter... Of course, she's Helena's daughter... Yes, now, we're having sherry.' She put the phone down and turned back to us. 'That'll bring him to heel, but he'll take an age to dress.'

'Dress?' I asked. Was he still in his pyjamas? I wondered.

'A gentleman cannot come to see three ladies without his tie — as seems to be the fashion these days, nor without a clean shirt, and his blazer and his buttonhole. I told you, he lives in the past.' Lily put another black cigarette into the amber holder. 'So do I, I suppose. One can't help it. It was so lovely. After the war I lived in Paris. We flew back and forth all the time.'

'You were married to a Frenchman,' I said.

'Was I?' She saw my face and laughed. 'Only teasing. It was wonderful while it lasted.'

Lily told me to top up our sherries and pour one for Jack. 'Too early for champagne,' she said, 'even for him.'

Then we heard the door and in came a dapper man with improbably black hair and a little moustache, dressed exactly as Lily had foretold. The buttonhole was a pink rosebud in a silver holder pinned to the lapel. Introductions were made; he kissed our hands and sat down with his sherry.

'Gerard Revell, Jack, Miss Revell wants to know about him.'

'Lord, Lil, that's going back.'

'You remember it all, Jacky, so don't pretend. Who was the fellow? Family and so on.'

'One didn't ask, you know. It wasn't done after the war. I mean, dash it, when a man had been out there, got a medal, one could hardly say, "Tell me about your people" as if he weren't quite the thing. We'd all been in it. One just accepted people — artists, actors, poets, scribblers and so forth, they all came to the parties. Dancing girls, even — pretty things. People whom my parents would have directed to the tradesman's entrance, but I had the flat — same one, actually — and I suppose Revell turned up. A poet, you see.' He paused to sip his drink. 'Queer things, those poems, haunted. But then plenty were. The things one saw… Revell, yes, had a job on a newspaper — don't know which one.'

'Oh, darling, surely there's something. You must have heard something.'

'Fill me up, old girl, while I'm thinking. You're all ahead of me.'

'You'll have to get it yourself and think while you do.'

Jack sat down again and crossed his legs. The creases were knife sharp. 'Aunt in Chelsea — no Chiswick — no Chelsea. Definitely Chelsea. Not that it mattered — she was dead. Orphan, old Revell — bit on the mournful side. Well, I suppose you would be. And the war — did his duty, and more. Never talked about it. None of us did — who'd understand, eh? Keep it under your hat, that was the ticket. Impossible to imagine unless… Revell inherited a country house —'

'Miss Revell knows that. She's come from there, but she was adopted, so she's wondering about her father.'

'Yes, well, I see you'd want to know, my dear. Dashed difficult — didn't know him, really. So many people came and went. One thing, though, saw him in Lobb's, buying hunting boots. Hand-made. Hadn't him down as that type. Didn't want to know me. I could tell that. I'm sorry, my dear, but that's all I know. Mystery man, Revell, eh?'

We said goodbye to the two of them and left them to their sherries. Lily invited us back. 'Any time,' she said. 'Helena loved you, Joanna, she really did.'

We went back towards the British Museum where nearby we found a café where we ordered poached eggs on toast.

'And a decent cup of tea,' Joan had said when I suggested it. She was smiling. 'Good gracious, scented tea, indeed.'

'You drank two cups.'

'I wasn't going to look like someone who'd been brought up in a canteen. I didn't mind Lily, though, after a bit. You couldn't help admiring her and she was genuinely fond of my mother. She took her in, and she was right about Gerard Revell.'

'Mystery man,' I said.

'He was that. Helena didn't seem to know anything about him, except that aunt in Chelsea. I wonder if there are any Revells in Chelsea.'

'We could look in the telephone book — just in case. It's not a common name. I'll ask at the counter if they have one.'

We looked. There was an A. Revell in Chelsea. 'The Flat, 27 Paultons Street — I'll have to get a map.'

We decided to make the journey out to Chertsey first and then to explore the link with Chelsea once we returned to London. We got a taxi from Chertsey station to Middlestone, a lovely quiet little village with a duck pond and a very old, grey church where we asked a woman for directions to The Lantern House which was just along the lane by the church. I asked the taxi driver to wait — we would not be long, I thought, and I didn't know how we'd get back otherwise.

We stood by the hedge opposite the house. I couldn't imagine what Joan was thinking about the house her mother had grown up in and loved. It was an old house from a story book, perfectly symmetrical with four windows on each side of a porch and four on each side above, red brick walls over which the deep red Virginia creeper grew, and a few late roses scrambled up the porch. An iron gate led into a garden bisected by a brick path. Everything was perfectly still and quiet as if a spell had been cast over the house in the gathering twilight. But not a malign spell like the spell cast over Foulstone where I'd thought it impossible that a happy family could have lived there, and the twilight smelt clean and sharp, with a kind of sweetness in the air, and I saw tiny yellow flowers by the gate that looked like stars.

But then, a lamp was lit in a downstairs window. We saw a hand raised briefly. Then a sudden flickering of light — a fire being lit, perhaps. I thought of Helena Lovelace, as she had been then, at home here. It looked somehow very peaceful — somewhere you'd be glad to get home to. There was an old-fashioned lantern lit by the front porch. Someone expected, perhaps, a light to guide them in the dark, the fire warmly glowing, and tea laid by it. The house did not look as if it had changed since the 1900s when Helena had lived there, a treasured daughter. I felt suddenly cold — shut out, I suppose. Two strangers in a darkening lane.

We heard a car coming along. It was time to go back to the church. Joan didn't say anything. Neither did I.

It wasn't yet quite dark, but the light was fading, and it was getting colder, but we found the grave and stood there in silence. I felt tears start to my eyes. It was very simple and very touching. We had read about them, but they had lived and loved and been loved. They had been good people. All of them gone.

In Loving Memory
Joanna Lovelace 1875–1916
Thomas John Lovelace 1870–1920
And their beloved daughter, Helena Revell, died 1924

'I wish I had brought flowers,' Joan said. 'I used to take flowers to William and Mary's graves. No one has been here since Lily came to the funeral. It's —'

Very nearly unbearable, I thought, hearing the catch in her throat, but I didn't look at her. I thought I would weep myself. I only said, 'We could come back tomorrow with some.'

'No, thank you, it's too late.'

I didn't know if she meant we wouldn't have time or that it was too late to be putting flowers on the grave. Too late for everything. 'I'll come when I'm back in London. I'll bring flowers for you. They won't be forgotten.'

She squeezed my hand. 'You're a good girl, Amanda. I do appreciate what you're doing.'

21

Amanda

On the train from Chertsey, we were quiet. It was dark now, far too late to be going to Chelsea, if that's what Joan wanted to do. I'd booked our hotel for two nights. We would have time to go to Paultons Street by bus early tomorrow morning and get the train to Oxenholme in the afternoon, but I'd wait for Joan to decide, and I waited for her to speak of what we had seen in Middlestone.

'I'm glad we found her, and you were right, and so was Lily. Helena did love the little girl, Joanna. It's eased something in me, but there's loss, too. I wish I'd known long ago. Outside that house, I felt shut out — I wish I could have — but, of course, her parents were dead by the time I was born. Too late. Poor Helena — to find herself at Foulstone with him.'

'She hardly knew him — she found herself married to a stranger. That's terrible — she seemed so lonely.'

'Such a pity Mr Dearlove died. She might have had more time. Gerard Revell might have been different. Oh, might, Amanda, life is so full of mights. Mary Goss, for example, things might have been different for me if she had told me about Helena. Why didn't she tell me that my mother had died in childbirth? Helena told her to tell me something. "Tell Joanna that I haven't", those were the words in the diary, and she never told me.'

'Was she going to say that Mary must tell you that she hadn't abandoned you? I can't understand it, either, unless it's to do with him. Mary Goss didn't want you asking questions.'

'I suppose so — and I was meant to be her sister's child, but that's odd, too. Why was that necessary?'

'So that other people didn't ask questions.'

'That'd be Mary, all right. But not to tell me — I mean when I got older. Too late then, I suppose. Oh, well — have we time to go to Chelsea tomorrow before the train?'

'Yes, we can go by bus.'

I knew Chelsea, of course. I wondered what Joan would make of the King's Road with its boutiques and cafes and all the riot of colour and bizarre clothes and hairstyles. Paultons Street was just off the King's Road, according to my map.

It was very crowded, as we threaded our way past the shops. Three girls in floppy hats, smoking, a boy wearing what looked like a dog's studded collar, a young man with his hair tied back in a ponytail. Joan looked very startled as something like an open-topped jeep screeched past us with four young men inside, all wearing bowler hats and flowered jackets, one perched on the door, but I stopped her just before she stepped off the kerb. A young woman came towards us, a young woman with long golden hair held back with a golden Alice band and a long fringe, wearing a honey-coloured fur coat and leading a honey-coloured Afghan hound on a golden lead.

I laughed out loud when Joan said, 'Is that her dog or her twin?'

We eventually came to the turning to Paultons Square and went down to Paultons Street where we walked along looking at the numbers. It was very quiet, such a contrast to King's Road. We stopped at number 27.

Joan looked nervous. 'You knock.'

'Right — I'll just ask, shall I? I mean ask about Gerard Revell.'

Just then the door opened and a young woman in a white coat, a white fur hat, and long legs in long white boots came out. She looked very polished and glamorous — like a model. She looked down at us with wide brown eyes and great long lashes which owed nothing to nature, I thought, spitefully, aware of looking dowdy with my hair scraped back into a ponytail and no mascara or lipstick.

'Oh,' she said. 'Did you want me?' As if every passing stranger would be seeking her out. I expected they would be. 'I wasn't expecting you until tomorrow.'

That threw me. I just gaped up at her. She spoke again. 'Your mother —' she threw a glance at Joan — 'she was to come tomorrow about the charlady's job. I'm awfully sorry but I can't do it now.'

'No, we're not — we're looking for a Mr Revell.'

'So am I — well, he won't be called Revell, but you know what I mean. Mr Right, I hope.' She laughed delightedly.

I didn't think for a moment that Mr Wrong would come, but I ploughed on before Mr Right came for her in a Rolls-Royce or something. A gleaming sports car, probably driven by an impossibly handsome man. 'No, you see, we wondered if the Revell family lived here. There was an aunt —' I was conscious of sounding a bit mad.

'I've an aunt, but she's Smith. No real Revells here. My name is Annabel Smith — Revell's my professional name. I'm a model and an actress.' She would be, I thought. 'Saw it on a gravestone in Chelsea Old Church. My agent liked it because it's unusual — a stage name, you see.'

'And there have never been any Revells here?'

'No, as I say, it's my aunt's house — she's lived here forever and her parents before her. More than fifty years. I'm in the flat upstairs. Sorry, I can't help. Oh, here's my lift.'

A car came along — a white sports car, of course, and the handsome man, and away Annabel Revell went with a screech of tires and a cheery wave.

'It's this hat,' Joan said, grinning, 'I suppose I do look like a char. However, I'm not proud as Mary would say. What now?'

'Chelsea Old Church. It's just down the road on Cheyne Walk — a few minutes away.'

We spent ages looking round. Fortunately, it wasn't very big and there did not seem to be any gravestones later than 1930. I saw the name, though, and called out to Joan. We stood looking at the grave of Gerard Revell.

But it wasn't our Gerard Revell. The dates were 1890–1893. A three-year-old boy, long, long dead.

We caught the train from Euston Station with more questions than we had posed before we had left for London.

Was Gerard Revell really Gerard Revell or had he taken on a fake name like that actress? It would take some thinking about. Once we had settled into our seats, Joan closed her eyes. I knew she'd had enough of talking — of the circles we'd gone round on the way back from Chelsea.

I was wide awake. I took my notepad and biro out of my handbag. It was time to think logically. Suppose Gerard Revell was actually someone else? Lily Mountjoy-Smythe knew nothing about him. Ditto Jack Fournier who had just accepted him into his circle. Apparently, one did not ask questions about a man's "people" after the war. A lot of people would have had secrets after the war — things they wouldn't want to confess to—

Samuel Bate popped into my mind. He had disappeared. He could have taken another name, gone to Scotland or America, gone off with his "fancy woman" as Mrs Bate had called her.

Alias Samuel Bate, or rather Samuel Bate, alias X. You read about criminals with aliases.

Joan opened her eyes. 'Samuel Bate,' she said, 'what's he got to do with it all, I wonder?'

'I was just thinking about him, thinking that he could have changed his name when he disappeared.'

'Perhaps Gerard Revell really did take that name from the grave.'

'It does seem a funny coincidence that the name of a three-year-old child in 1893 was Gerard Revell — on a gravestone in Chelsea.'

'He'd be about the same age. I mean if that boy had lived, though I don't know how old our Gerard Revell was. In his twenties when he went to war, maybe.'

'Perhaps he did have an aunt in Chelsea, but she was called something else.'

Joan shook her head and tutted. 'Oh, I can't make it out, Amanda — why would he change his name?'

'That girl, Annabel Smith, wanted a name that sounded better than hers. He was a poet — maybe he just thought Gerard Revell sounded like a poet's name — perhaps his name was Smith like hers. I was thinking about what Gerard Revell said about Bate — that he was a crook. He probably had things to hide. Why were you thinking about him?'

'Gerard Revell and Nowell Dearlove served together, and Samuel Bate went to Foulstone — he must have known him, surely. He wouldn't go all that way to see someone he didn't know.'

'But he was writing to Mr Dearlove — or that's what Helena assumed from that bit of a letter Mrs Bate had. I wonder if Bate's mentioned in Gerard's papers.'

'Or, if there's anything about the aunt — if she existed.'

22

Amanda

'What are you looking for?' Joan asked when we were sitting at her kitchen table after breakfast the next morning. I had Helena's diary open.

'Mrs Bate's address.' I slipped my fingers down into the back pocket and drew out a yellowed piece of paper. Helena's writing.

'You're not thinking of going back to London?'

'I'm thinking it's an odd story. Helena sees a man in the woods — a ghost of sorts, she said, and he just stared at her. What was he seeing?'

'I don't know.'

'I wonder if it was Bate. She saw him on the lawn in the night.'

'But he wasn't missing then.'

'Oh, I'd forgotten that. Let me look at what Mrs Bate said. "He'd go off for days at a time." He didn't tell her where. He only told her he was coming to Kendal because they had a row. Suppose he did come here before that last time when we think she saw him under the bridge and had the miscarriage. Then Mrs Bate comes, Gerard is furious, and Helena wonders —'

'If Gerard knew him.'

'We need to see if there's anything about Bate in Gerard's papers.'

There was no diary for Gerard Revell, just a few bundles of papers we had found in the top drawer of his desk. Bills mostly

— for boots, jackets, breeches, all the things he had needed for his hunting, shooting, and fishing.

'Expensive,' Joan said, her lips folding rather tightly.

There were a few copies of *The London Mercury* where we found his poems. Helena had mentioned the one called 'The Ghost'. We read that. I noted again those words, "You were the one/ The truest and the best." Nowell had meant a lot to Gerard Revell. Had he loved him in a way that he could not love Helena?

They were quite haunting poems. I wondered why he had not continued writing. Nothing to say after the war, perhaps.

'Nowell,' Joan says, 'it sounds as if Gerard's looking for Nowell, yet it's Helena who sees him. I wonder if he thought Helena was Nowell in the garden. He told her Nowell was nothing to do with her — as if Nowell had to be his. His friend — like the house. It was his. She was just there to produce another Nowell — for him. Selfish — that's what he was.'

I didn't tell her my thoughts about Gerard and Nowell. 'I suppose it was what happened in the war. No one else could share it.'

Joan didn't answer. She was turning over more sheets. 'Here's something. It's about what happened to Nowell.'

I could see that Gerard had written it out several times. The first two versions were heavily crossed out with words in the margin. We couldn't read what he had crossed out. Perhaps he had been preparing for some kind of memoir. It was written in the first person.

In front of our trenches about three or four hundred yards away, there was a bulge in the German line — a nuisance to us, overlooking the next-door battalion — meaning that the Germans could fire down the length of their trench — dangerous, of course. Our Colonel wanted it captured. We were sent out on what we called a stunt, starting from an old gun emplacement. We'd not got far when an inferno suddenly erupted, machine-gun fire, bursting shells, Very lights, smoke — the lot. We all got separated. I was blown into a shell hole and crawled back up. I saw Nowell fall, and in a lull, I crawled to where I thought he was — it wasn't far, and I managed to drag him back. He'd been shot, but he was alive. We were there all night — I don't really know — I must have been unconscious. When I came to, Nowell was gone — the water, you see, the mud…

It ended there, apart from a few words further down the page which read, '*I should have — I can't —*'

'He couldn't go on with it, perhaps,' I said, 'too painful to remember. He sounds as if he felt guilty that Nowell had died in the mud. I mean it was a terrible thing to wake and find him gone.'

'It was, I can understand that,' Joan said, 'I suppose you might be right about him. The war destroyed him. He shouldn't have married, though. He wasn't fit.'

'Perhaps he thought marriage and children might be a future that would — I don't know — make things better, but he couldn't forget.'

'Hm… Lily didn't believe in him.' Joan, I could see, still had her doubts about Gerard Revell.

'But she didn't like him. Prejudiced, perhaps, because of what happened to Helena?'

'Jack Fournier said the same thing. They couldn't make him out.'

'He had things to hide, though — his name, perhaps. He didn't want people to know he was really someone else. That's what made him odd, not that he was faking his feelings.'

'What about Samuel Bate? Anything about him?'

I turned over and there were lists of sentences — Gerard seemed to be trying out descriptions of the war, but they weren't very coherent, just scraps of unconnected phrases.

The old lie. I recognised that from Wilfred Owen's poem about the gas attack. It was the line that refuted the idea of noble sacrifice. Other phrases were descriptive of the front line. Gerard Revell wrote of 'a torn land, Hell let loose, the howling fury of shells, a blood-soaked dawn, a gouged sky' … all random jottings. Ideas for poems, perhaps.

Joan read aloud, '*Oh, merciful father … he went to his death with a curse on his lips… Good Lord, deliver us … from battle and murder … the world, the flesh, and the devil…* I can't make any sense of this. He must have lost his mind.'

I looked at the rest of the words: *earth, sky, hell…* 'I don't know, Auntie Joan. Maybe he was just jotting down ideas for poems about the war.'

She turned over another page. There was a list of names: *Lieutenant Frank Pelham (d); 2nd Lieutenant Henry Worsley (d); Sergeant Corley (d); Corporal Henshaw (d); Pte Morton (d).*

'All dead?' Joan asked.

'Yes, that's what the "d" means, and there's another over the page — Private O'Dowd — dead, too. Oh, here's Bate.'

At the end of the page the name Bate was written over and over again, and overleaf the words: *Private Bate — not dead.*

And there was more: *Bate, Bate, Bate. That cursed man. A worthless thing, a shirker and a coward, haunting me like a demon. My evil genius.*

'He did know him.'

'And he didn't like him one bit,' Joan said.

'I wonder if he was in the action when Nowell was killed — odd that Gerard doesn't write Nowell on his list.'

'I suppose he might have found that too painful,' Joan conceded. 'I understand that, even if I'm puzzled by what Lily and Jack said about him. Nowell was his best friend.'

'The poem shows how much he missed him. But all this does sound as though Bate was in their company or platoon or whatever. Gerard calls him a coward here, too, and Mrs Bate told Helena that he was a deserter.'

There was more on another page. *How can a man be dead and live? I have seen a dead man rise. I know when one is dead and when one lives.* And then a fragment of a poem: *But he is drowned/ Full fathom five my brother lies/ where rats gnaw his bones.*

I recognised the quotation from Shakespeare, but Shakespeare's Ferdinand says "father", not brother, so Gerard meant Nowell who had drowned in that shell hole. Gerard might have been mad, but I could understand it — the random phrases all added up to a nightmare picture for me. It did sound as if Gerard Revell had really suffered.

On the next page, there was just one line. I recognised that, too, from *King Lear*. The benefits of A-level English.

Why should a dog, a horse, a rat, have life, and thou no breath at all?

'This is about Nowell,' Joan said, 'not Helena.'

'I think so. This is from *King Lear*. Lear's words after his fool is dead.'

'Fool's a queer word to use.'

'A king's fool — like a jester. In the play, the fool is close to the king and tells him the truth. Gerard was close to Nowell. Nowell looked up to him. Maybe it's the word rat that's important. He's underlined it.'

'So, Bate's the rat — who survived when Nowell didn't.'

Back to Bate again. Gerard despised the man. Was it only because Bate had been a coward and a shirker who had survived when a finer man had not? I could imagine Gerard

Revell's fury if Bate had come to ask for money, but why did Bate choose Gerard? He must have known Gerard loathed him.

Joan was ahead of me. 'Did Samuel Bate know something about Gerard Revell? Did he know that Gerard Revell was not who he said he was?'

'Gerard says he was haunted by Bate. Bate, the demon. Let's see if he says anything more — about Bate coming, for example.'

I turned over some more papers, but they were just household accounts, bills for coal, for oil, one from a bookshop in Kendal. I looked at the titles Gerard had ordered. *The Poems of Wilfred Owen* — so he had read them. And then there was another sheet with his familiar spiky black writing.

'What's that?'

'Looks like a poem.' I put it down so Joan could see it. Its title was 'The Third'. I read it aloud:

One walks alone in the woods.
Who is the one in the woods?
Leaving no print in the snow,
No sound in the frosted air.

Two walk. A pair in the moonlit trees.
Who are the two in the trees?
Leaving no mark in the earth,
No shadow cast before.

Three walk light on the leaves.
Who are the three on the leaves?
Leaving no trace on the path,
No breath in the Autumn air.

Three tread light in the woods.
Who is the third that walks behind you?
Deaf to his whisper, blind to his tears.

'What's it all about?' Joan asked. 'The third — sounds a bit rum to me.'

'Nowell and Bate? Bate was in the woods. Maybe, Gerard did see him as well as Helena. Helena thought she saw a grey figure in a cape on the lawn. Were they both seeing ghosts?'

Joan was silent for a moment. 'But Bate was alive.'

'Whatever it means, it's all tied up with the war. Did Gerard think Bate was dead in that action when Nowell died and then he turned up? He says, "I have seen a dead man rise." He thought he was a ghost?'

'A man he hated. A man he didn't want to see.'

'Mrs Bate said he came for money.' I hardly dared say what I thought next. 'Blackmail?'

'If Bate knew that Gerard was an imposter — and — oh, Amanda, those letters that Helena referred to — the one he said was from his publisher and the one he stuffed into his pocket.'

'The cheap paper. And off he went to London. To see Bate? To pay him off. Blackmailers always want more —'

'It seems too far-fetched — I mean — blackmail? Aren't we letting our imaginations run a bit — wild?'

'No more fantastic than believing Gerard Revell stole a name from a graveyard.'

'What's that address?'

'Bate lived in Battersea, somewhere called Searle Street. Not that it helps. I don't know Battersea. It's south of the river, though. There's a bridge, the Albert Bridge, that goes right across to Chelsea.'

'Mrs Bate is probably dead now.'

'She might have had children. Bate might have gone home again. Is it worth a try?'

'I couldn't face London again — all that traffic. Once was enough for me.'

'I could go and stay with my parents — but I'd have to tell them something, Auntie Joan, I couldn't lie about why I'm there.'

'I know and I wouldn't want you to. You tell them whatever you think they need to know. I'll trust you, and what does it matter what they think about me?'

'But they won't think anything about you — this is about Gerard and Helena. My mum's always been fond of you — you were friends.'

'A poor friend, I've been.'

23

Joan

I meant what I'd said. All this nonsense about hiding everything and avoiding people. Sheila had been a good friend. All those invitations to London and I'd made excuses. That was Mary Goss, I suppose, keeping all the secrets and I'd got into the habit. It's what comes of not talking about things, but that was the way then as I'd told Amanda. Really, Mary could have told me about my mother. Surely, to die in childbirth wasn't something to be ashamed of, but, of course, she didn't want me asking awkward questions. People didn't talk about childbirth then. "The stork's been to number twenty-four." Dear Lord — and when I found out at school that there was no stork, I suppose I thought it was shameful. Too much whispering.

Well, now I'd been to London, and a cat was out of its bag, though quite what sort of cat, I didn't really know. Gerard Revell didn't add up for me, either. All right, I could understand that the death of Nowell had — well, let's say broken his heart, but shouldn't that have made him kinder to his wife?

Amanda went off in her orange car to the station that afternoon. She couldn't say when she'd be back, but she'd send a letter as soon as she found out anything.

I kept thinking of those papers spread out on Amanda's table. Talk about haunted. That spidery writing, all those bits of words here and there. What on earth was he about, that man? Driving himself mad, it looked like to me.

I spent the rest of the day cleaning and doing laundry. Anything to stop thinking about Gerard Revell staring at me through a cracked window. Of course, when I swept the stairs and dusted the windowsill, I couldn't help looking out at Foulstone Manor. I was sure I could smell it again — I hadn't smelt it in London or when we'd gone through the papers, but it was here again. Faint, granted, but Foulstone wasn't going to leave me alone. Unfinished business, I thought. And if Amanda didn't find out anything about Bate, would I ever be at peace? Amanda would go eventually, and I'd be here and that place looming over me. I think I'd have gone up there and set it on fire at that moment if I hadn't thought of the police and the fire brigade and questions.

I walked up to town — very briskly. I thought I'd go to the grocer's and get a few things. I'd need to feed Amanda when she got back. I thought I'd make a cake as well. A tin of peaches, perhaps, some cheese. They had sherry at the Co-op. Why not? I could say it was for a trifle. As if anyone would ask. What did I think? That Mr Mason would tell his wife that Miss Goss was buying sherry. Had she taken to drink?

No one paid the slightest attention, though I admit I bought a packet of jelly and some sponge fingers to go with the sherry — just in case anyone thought. And on the way back, I did laugh at myself. They really would have something to say if they knew the goings-on at Foulstone.

Passing the churchyard, I had an idea to go in and look at the War Memorial. I'd never looked at it before. I'm not a churchgoer. I thought I'd have to be sociable — tea parties, whist drives, jumble sales and all that. Good gracious, when I think about myself, I wonder. All these years spent running away.

Nowell Dearlove was there. And names I recognised from the town. People I didn't know, but who had lost someone in that war. "Their name liveth for evermore". So they would, as long as this memorial stood there. Comforting, I supposed, though Arthur Dearlove may never have seen his only son's name. They'd had no life at all — none of them. And it was the same for those who fought in the second war and for those who'd been bombed and killed in the raids. No life at all — and I'd wasted mine.

Arthur and Nowell Dearlove. I thought of what my mother had written in her diary. Mary had told her that Gerard had put all the Dearloves' belongings in the attic rooms. I wondered what Arthur Dearlove had to say about Gerard Revell. Perhaps there would be something in those boxes. But that would mean — I couldn't go there on my own.

Why not? I chided myself. It was my house. What was there to be frightened of? I'd been in with Amanda, and I hadn't died, only felt the queerness of it, and the cold, and that sense that the house knew something it wasn't telling. Well, now I knew some of those secrets and they hadn't killed me.

And, dear Amanda, off to London to search for Samuel Bate, doing me a favour. She didn't have to. So, I'd just wait, would I? Let it all happen around me as usual. Weak as water, Mary would say about someone who complained about a slight cold or having to walk because the bus didn't come. Weak as water — that'd be me if I didn't shape myself.

I took the keys out of the drawer when I got back and put them by the front door. I didn't take off my coat but put the shopping in the larder and put the kettle on. I drank my tea and watched the sky darkening outside the window. Tomorrow then, I thought. Not in the dark. I couldn't shape myself enough for that. All that talk of ghosts. A few shadows in a gloomy old house and a bad dream. But what was my smell then? Was that a ghost in its way?

It was no use thinking, so I made the trifle instead and used up some of the sherry. My conscience was clear. Then I ate sardines on toast on my knee by the fire and listened to the wireless. I took up my knitting. It's a very soothing occupation — if you're good at it. Which I am, though I say it myself. I was knitting a scarf for Amanda — I'd got some black wool. I'd thought of buying blue, but then I'd thought that a black woollen scarf was harmless. You couldn't not like a black scarf. It'd keep for a funeral, I thought, not that Amanda ought to be going to funerals at her age. Good gracious, thinking of funerals now. It's what came of poking about in graveyards.

I knitted through Radio Three. There was a ghost story. Not for me, I thought, as the haunting music came to introduce the story. *The Inheritance of Mr Humphreys* — whoever he was, then footsteps — someone walking through Autumn leaves, the sound of a bell tolling — a passing bell. I remembered that — how they used to ring a bell so many times when someone died. Funerals, I remember thinking...

I woke up to the sound of music — like something faraway. For a moment I didn't know where I was. My knitting was on my knee, the ball of wool had rolled across the floor, and the fire was nearly out. I must have fallen asleep — all that chasing about in London. I heard the Westminster chimes introducing the news. Ten strokes. Gracious, I'd slept through the play — probably woken up just in time for that music at the end.

I went to open the front door and get a breath of air. The keys were on the table where I'd left them. Tomorrow when it was light. I stepped out onto the path and walked a few paces to ease my stiffness. Amanda's cottage in darkness, of course. Gerard Revell's papers inside on her table.

"Who is the third that walks behind you?" What a peculiar poem that was. Amanda seemed to make sense of it, but she was a clever girl. Knew poetry and Shakespeare. She thought Nowell and Bate were the two in the woods and that Gerard had seen them.

After what we'd read in his papers, I could sort of understand Gerard seeing the ghost of Nowell. Queer things happened in the mind. And that Bate had sounded a bit ghostly when Helena had described him. The third person walking behind them must be Gerard Revell. Why behind them? Because he was alive, and they were dead. But Bate wasn't dead. Unless he was — by the time Gerard wrote the poem. How would Gerard Revell know that? Bate had disappeared.

I hoped that Amanda would come back with some news about Bate. He might be in Arthur's and Nowell's papers. I'd got round the back of the cottages by then and stood looking at the house in the moonlight.

I wasn't frightened. I didn't feel anything, not even the cold, though I'd only gone out in my slippers for that breath of fresh air. I had no coat either. By rights, I should have been in bed with pneumonia afterwards.

I told you about the moon — how sometimes it was bright enough to light your way. Well, I must have walked across that field on the frosted grass, or I'd dreamt it. The woods seemed very black under the moon. The air was very still. The scene was like a painting of the night, of an old house in a wood lit by the moon. It didn't look real, as if it might disappear if you looked away. That's why I didn't know if any of it was real.

I think I walked up to the gate which led into the woods. I looked along the empty path. Then they were there, coming towards me. Three of them, two in front, side by side, all grey in the moonlight, and one behind.

And that was it. They were gone. In a second. And I stood there, not feeling anything. I can't really say if I saw them.

I don't know how I got back. I only know that my feet were wet, and that I didn't sleep much that night.

And that I felt dreadful in the morning, not knowing at first if I'd dreamed the whole thing. I had been out, though. My slippers were not tucked under the bedside cabinet where I always placed them before I got into bed. They were on the hearth where I must have left them to dry, and there was a cup and saucer on the table by the fire. Cocoa dregs. I hadn't washed up.

And I remembered the moon and the path, and the three.

I stared at the slippers for ages, thinking back. I had been out. The slippers were proof, but whether I'd seen those three, I couldn't say for sure. Had I been still half asleep? I'd dreamed of Gerard Revell before. I saw him looking at me that night after we'd read Helena's diary. And I had been listening to the opening of that ghost story on the radio. And I'd been thinking of that poem. "Who is the third?" No wonder my head was muddled. I thought that was it, and London and all those trains and buses, and graveyards.

I washed the cup and saucer and I thought about all of it, how much I'd been shaken up, turned inside out, so to speak. Graveyards, indeed, ghost stories, madness, poems, hauntings. It was enough to make any sane person see things. You didn't have to be mad to imagine things.

And so, I made my tea and toast and reasoned it all out. And about that smell. I thought about that, too. I saw him by that door when I was a child. Maybe it had been when Helena was in the nursing home after the miscarriage and William and

Mary had not been in the house, or after my mother had gone. I would have known she wasn't there. I would have been in a state — and he, looming over me, grasping my arm. He had terrified me. And that door must have been the cellar door, the cellar which smelt of damp and rot. Mary had said so.

One thing at a time, I told myself, as I stood at the oak door again with the keys in my hand. I'd waited for the rain to pass and now in the sunshine, I contemplated the house. I thought what a wreck it looked, and what was I going to do with it. I couldn't think that far ahead. It was enough to get in and find out about Arthur and Nowell.

I looked in the old stick stand for something to prop open the front door. I took one — a stick with a dog's head. The wood felt warm to the touch and the little carved head looked friendly. I could see the carved fur and it had amber-coloured glass eyes. I wondered whose it was. Arthur Dearlove's, I decided — not Gerard Revell's. I liked the feel of it. I'd take it with me. I found an iron weight — clearly once a doorstop — and used that instead to prop open the door. In case I had to hurry out.

I couldn't help laughing at myself a bit. What was I thinking? That I'd bash a ghost over the head. Still, I kept the stick. My heart was beating very fast as I looked again up that shadowy staircase.

I didn't linger in the hall or on the first floor. I went up to the nursery floor, gripping my dog's head, and took the narrow staircase that led to the attics. I had never been up there before, and I was surprised to see two doors facing me, both of them unlocked. I took a deep breath and opened the first. Light came from a window in the ceiling, enough light to make out the dust everywhere and the thick cobwebs hanging in the corners. There was the smell of damp, of course, and I could see a stain by the skylight where the rain had come in. But there was nothing sinister in the room — no sense that it was — well, haunted.

In fact, it was all very tidy for an attic room. Mary Goss, I wondered, thinking of the stripped beds downstairs. Had she come after he'd died to tidy everything up? Boxes were stacked up carefully against the walls, and some tea chests and wooden crates. There was a table in the centre of the room with books in neat piles. There was a trunk in one corner on which I could see the initials N.A.D. There was a long bag with leather handles next to it and a tennis racket in a press and then something that looked like a kit bag. The war, I thought. Nowell's. A tea chest was labelled, "Revell War". I needed Amanda with me for that.

I didn't know where to start, but then I realised that the other boxes and tea chests had writing on them. William's writing. He and Mary had been here, perhaps. Sometime after Gerard had shot himself. When I was at school — that'd be it. They'd have come for days, I supposed, tidying up. Perhaps, they had come over the years to keep their eye on the place. No need to mention it to me.

I read *Dining Room Silver* on one and there were others labelled glassware, decanters, bed linen. Then there was another tea chest tied with string, but the writing was different. The label said *Study*. I couldn't tell if it was Gerard's writing, but he had put Arthur Dearlove's things up here. The string was rotten and easy to untie.

The tea chest was full of books at first sight. I took them out carefully. They were mostly history books about Westmorland and Cumberland and underneath there was a leather blotter with the blotting paper still in it and under that there were papers — documents, I supposed.

I opened a leather folder and saw inside papers labelled *Foulstone*. There were thick parchment papers folded and labelled "Last Will and Testament" and the address of a solicitor in Kendal.

I opened one very carefully. The paper crackled at my touch. I scanned the words until I found the name Gerard Revell. Arthur Dearlove's will left the house and its contents to Gerard and thereafter to his heirs. In the event that Gerard Revell had no heirs and pre-deceased his wife, then she would have a life interest in the property. After her death, the property would be sold, and the proceeds donated to various charities — The National Association for Discharged Sailors and Soldiers, The British Red Cross Society, the Save the Children Fund. A good man, I thought.

Gerard Revell didn't want Helena to have it after his death. She wasn't to have any life interest in Foulstone. That was my first thought. He wanted her to be mad. Only a son could inherit.

I was not to be his heir. I was to be given away to Mary and William Goss. I wondered if Gerard Revell had made a will which cut out Helena and me. But I had inherited Foulstone. Perhaps he had thought about me before he killed himself. I thought about that, but it was impossible to decide. More likely, he didn't care by then.

What was it that had driven him to shoot himself? Grief, as Amanda's newspaper piece had speculated? Helena had died four years before him. It couldn't be guilt about that. The date of his death was ten years to the day after Nowell's death — something to do with Nowell then. Nowell whose things were still here. I looked round again. There was no box labelled *Helena Revell*. There had been only empty hangers in her wardrobe. Had he got rid of her things? Was she to be got rid of? Like his daughter?

It was no use going round in circles. I laid the folder to one side and delved deeper until I came to more books. A set of diaries with dates embossed in gold on the spines. They'd tell the story of Foulstone Manor before the war. The story of the Dearlove family. They started in 1900. The last one was dated 1918 — of course, it wasn't finished. Arthur Dearlove had died in 1920. I'd take that with me.

I went downstairs to where the sunlight was coming through the open door. I looked down the kitchen corridor where the cold wind had come from on the day I had entered Foulstone for the first time in nearly fifty years, where the plaster had fallen from the walls and frightened us half to death.

No, I couldn't face that dark corridor. I moved the iron doorstop and struggled with the door, having to push it open again when it wouldn't shut properly. I'd have to try to slam it shut. The cold wind blew and with it came the smell of rot and decay — and death. And I felt the sickness and metallic taste on my lips — just as Helena had all those years ago.

He was there.

24

Amanda

'Course, I remember.' I didn't doubt it. The old lady's eyes were very piercing as she answered my question about Mrs Bate, her former neighbour from nearly fifty years before. Mrs Bate was not to be found in the little terraced house in Searle Street, but the present occupant had pointed us next door.

'I might be eighty-six, Miss, but I've got all me marbles. I can look after meself, thank you. But you can make us a cup of tea.'

I followed her directions to the kitchen and returned with the tea.

'So, Mrs Rudd, I was asking about your neighbour, Mrs Emily Bate. I know it was years ago, but my godmother wanted to get in touch with her or anyone who knew her.'

'Poor Emily Bate, you'll have to hold a séance to get in touch with 'er.' There was a satisfied gleam in her eye as she said that.

'She's dead?'

'As a doornail, Miss, but make no mistake, I can remember 'er. Unlucky woman.'

'Did you know her husband?'

'You mean the one what disappeared.' I nodded. 'Rum do that. Saw 'im go, I did, in 'is raincoat an' 'at, an' a bit of a fancy leather suitcase. 'E ain't comin' back, I thought. 'Eard 'em, see, rowin'. They was allus at it, but that mornin' I 'eard 'er tellin' 'im 'e needn't come back. Bate was a nasty piece of work. Hit 'er, many a time, always cussin' an' swearin'. Wouldn't give you the time o' day. Deserter, 'e was, in the first war. They made

171

'im go back an' served 'im right. Survived, though, an' better men than 'im copped it. My boy...'

Her eyes clouded as she turned to a photograph of a young and handsome man on the mantelpiece. He looked about eighteen, very serious, but with a hint of a smile about the eyes. He looked very smart and very innocent, but hopeful. He had had no idea of what was to come. I thought of Nowell Dearlove and felt the tears prick my eyes.

'That's my Teddy. 'E was a lovely boy to me — a clever boy. Could 'ave done anythin'... I was that proud when 'e went. We all was. They cheered in the streets. Like a pageant it was. Give them flowers. Little did I know... Think an old woman like me don't remember. I remember that telegram as if it was yesterday. Lots o' women 'ad them — sons, husbands, brothers... An' what was it all for, eh? An' it all 'appened again. All them bombs... Now, where was I?'

'Mr Bate.'

'Never came back. Mind, she was well rid. Took every penny she 'ad and that wasn't much. Kept a few quid in the teapot — fer the rent an' that. All gone. Some fancy woman, Emily thought. In some racket, I'll bet. My 'usband, Billy, used ter 'ave a drink with Sam Bate — sometimes 'ad a wad o' cash. Where's a bloke like that get so much cash? Billy used ter ask. 'Ere and there, Bate said. That's why 'e went off, I thought — some money-makin' racket. See no one 'ad anything — there was men without legs or arms dependin' on charity, widows 'avin ter beg fer a pension. Bate'd got that cash crooked, no doubt about it, an' Emily Bate 'ad nothin' 'cept a few shillin's from the fish shop when 'e went off.'

'Where did Mrs Bate move to?'

'Rooms — see their 'ouse was rented an' she couldn't afford it.'

'How did she die?'

'Terrible thing — not that I was there. She'd moved again by then, but I saw it once when I was a kiddie.'

'What did you see?'

'A woman fell out of a window — same as Emily Bate. Women still do it, though — sit on the windowsill to clean the windows. Poor Emily musta lost 'er balance.'

'Was she alone?'

There was that piercing look again, but she chuckled. 'Think Bate came back and did 'er in? Wouldn't'a put it past 'im. But, no, it was much later, 1942. Her husband was at the fish shop.'

'She married again?'

'Not exactly. I mean no one said anythin'. We all felt good riddance ter Bate, but you 'ad ter wait seven years when someone was missin'. Why should she do that? No, they lived together, Emily an' Phil Crabbe — in the fish trade after the war. We used to laugh about 'is name, but 'e's a good sort is — '

'He's alive?'

'Jest round the corner. You'll 'ave ter speak up. He's a bit deaf. Mind, 'e's eighty-five, though nothin' wrong with my ears.'

I left her to her memories and went out to find Mr Crabbe who I hoped might be able to tell me more, but I couldn't think what.

The story was pretty much the same. I told Mr Crabbe the story about my godmother wanting information about Samuel Bate who had visited a house called Foulstone up in Westmorland. Mr Crabbe knew all about that from Emily Bate. He also confirmed what Mrs Rudd had said about Bate's criminality and his all-round worthlessness. Mr Crabbe had been in the war and told me about those who made a habit of thieving from dead soldiers — their own and the Germans, and who ran rackets in cigarettes, rum, chocolate, and stolen food. Bate had a reputation, it seemed.

'They wasn't all heroes — not the likes of Bate, though he wasn't afraid, I'll give him that. Hard as nails, though. Swore his way through it all. Some couldn't stick it — shell shock, they called it. Not him. His temper was the drink an' resentment. Not nerves. Raring to get home he was — time for a reckoning, he said. Most of us was just weary, bone weary, after what we'd seen. Not him. Time for pay day, he said. See, he'd been concussed in an explosion, but they made him go back. Bitter about that. Hated the officers worse than the Jerries — said he'd been left to die in a shell hole by some b — well you knows what he meant.'

I couldn't think that Nowell Dearlove would have abandoned one of his men. Gerard Revell? Haunted by two men he'd seen die? He had thought Bate was dead. But Bate had never mentioned Revell. I asked another question. 'He wrote Mr Dearlove's name on a piece of paper. Mr Dearlove's son was killed. Did Bate think Mr Dearlove would give him money?'

'I couldn't fathom that, Miss, I mean go all the way up north to ask a dead officer's father for money. No, mark my words, he was up to something else — runnin' from a load o' crooks, I'd wager. That's all he ever thought about, money. Course, no one had any those days after the war, except Sam Bate — in any kind of racket, I'd say, but there was some hard types around, Italian brothers into drugs, booze, gamblin', extortion, and if Sam Bate got in with folk like that, he was makin' a big mistake. These gangs stick together, see, and Bate was the type that thought he was big enough. Clever devil, Bate, saw that in the war, skin a louse for its pelt. Clever enough to make a packet out of other men's bad luck, but mebbe not clever enough for the big time.'

'Did Emily know anything about all this?'

'She thought he was up to no good with some woman — an' I believed that, too, though what sort o' woman would want him, I don't know. An' after she'd tried to find him, we got together an' I told my Em to forget him. It wasn't our business. Said I'd look after her. We'd to get on with our lives an' we did until… I told her not to sit on that windowsill, but they all did it. Still, we had happy times, though we never had much, an' I've got me daughter. She's married now an' I've got the grandkids and their kiddies. No wars for them, I hopes.'

I was glad that Mrs Bate had found happiness, and that Mr Crabbe had his grandchildren and great-grandchildren in his old age. Mrs Rudd hadn't mentioned any other children other than Teddy. All those women receiving those telegrams. How that war and the last one cast such long shadows. And Joan — her life so bleak because of that first war. Helena's life. Gerard Revell.

'Did he ever mention the name Gerard Revell?'

'That was the name of that lady she saw at that house — but Em said not. She didn't know that name.'

I didn't think I'd learn anything more. I stood up to go, but Mr Crabbe stopped me.

'Somethin' I've thought. It didn't seem much at the time. Hettie Rudd always said she knew he'd not come back. She said he had a suitcase with him and Em found an old cardboard one he'd used in the war. Mrs Rudd said he had a small leather one — looked new. Scarpering with his ill-gotten gains, I think. He wasn't never coming back, was he? Goin' to

America from Liverpool, I'll bet — thought he'd be a big shot over there. He'll not have lasted. I reckon he's long dead.'

I could smell cooking as Joan let me in. Roast chicken. 'Smells good,' I said.

'I thought if you didn't come today, we could have it cold tomorrow, but now it'll be a nice roast dinner. I've made a sherry trifle —'

'Oh, you bought more.'

'Oh, yes, nothing to it — except it made the basket heavy to carry back.'

She went out to make tea and I sat by the fire. I was glad to be back, and Joan had looked so pleased to see me.

'Did you find out anything?' she asked when the tea was poured, and we each had a bourbon biscuit.

I told her all about Hettie Rudd and Phil Crabbe and Mrs Bate's death and what they'd said about Samuel Bate.

'He was an awful man then. I wonder if he got money from Gerard Revell and then went off as that Mr Crabbe said, especially if he was on the run from a gang of crooks.'

'Sounds like he was capable of blackmail. I did have a thought about him, though. He had a suitcase with him. Mrs Rudd and Mr Crabbe thought he wasn't coming back, and I wondered where he stayed. We think Helena saw him at the bridge in the morning, but he was seen at the station the night before.'

'Took a room somewhere? We can't go about asking in town about someone who came here fifty years ago. It was in the paper you read, and no one came forward then. Slept in a ditch, maybe.'

'Yes, you're probably right. I think we have to accept that he vanished, and we'll never know what his relationship with Gerard Revell was.'

'There's something else. I found a diary belonging to Arthur Dearlove.'

'Where?'

'Up at Foulstone.'

I was astonished. 'You went up there on your own?'

Joan smiled as she answered, 'You went to London on your own. I thought I'd better shape myself and do something a bit more courageous than buying a bottle of sherry.'

'Have you read it?'

'I have.'

'And?'

'I want you to take it with you next door after we've had our chicken. You can tell me what you think tomorrow. I'll make us a good breakfast.'

PART FOUR: 1919

25

1919

Arthur Dearlove always felt the emptiness of his house on this day. Dear Mary Goss was no doubt shopping and William Goss in the garden, but had they been with him, it would have made no difference. September, he thought, a lovely month, the trees turning to gold, the creeper turning to scarlet, a few late roses still blooming, and beyond the fence, the sheep taking in the warmth of the sun after days of unseasonably bitter cold. The fells were burnished with bracken, all copper and russet under the clear Wedgwood blue sky. He looked at the letter in his hand. The war, he thought. On a golden day like this, you would hardly think that such things had happened. The war was over — for some, for many, and he did not begrudge them their joy, their hope, and their future.

But there was only a maimed future for him. The future he had planned erased completely since he had had the dreadful news, a year ago to the day. He had known. People said they knew as soon as the telegram boy came up their drive or path on his bike. He had known what news was in the leather pouch on the boy's belt. The boy had known, too, his very young face serious under his pillbox cap. The uniform of the King. A boy in man's clothes, like those out there in Flanders.

Arthur had been walking up on the fell and had lingered by the roses when he came down, leaning on his stick with the dog's head which Nowell head given him one Christmas. It was one of the very few dry days of that other unseasonable September. Of course, he had been thinking about Nowell out in the rain and mud. And he had been thinking of Flanders, of Ypres, in particular. Nowell was there somewhere. The newspapers had told how the troops were in good heart and fighting splendidly. In April 1918, the order from Field Marshal Haig had been that 'Every position must be held to the last man.' What a chill there had been in those words.

The boy had handed him the envelope. Arthur Dearlove knew by the mark on the envelope that it was bad news. The boy knew there would be no reply. He had delivered such messages before. Mechanically, Arthur reached in his pocket for a coin. The boy shook his head. Then he rode away. He did not look back at the man standing on the path in the rain that was now falling. One of those showers that came without warning over the Westmorland fells.

Arthur did not notice the rain. He didn't need to read those words again, "Deeply regret to inform you Lieut. NA Dearlove killed in action. Flanders September 24th."

Mary Goss had stood at the front door waiting. She knew, too. He went into the cool panelled hall. He remembered the yellow roses on the chest glowing very bright. Down the corridor, Nowell's dog was barking. Alive, alive, he had thought, and my boy dead. Mrs Goss touched his arm, her face very white in the gloom, and the tears starting in her kind eyes. He shook his head and went upstairs to sit at his desk and look at the photograph of his beloved only son whose face looked back — the dear, handsome face that he would never see again creased in laughter. Remembering the lithe figure striding down from the fell with the dog at his side, his face flushed with the wind, his brown eyes warm with affection for his father and his home where he was cherished as he had every right to be.

A fine-featured face, serious, of course in the next photograph in which he was in uniform. Eyes that looked straight at you, candid and determined. Nowell had never hidden things — he always admitted wrong-doing. A broken window, a fall from a forbidden tree, a sneaking taste at the port decanter — small things, but his frankness counted, and his apologies were manly. Arthur had been proud of him. Nowell was like his dead mother in looks. The same brown eyes, the same nose, very straight and narrow. A little cleft in the chin. Arthur's wife had not been a beauty; she had been ordinary, with mid-brown hair, but with humour in that cleft chin and those warm eyes and he had loved her as deeply as they had both loved their son. Nowell had turned into a handsome young man with his father's height, his mother's eyes, and something of his own, of course, that neither Arthur nor his wife could trace. Perhaps, they came from way back, the golden hair, the finely modelled mouth, and straight white teeth.

Arthur looked at the photograph now. His son frozen in time, unchanged. But he had changed, Arthur knew that. He'd had a few glimpses of the toll the war had taken — the sudden anguish of a start at a crash in the kitchen. An occasional comment. 'No Man's Land, they've got that right. Fit for man nor beast, nor bird, nor any thing that liveth.' 'Obstinate hopelessness,' he had said one morning, 'that's what we feel.' Then he had gone out, whistling the tune of that old song "Smile, Smile, Smile". What's the use of worrying? Those were the words he heard in his head.

Mrs Bents, the milkwoman, whistled — a cheerful woman with a weather-hardened face, a friendly smile, and raw hands from the milking. She worked for a farmer and lived down near the mill with her daughter.

'For her, I suppose,' Nowell had said, flinching at the clatter of the tailboard of Mrs Bents's cart and the metallic clash of the churns. 'For sturdy, uncomplaining Mrs Bents, and for all those like her, just ordinary, but full of goodness somehow. Decent and honest. And for you, Pa.'

And whenever Arthur heard someone whistling, his heart was pierced with such agony that he could hardly breathe. Mrs Bents still whistled, even though her husband had died in the flu epidemic. The postman, the boy who brought the eggs from the farm, all whistled, but never William Goss. He had stopped whistling on the day that telegram came. Mary Goss still made bread, but never Nowell's favourite gingerbread or tea cakes. Tea at four o'clock came with a sandwich and a sponge cake. Full of goodness, Mr and Mrs Goss. Nowell had died for them and their kind. 'And for you, Pa,' Nowell had said, winking at him, turning the pain to laughter just for a moment. Arthur would rather have died for him.

Oh, but it was agony now to remember. Nowell at the station, coming home in his crumpled uniform with his khaki knapsack. Nowell taking his baths. William Goss never minded firing up the range for the hot water. William and Mary Goss would have done anything for Nowell, hot water, fresh towels, clean sheets, clean clothes. Mary Goss cleaning and pressing Nowell's muddy Burberry, his service jacket, his breeches, his shirts. They were there now in the kitbag in Nowell's wardrobe. The sarcophagus, Nowell had joked as a boy, peering into its gloomy depths. When he was a little boy, Arthur had always looked inside to check for ghosts. Not now. Not ever, perhaps.

Mary Goss knitted night and day. She could do it with one hand, without looking, the knitting stick in her belt, and stirring soup with another. Scarves, socks, gloves, sweaters, made of what she called bump — oiled wool from Kendal, which she was sure would keep him warm and dry — they all went back with him and bars of Kendal Mint Cake. Bull's Eye sweets, too, good for chills or a sore throat.

She used to bake a fresh loaf for his breakfast every day and never minded if he ate it all. 'Frozen bread over there, Mrs G., grey as the mud and hard as bullets.' And another loaf, or tea cakes, or gingerbread, or all three would appear for tea for which Nowell would come down glowing, his hair still wet. 'Lord, Pa,' he'd say, 'you've no idea how good it is to be clean.' And then he'd suggest a game of cards, or chess, and after dinner, some light music on the gramophone. 'No Chopin mayonnaise,' he'd say. An old joke — a charwoman they'd had once said it.

That last leave he had brought his friend, Gerard Revell, another fine young man. A lonely young man, Arthur had thought, serious and thoughtful, whose friendship Nowell had so valued. Gerard Revell had no family, it seemed. Arthur was glad to have him there. They didn't talk much of the Front, but Arthur knew when his son's troubled eyes caught his. Arthur read the papers; he could read between the lines, and he had seen the casualty lists. Only once had he caught the murmur of voices as he entered the room. Nowell's voice, low and mournful, quoting a line from his favourite poet, Walter de la Mare. 'Hating thy journey, homeless, home.' He had been pierced with anguish. No wonder, though, that these boys were haunted by the spectre, death. It was all about them, day and night. They would feel its foetid breath at their necks. He passed a hand over his eyes to banish the image.

Going into the room, he had taken some comfort from the idea that Nowell and Gerard had each other. The talk was of the walk they would have tomorrow when Nowell would take

Gerard up to Firbank Fell where George Fox had started his Quaker movement and had spoken of peace. Perhaps, they would find some solace in that remote spot, out in the fresh air, hearing the sweetness of the larks and the bubbling curlews, and resting their haunted eyes on the green hills.

Nowell and Gerard at the station, their uniforms smart again. One of Mary Goss's fruitcakes in a tin. 'It'll keep well,' she had told them. She'd never made one again. Arthur sometimes thought of that cake — had Nowell ever tasted it and thought of home? And then had the night come? And the order to go to his death?

Nowell waving from the window. The train disappearing round the curve, the sound of the engine fading, the smoke still hanging on the platform. A woman weeping. Had her son come home? he wondered now.

Arthur kept the telegram in a box in his desk, and the letter from the chaplain, kinder words than those in the telegram. He didn't need to read them today. He had them by heart. There was comfort in them. He had shown the letter to Mary and William Goss and then he had read it over and over in the quiet of his room, the letter which told him about Nowell's gallant part in the raid against the German position:

I cannot tell you how sorry I am. I can assure you that there is not one who does not feel his death as a personal blow...

I wish I could help to soften the hardness of your sorrow. I know that Nowell was your only son. The only comfort lies in knowing that he gave his life in a sacred cause, fighting for Right and Justice. It is the greatest sacrifice that a man can make. I am sure that Captain Revell will write to you. He, too, is the finest of men and risked his own life to find your son. Alas, he could not save him.

All those who have fallen in the field of honour in this world war are following the path of self-sacrifice and of duty which our Lord himself once trod...

He had tried to believe it, though it was very hard. There were thousands like him, he knew. Mothers who had lost two or three sons; other fathers who had lost their only sons; wives who had lost their husbands; children who had lost their fathers. And what of those who had returned to find no home or no employment to reward them?

The winter was a hard and bitter one. Snow fell thickly on the fells, blotting out the landscape. The nights were long and dark, and he sat very often simply looking into the fire, not bothering to light the lamps. Even the spring was cold, and the snow continued to fall. There was no getting out for a walk, though he struggled up to church whenever he could. He sat alone there sometimes to pray for his boy and for all those others who had died out there, and for those who grieved as he did. He could have gone to the school chapel where Nowell had sung and prayed — but it was too soon for that. The sight of the new generation of boys was too painful, though he was glad that their fresh, eager faces would not see what his boy had seen.

He read the chaplain's letter again and again and took some solace from that, but nothing could erase the truths that he had learned since 1918. He had read extracts from the memoirs of a young soldier called Dudley Howard-Tripp. Tripp had lost his best friend, too, after which "war loomed like a monstrous nightmare of injustice and degradation around and above me, and a band of ice seemed to gather my soul into its grip, crushing and mortifying."

The words had seared him, but Arthur had felt the truth of them. Tripp had gone on to write that one blinded or crippled boy robbed war of all its glory. And, he had thought about those whose minds were maimed. What they had suffered. What Nowell had suffered. Arthur had chanced upon Walter de la Mare's new collection — he thought to buy it in remembrance of Nowell's love for the poet, but one line in the poem 'Motley' had filled him with horror. De la Mare had written of "A measureless Beast with eyes like one from filthy dreams awoke." His eyes had filled. His boy, his innocent boy, who had looked into the eyes of a beast and seen degradation. He had put down the book, left the shop, and wept alone in his study.

Grief, pity, horror, and guilt, too. He should have stopped Nowell — but no one knew what was to come. Everyone thought victory would be achieved easily — over by Christmas, they said. And when victory did not come with trumpets and drums, young men like Nowell thought it was their duty to fight for King and Country. Honour, was the clarion call of the newspapers. Honour was sacred. The nation's sword was drawn in defence of honour.

The Officer Training Corps at the school. A photograph that he could not bear to look at now — the school monitors in 1914, several of them in uniform. Seventeen-year-old Nowell. Battalion drill, tactical exercises, route marches, bivouacking up on the fells, trench digging — boys playing at war. "Play up! Play up! And play the game." How ironic those familiar words seemed now. Boys preparing for the great adventure. They revelled in it. They had to go. It was their duty. Nowell would have looked at him as if he were mad had his father suggested otherwise. And he had not. He had believed, too.

Now he looked again at this new letter. Gerard Revell was coming at last, and Arthur would know another truth that he longed to know. Nowell had never been found. Nothing remained of him. That had been very difficult to come to terms with — no honoured grave to visit, either in the quiet churchyard here or in Flanders. An M.P. had spoken at the beginning of the many young men who would go down in the struggle — for duty's sake. Down, down, he thought now, down into the mud.

Nowell's bedroom was unaltered. Mary Goss kept it clean, but she did not change anything. His Bible was there, too, and the photograph of his mother. The school photographs on the wall, the cricket bat propped against the chair, the clothes in the wardrobe, the cricket blazer and tie, the cricket sweater which still smelt of him — though it was fading now. Soon it would be gone, and those faint traces of his son's being would vanish. And his army kitbag, returned. In the sarcophagus. Ghosts of a kind.

The book of de la Mare's poems was still on his bedside table, its bookmark in the place where he had last finished reading. He had read the last words that Nowell had read at Foulstone Manor, the words he had underlined, and thought his heart would break. "Homeless, home."

This room was where he felt Nowell most keenly, where he expected Nowell to be when he opened the door. Sometimes, he thought he glimpsed a golden head just at the end of the corridor or he thought he heard someone whistling. Laughter sometimes and his heart would leap. He would go into the room then and sit on the bed, waiting for his heart to stop its wild beating. Oh, Nowell, my boy, he would cry. And then he would wipe his eyes, take up Nowell's Bible to look at the page marked by the thin silk ribbon. Nowell's favourite Psalm 23.

Oh, those prescient words: "Yea, though I walk through the valley of the shadow of death, I will fear no evil: for thou art with me." Arthur would read them aloud and pray for strength, too, for acceptance, and for the certainty that the Lord had been with his boy when he passed through that valley of death.

It was hard won, but it came only to ease his agony for pain would always be there — a burden he would have to carry. Nowell had used the word endurance. Well, he must endure, too. Otherwise, Nowell's death would count for nothing at all.

Gerard Revell could tell him exactly what had happened to his son, and then he would find a measure of peace. His house would still be empty, his future a blank, but he would live it as best he could, with at least some small comfort that he might know where his boy lay and how he had died.

Arthur Dearlove hoped that his own son, Nowell, would have felt as deeply if Gerard had been killed. He thought of Dudley Tripp and his lost friend, and he could hardly bear to look at the anguish in the young man's eyes as he told the dreadful story.

'In front of our trenches about three or four hundred yards away, there was a bulge in the German line — a nuisance to us, overlooking the next-door battalion — meaning that the Germans could fire down the length of their trench — dangerous, of course. Our Colonel wanted it captured. We were sent out on what we called a stunt, starting from an old gun emplacement. We'd not got far when an inferno suddenly erupted, machine-gun fire, bursting shells, Very lights, smoke — the lot. We all got separated. I was blown into a shell hole and crawled back up. I saw Nowell fall, and in a lull, I crawled to where I thought he was — it wasn't far, and I managed to drag him back. He'd been shot, but he was alive. We were there all night — I don't really know — I must have been unconscious. When I came to, Nowell was gone — the water, you see, the mud — I should have — I can't…'

Down, down, as he had thought, but this young man needed comfort, too. 'Of course, you can't. I understand. At least I know.'

'He didn't falter, sir — he carried on under fire…'

He need not have come, Arthur thought. He might just have written, but he had come to face Nowell's father and to tell him all the painful truth of it, that he had tried to save Nowell, but that he could not. What a burden that was. But a burden this suffering young man should not have to bear. Nowell had been shot, and though Gerard had brought him back at the risk of his own life, Nowell might have died of his wounds. The guilt was not Gerard's. It was the war's guilt.

Gerard told Arthur Dearlove that he must go back to London. He had a job on a newspaper — nothing grand, but it would be a living. Gerard had no people. There was no country house to which he could go back. No one to look after him. Arthur made up his mind.

'Stay here for a while, my boy. You need looking after, feeding up. Mrs Goss will do that. You can do as you please — take some long walks, sleep in, read the paper, read the books in the library.'

'I don't think I…'

'A week or so. It will do you the world of good — and me. You were my boy's greatest friend. He said so in his letters. He could not have managed without you — you saved his life, he said, so often when it was unbearable. I don't know how to thank you for all that.'

Gerard Revell turned away. 'I let him down — at the end — I failed —'

189

Arthur had seen the anguish in the young man's eyes. 'But it was impossible. I know. I've read enough about it, but you risked your own life, and before — his strength and stay, he said you were.'

Gerard Revell stayed for three weeks. He grew to love the quiet manor house with its panelled rooms, its stone floors, the mullioned windows, the bedroom with its view over the woods and hills beyond where he walked alone. He played chess with Arthur Dearlove, but they didn't talk about Nowell. Arthur regretted this, but he had no wish to force the matter. After all, Gerard had been through it, had suffered its horrors. It was not for him to insist, and there would be other times to be sure in the future when Gerard came again, and they could talk about Nowell when the pain was less raw — for both of them.

On leave, in one of their quiet moments Nowell had said that it was hell, and that he was afraid only that he might prove a coward. Thank God for Gerard Revell, he had said, Gerard whom he thought was finer than he, braver, more daring. Gerard would prove a hero — and so he had, Arthur believed, but his own boy had been a hero, too, had not run away, had faced it, and had died facing it.

Arthur watched Gerard from his study window. He had watched him walk away to the woods, his shoulders hunched, his head bent, and his heart had been wrung with pity for the lonely young man. He looked as if he bore all the injustice and degradation of that monstrous time. He made a decision. He would do something for Gerard. He told him so on a night when they smoked a cigar on the terrace.

'It is not all over, Gerard. Come back and tell me you are going to be married. Then you shall come back for good and live here with a pretty wife and a couple of children — a boy to have this so that I'll know it's in good hands. It will belong to you when I am gone. No, don't say anything — I cannot leave it to Nowell or Nowell's son. That was not to be. Who else should have it but you and the family you must have — for Nowell's sake? Promise me and you shall have it for your son whom you will, I hope, call Nowell, and he will live on in your boy. And if that is too much to ask, I shall understand, but bring him to see me, and the years ahead will not be so empty. We shall have hope in the future.'

PART FIVE: 1970

26

Amanda

I sat up late by the fire after I had read Arthur Dearlove's story, listening to the wind and rain outside. I knew I wouldn't sleep, though I was exhausted by what I had read. It was so moving, as if he were speaking to me from fifty years ago, telling me what he had suffered. How he had grieved when Nowell was killed. And Nowell — what he had endured. What he had seen. I could hardly bear to think of it. That image of the beast and the filthy dreams. It shouldn't have happened to him — or millions more.

Nowell sounded so — so young and so untouched before the war, so loving to his father and so fond of William and Mary Goss. I could imagine him as his father had seen him, handsome, so alive, open-faced, whistling — just as Helena had glimpsed him. And then she had not seen him again after her miscarriage, after she had seen Samuel Bate under the bridge. If it had been he.

She had been haunted by both of them in a way. It was as if the war had haunted Foulstone Manor and that was something to do with Gerard Revell. I couldn't really puzzle it out. That poem of Gerard's, 'The Ghost', showed that he was haunted by Nowell and then the poem 'The Third' — the woods haunted by Nowell and Bate. Perhaps Bate hadn't gone to America. Perhaps he had died. My thoughts circled round.

I could understand Helena's dreams after she had seen Bate in the woods and possibly on the lawn in the night, but could dreams be more than just images in the mind? I suppose I was asking if there were such things as ghosts. I'd read enough about them, but to contemplate the fact of them was overwhelming. I thought I'd seen a figure in the corridor at Foulstone and I'd felt a moment of real terror. Was that Gerard Revell haunting the place where he had killed himself?

What had Gerard Revell been remembering when he shot himself? I looked again at the account he had written of Nowell's death. He had written it out three times. I'd thought he was perfecting it for a memoir, but he had never published it. There were only the fragments we had seen and the paragraph he had repeated to Arthur Dearlove —

A thought struck me then, a rather frightening one. Gerard had repeated the story to Arthur Dearlove. Why had he needed to write it down three times? The events must have been seared into his brain. I rifled through Gerard's papers to find the written accounts and then I compared the final version with what he had told Arthur. It was exactly as Arthur had written it down in his account of the conversation — every word that Gerard spoke precious to him. I could understand that, but Gerard had included the phrase "you see" in his written version, as if — as if he were talking to someone. And then the words "I should have... I can't..."

How odd to have written those as if he were learning his part. Working out what he would say and how he would finish. The first two versions with their crossings out were trial runs. And he was word perfect for Arthur Dearlove. He had even put in the three dots after the word "mud" — that was where he would break off because it was too dreadful to remember. Then he had added those two phrases nearer the end of the page. He would say that he could not go on.

I could hardly take it in. Could it possibly be that they were not meant for any memoir? That he was rehearsing. That the last phrases were meant to show that he was so broken that he could say no more and Arthur Dearlove, in the goodness of his heart, had accepted that Gerard was not able to tell him anything more — not even to speak of it. Arthur Dearlove had hoped that he and Gerard would talk again, but Gerard could not — would not open up.

I felt shaken to the core at the enormity of what I was thinking. Gerard Revell's version was not the truth.

I remembered what Mr Crabbe had said about Bate — that he had hated the officers and that he had been left in a shell hole to die. Had Bate been there when Nowell died and had he seen something? Gerard Revell had seen a dead man walking — perhaps, as we had thought, he had believed Bate was dead and then he came back, the coward and the shirker, to blackmail him — to tell him that he would expose the truth of what he had seen unless he was paid.

It was a horrible idea that Gerard Revell had lied to Arthur Dearlove, to present himself as a hero and to take Foulstone Manor as his reward.

I listened to the wind, stronger now, and the rattle of rain on the windows and I found I was trembling. It was bad enough that Gerard Revell had stolen a name, but this was monstrous. I found that I could believe in his tormented ghost at Foulstone, and in that smell. It was as if the place was rotten and corrupt. The lie had tainted Foulstone, had infected poor Helena, and Joan. It came down the years, the smell a horrible echo of that lie. I could not bear to think of going there again.

A great gust of wind shook the house, and the front door flew open; my lamp and candles flickered and the dying fire leapt up. I stood up, terrified. I think I thought that it was he, Gerard Revell, that he knew I'd found out. There was someone there — a figure in white stepped in. I don't know how I stopped myself from screaming.

It was Joan in her nightdress, her grey hair swept by the wind. She looked terrified, too. We just stared at each other and then Joan spoke.

'Oh, Amanda. I'm so sorry — I don't know what —'

I brought her in, slammed the door and bolted it, and took her to the fire and threw on a log as I sat her down. She was in her slippers. My sheepskin coat was on the back of a chair, and I put it round her.

'What is it? What's happened?'

'Nothing — at least, I don't know. I must have been dreaming. I was thinking of Nowell and what I'd read in the diary. I couldn't get his death out of my mind. Drowning in the mud — what a terrible thing. And Helena thinking she'd seen him — remember she saw him covered with mud as if he had lain in it, and she smelt mud and decay and something like gas. I smelt it again then. I must have fallen asleep, yet I could hear the wind in my sleep, and the smell was in my mouth, or maybe I was awake. I heard something and now I'm here. It's happened before when I haven't known if I was awake or asleep. I thought I saw him looking at me through a cracked window. You don't think I'm going mad, do you?'

I'd mastered my own terror by now, seeing Joan and knowing she was not him. 'No, no,' I said, 'it's all been too much — these last days. We haven't stopped thinking about it all, and hearing about Bate, reading all this stuff. Look at me, I couldn't stop thinking about — it's like we're haunted.'

'I saw them — the three. I went in the night, and they were there in the woods. I wasn't going to tell you — but now, this. Me here. In my nightdress for goodness' sake. What's happening to me?'

'It's not just you. I saw something. I wasn't going to tell you — I thought I'd imagined it. At Foulstone. Remember when I dropped my torch, I thought I saw someone in that corridor where the plaster fell... And that time in his study, I felt frightened — I thought there was the smell.'

Joan's colour was coming back. I was kneeling in front of her, holding her hands which did feel warmer despite the tremor I felt there. And there was relief in her eyes.

'Gerard Revell, do you think it was him?'

'Or Nowell, I don't know, it was only for a moment.'

'So was mine. I saw them on the woodland path. A second or two. I don't know if it was real.'

'I don't know, either. Oh, Auntie Joan, I don't know what to believe. Helena saw Nowell in the woods — was she seeing a ghost? Were we? Or is it just that we are so caught up in it all that we're imagining. I wish I knew more about these things — apart from what I've read in fiction. Those kinds of ghost are frightening, but you know they're not real. Then again, lots of people say they've seen them. I remember stories about the Tower of London — all sorts of accounts by ghost hunters.'

Joan looked sceptical. She was recovering. 'They want to see them, so they do, but in our case, we've not gone out ghost hunting.'

'But tonight —'

'You were reading Arthur's story. Something in it frightened you. Not just me coming in with the wind. You did look terrified.'

'I was. I thought of something that made me believe that Gerard Revell — that they are haunting Foulstone.'

'Tea,' Joan said, 'I need tea or sherry or something before I hear this.'

I wished I had some brandy, but I made the tea instead while Joan built up the fire. I made toast, too. Something familiar and comforting. And then I told her what I had thought about Gerard Revell's account of Nowell's death, the way he had practised what he was going to say, and I added something else to my own thoughts.

'Gerard Revell killed himself on the tenth anniversary of Nowell's death.'

Joan looked as horrified as I had felt. 'He told Arthur Dearlove a lie,' she said, 'a terrible lie to that good man who believed it all and pitied him. Oh, God, Amanda, he is worse than we ever thought. Even we thought that his suffering was the cause of what he did to Helena.'

'And Bate knew. When he turned up, Gerard Revell thought he had seen a dead man come back to life.'

'He met him in the park that time — Helena thought so. She saw Gerard give the man something — she loved him for that. Oh, Amanda, lie upon lie.'

'I found something else in Arthur's diary. A letter from Gerard Revell to Arthur Dearlove. You'll see that the address is The Naval and Military Club, Piccadilly. It was written in September of 1920. I think it says a lot about him.'

I knelt by Joan, and we read it together.

My Dear Mr Dearlove,

I have good news. My promise is kept, I am delighted to say. I shall be bringing my bride to Foulstone Manor to see you. Her name is Helena Lovelace. She lives with her father, a gentleman of private means of The Lantern House in the quiet village of Middlestone, near Chertsey.

I met her through mutual friends, the Mountjoy-Smythes of Ferndean Court, Berkshire.

She is a quiet girl who suits me very well — and I hope I suit her. Her quietness is soothing to my soul, and I believe that the future you envisaged for me will come true at last. You gave me hope, sir, and I shall be ever in your debt.

Miss Lovelace and I share the same interests in poetry, art, and music. And we both like to walk in the parks and on Hampstead Heath. I am certain that she will love Foulstone Manor. A quiet life in the country will suit her very well.

You will like her, sir, I am sure. She will take care of Foulstone Manor for our son — when he comes. He shall be called Nowell as you wished.

We have not yet set a date for the wedding, but I hope that you will be able to come to celebrate with us. Mr Lovelace has given us his blessing and I hope we may have yours.

I am, Mr Dearlove, your most grateful friend,
Gerard Revell

'It's all about him,' was Joan's first comment. And she was right. Helena would suit him, and then that afterthought that he hoped he suited her. She'd like a quiet life — all right, she did choose that, but the letter sounded to me as if it was all decided for her, and then she would look after Foulstone and the son.

'The son he was sure he would have,' I said, 'the son who would be Nowell and inherit Foulstone. Perhaps Gerard Revell thought that would atone for what he had done.'

Joan was looking thoughtful. 'But this letter sounds — so — I don't know — calculating. Is that the word? I didn't get the impression that he knew the Mountjoy-Smythes all that well, and we know that Lily didn't like him much. He makes it sound as if —'

'Of Ferndean Court, as if he knew it, wanted to impress Mr Dearlove with his credentials, so to speak, and that bit about

Mr Lovelace, a gentleman of private means, of The Lantern House. He didn't give his own address, but The Naval and Military Club sounds the sort of place where Captain Gerard Revell would be a member.'

'September 1920,' Joan said. 'Helena met him in the summer of 1920, but he didn't propose until October 1920.'

'He told Arthur Dearlove that she had accepted him before he proposed. He had it all worked out — getting her father on his side. Maybe her father told him that he had not long to live and that he wanted Helena taken care of. Gerard Revell knew she wouldn't refuse him if her father persuaded her.'

'No photographs of that wedding — accident with the camera. I don't believe that. He didn't care tuppence about it. He just wanted that house. He's a devil.'

'And a lucky one. I bet Arthur Dearlove made his will when he got that letter and then he died in September – he fell down those stairs.'

Joan looked at me. ' You're not thinking —'

'No, no, of course not. I couldn't — he wouldn't — not that.' I didn't dare say the word out loud.

Neither of us spoke for a minute or two. The fire crackled and the wind roared outside, and still the rain rattled on the windows. I put my hand on Joan's knee and she covered it with her own. It was as if a great abyss had opened before us, some huge, dark place to which we dared not go.

'Good Lord, deliver us from battle and murder,' Joan said. 'That's what he wrote.'

'Did he leave Nowell and Bate to die? That it was a kind of murder?'

'He came to Foulstone to see Arthur Dearlove. Presumably Arthur had written to ask him to tell what happened. Gerard couldn't refuse and if he *had* left them, he couldn't tell Arthur that.'

'How could he? To tell the truth was impossible. I can see that.'

'So can I — I don't hold much sympathy for him, but I can understand that. Anyway, it wouldn't have helped Arthur to know the truth, but to accept Foulstone and marry my mother for it, that's unforgiveable —'

She stopped at that word. We both knew that there might be something even more unforgiveable and in the next silence I thought about Arthur Dearlove's convenient death. 'We have no evidence — the inquest found that it was an accident. Mary Goss found him. There was no mention of anyone else in the house. It can't be. I'm sorry I thought it — it was a dreadful thing to think.'

I heard Joan exhale a deep breath. 'I thought it, too. We're overwrought — me sleepwalking, both of us seeing ghosts. Letting our imaginations run riot.'

'What do you want to do?'

Joan gave me a half smile. 'Sleep — without dreaming.'

I felt guilty. What had I started? Where it had taken us — to contemplating blackmail and murder, and nothing finished, so many loose ends. It's not a novel, I thought, it's not even a ghost story. They have endings. Of course, they do often leave the reader unsettled, not knowing whether the apparition was true. But the reader can close the book and it's over. You can even laugh at the preposterousness of it all, but this … we'd both seen something.

Joan was watching me. She looked anxious. 'Don't think it's your fault. Perhaps, I'd have gone up to Foulstone anyway. Perhaps, I'd have opened Mary's boxes and let something out.

But I've had you and I'm glad, Amanda, even though I've no idea what to do next — if anything.'

'I don't know. What if we see them again and again? In the woods or in the house?'

'I felt the other night that I'd like to burn it down, but that's a daft idea, I know. What do people mean when they talk about laying ghosts?'

'If it's a memory then come to terms with it — find out what happened and accept it — sounds easy, doesn't it?'

'Be said — that's what Mary Goss used to say, meaning that's enough — be satisfied as if that was the end of whatever the problem was. But it's not enough just now. I can't stand the thought of that place haunting my dreams —'

'Exorcism — the church does it. A vicar says prayers and they sprinkle holy water and tell the ghost to go.'

'Gracious — I don't think I'd like to be telling a vicar what we think we've seen. No, thanks.'

'Then we'll have to lay them ourselves.'

'How do we do that?'

'Haven't a clue,' I said.

We both laughed and felt better. Even the wind had dropped, and the lamps had stopped flickering.

'We've found out a lot,' Joan said. 'I think it would help if we tried to find out who Gerard Revell was, and then we'd kind of feel we'd done all we could. Maybe that would be it — we'd stop imagining. We'd lay the ghost.'

27

Joan

We needed to go back to London. While I was planting the bulbs after all that wind and rain last night, I'd been thinking of Foulstone, worrying about the storm, the chimneys, the roof, water flooding in, and not knowing what I was going to do about any of it. It seemed such a burden, and I'll admit, I was thinking about ghosts and if I would ever have the courage to open that heavy front door again and step into that hall, see those stairs, and feel that cold wind from the kitchen passage.

I'd heard the wind in my dreams and seeing that cellar door open, inviting me to go down into the dark to a place I could smell but not see, where a figure wearing something long and dark stood at the bottom of a set of wooden stairs which were all broken and rotten so that I knew I would fall — and I was falling.

I'd woken then — something had hit the window, I thought, a branch maybe. But the smell was in my mouth and a sense that someone was with me, something filling the room with a kind of darkness. I could feel it, thick and suffocating. It was as if the room had vanished. No walls, no window, no door to get out. Just blackness.

And that's when I must have got up. I don't remember going downstairs. I just remember standing in Amanda's parlour and her white face staring at me.

But that talk helped us both to get a grip on things. When I'd left her, I thought how I couldn't go on just letting things happen to me — just letting him — them — whoever —

haunt me forever. I would go mad, I thought, and Amanda shouldn't have to deal with that. It would take some doing, I knew that, but together we could deal with it. Hobson's choice, as Mary Goss would have it — whoever Hobson was. Not haunted by ghosts, I'll bet.

I closed the shutters on Foulstone Manor when I got back to my cottage, and I sat in bed and thought. The night I'd opened Mary's boxes, I'd done something. I'd been up to Foulstone. I'd been to London.

Amanda came round earlier and said she had spoken to her parents and they offered to have us stay. Sheila had had a good idea, it seemed. She thought about going to Chelsea Old Church to look at their records. That baby, Gerard Revell, who had died in 1893, might well have been christened there and there could be something about his parents — where they'd lived, perhaps. There might be another boy, born at the same time with a clue in his name.

I was looking forward to seeing Sheila again.

28

Amanda

'What your dad said — it's so true, Amanda. Shame's an awful thing, and it's really not my fault. I see that now. I think deep down, I was ashamed that he'd been such a terrible person.'

We were on the bus to Chelsea. Joan was talking about what Dad had told her. Of course, we'd talked about Gerard Revell and the Dearloves and Bate. Joan had been shy at first, but she'd been welcomed so warmly by Mum and Dad that she did relax. I showed her the guest room and where the bathroom was and left her to unpack, I wanted her to have time to settle in and get her breath.

Mum wore her old tweed skirt and kept her apron on while we had a cup of tea and when Dad came home, he changed into a sweater and corduroy trousers and kept his slippers on. I hadn't said anything, but they were like that — always sensitive to what other people might feel.

We had pork chops, mashed potatoes, peas, and carrots, and Dad asked Joan if she grew her own and said that homegrown tasted better. It was time they came north again, he said, and they would in the spring. They could stay at a bed and breakfast, perhaps, he thought. It would be good to see all the old places.

Joan seemed to be enjoying herself. I found that I couldn't help watching her to check if she was all right as you would a child in unfamiliar company. I felt protective of her and at the same time delighted that she was getting on so well.

The talk turned to what we were going to do the next day and Joan told the story of what we had found out so far, turning to me to help when she needed me. She wasn't used to an audience, but, as ever, she surprised me by saying, 'I don't know what to think about it all — Gerard Revell was a liar — we think he got his inheritance by lying about what happened to Nowell Dearlove in the war. He was my father — what am I to feel about that?'

That was when Dad said, 'Not ashamed, I hope, Joan. What he did was nothing to do with you. People do dreadful things. Murder, even, but we cannot transfer their actions to their children.'

Joan and I exchanged a glance — I think we both felt guilty about thinking Gerard Revell was a murderer.

'You don't think children inherit — well, the bad things from their parents?'

'No, Joan, I do not. In any case, I can't help thinking about the war — we expect every man to have been a hero, but that's impossible. Men saw dreadful things, did dreadful things. I'm not sure that we can judge any man's actions in those extreme situations. Suppose Gerard Revell saved himself instead of Nowell, who are we to say that we would not have done the same thing? That other men did not do the same thing. The instinct for survival is very strong in all of us. Otherwise, the human race would not have got very far.'

'We understood, though, Dad, that he wouldn't have been able to tell Arthur Dearlove the truth —'

'It still seems terrible to accept the house — and then he married my mother and wanted to have her put away.'

'Now, that is hard to justify, Joan, I admit. It seems to me that he did not ever get over the war and Nowell's death, perhaps.'

'Mr Crabbe — you know, Emily Bate's husband — he said they weren't all heroes. He talked about shell shock,' I said.

'It lasted, too,' Dad replied. 'Some men never got over it. I remember a doctor friend of mine who was terrified of his father who'd been in the last war. Such rages, he said. His mother was terrified, too. My friend said he just remembered a dark man who sat silently smoking in the corner for most of the time except when he erupted in such violence that he and his mother hid in a cupboard. However, my friend turned out to be a fine doctor and a good husband and father — nothing like his violent father. So, you see, Joan, it really isn't anything to do with you.'

We were too early at the church, of course. No one was about at nine o'clock in the morning and the church doors were very firmly closed, so we went to look again at the grave of the child, Gerard Revell, beloved son of Matthew Hardy Revell and his wife, Hannah.

'I wonder where they're buried,' I said. 'You'd think they'd be near their beloved child.' We looked, but there were no other Revells. 'Sad isn't it, that he should be left here all alone. They must be dead by now.'

'Perhaps that's why he chose the name — this Gerard Revell didn't seem to belong to anyone. A forgotten child. Who'd ask questions about him?'

'The parish register should tell us who he was and who his parents were — that is if they are kept here. Dad said that if a church hasn't a safe or something fireproof then the records go to the town hall or records office.'

'Let's hope there's something here, and that someone comes.'

We waited, looking down at the child's grave. It was very quiet apart from the hum of traffic which seemed oddly far away. I couldn't help wondering where his parents were and why they were not here. There didn't seem to be any burials after 1930 and then I remembered that the church had been bombed in the Second World War and rebuilt in the 1950s — that would be why then. They couldn't be buried here. They hadn't just left him, or just forgotten him. I couldn't imagine a mother doing that. Helena Revell had not forgotten her Joanna.

'The more I look,' said Joan, 'the more I feel the wrongness of it. To steal a child's name. It's so sly — I mean he must have thought that this Gerard Revell didn't matter, that he'd been forgotten. No one would care.'

'I wonder if he knew this church, or was he just passing? If his aunt did live in Chelsea, maybe he was baptized here.'

'Oh, I wish someone would come — perhaps nobody comes.'

'There'll be information in the porch about times of services and maybe a telephone number for someone.'

Just as we thought to investigate, a man in a dark suit and a bowler hat came up the path. I went up to ask him if we could see the registers.

He turned out to be a churchwarden, but we were disappointed to learn that the parish records were no longer kept at the church.

'The war, you see. The church was almost wholly destroyed. April 1941. I was a younger man then, a fire watcher. I remember it as if it were yesterday. Fire watchers dealt with the incendiary bombs with our pumps and buckets. There were shelters in Paultons Square and in the rectory gardens. We could hear the bombers droning across and the people came out of their houses to the shelters. There was an explosion by the river — we knew it was bad. My Fire Party left the church, and we walked along Cheyne Walk. Another mighty explosion. Twenty-past one, it was, and Danvers Street on fire — a gas main, and then we knew — oh, I am terribly sorry. You don't want to know —'

'No, no, please don't apologise.'

'My mother was killed.'

I couldn't help thinking of that second war — not so long ago as the first, and this elderly man reliving it for a few moments and remembering his mother. How lucky I was to have been untouched, to be young and have everything to look forward to. And, yet two wars. It was terrible to think of it. And not just bomb damage. Damage of every kind.

'Anyway, we salvaged some of the registers, but, of course, it was not safe to keep them in the ruins. Are you interested in a particular family?'

I told him that my godmother's father had been a Gerard Revell, that she had been adopted and wanted to find out about her real father who had been brought up by an aunt in Chelsea.

'You have seen the child's grave, I take it.' We nodded. 'Obviously he cannot have been that Gerard Revell's child and there are no other Revells buried here. The child's parents are buried in Brompton Cemetery, but there is a Miss Revell still living in Oakley Street. She is a member of our congregation and the sister of the little boy, Gerard Revell, and may be able to tell you if there ever was another Gerard Revell in the family. When was your father born?'

'In 1890, I think, but I don't know if he was born in Chelsea.'

'An unusual coincidence if he were. It is not a common name, however, and there may be some connection to Miss

Revell's family. It is number fifty-five Oakley Street which is just opposite Albert Bridge if you walk along Cheyne Walk.'

We thanked him and made our way out of the churchyard.

'Sister,' Joan said, 'I never expected that. She must have been born after the real Gerard Revell.'

'She might be eighty or so. I hope she won't mind our asking.'

Oakley Street was a wide, tree-lined road with rather grand houses, red brick on one side and white stucco on the other, some with handsome pillared porches on top of which were black wrought-iron balconies. Number fifty-five was tucked in beside a house with one of the pillared porches. A flight of steps led up to a black front door, a tall narrow house with three storeys above the ground floor. The windows of the first floor were topped with triangular pediments. It all looked very smart and well-cared for.

'Trust him to choose a moneyed family. I'll bet he didn't know about the sister.'

I went up the steps and pushed the bell. We heard it ringing in the house. No one came. I looked at Joan, feeling rather reluctant to ring again in case the lady of the house who might well be eighty needed a long time to come to the door.

Eventually we heard someone slide back the bolts. Then there was the sound of a key in the lock and finally the door opened to reveal a white-haired lady wearing a tweed skirt, a pale blue cardigan and matching blouse which looked like silk and under the collar of which rested a double string of pearls. She wore pearl earrings and looked very smart.

'I'm so sorry to take so long. I was upstairs and it's a long way down. How may I help you?'

I explained that we were looking into the history a man named Gerard Revell. 'Or,' I added hastily, seeing her puzzled frown, 'a man who called himself Gerard Revell.'

'How very mysterious. And you are?'

Joan answered. 'My name is Joan Goss, and this is my goddaughter, Amanda. It's a bit of a long tale, but I was led to believe that Gerard Revell was my father —'

'With the same name as my dead brother. That is odd. I should think you had better come in and tell me all about it. I am Miss Florence Revell.'

We followed her into a very lovely hall with black and white tiles on the floor and a chandelier descending from the ceiling and then upstairs into a sitting room — drawing room would have been a better description, I thought. It was very unlike Lily Mountjoy-Smythe's room, much more traditional with its green wallpaper decorated with birds, its comfortable sofas covered in heavy flower-patterned linen and tables with photographs in silver frames — wedding pictures, I thought, and some of children. There was a fire burning in the grate surrounded by white marble and a table was drawn up beside it on which lay a book and some knitting.

Miss Revell invited us to sit down and offered coffee which I declined, sensing that Joan wanted to get on with the story. After all, it was not an easy story to tell. Miss Revell looked at us expectantly.

'It is a long story, but I'll tell it as briefly as I can.'

Joan was surprisingly brisk, telling Miss Revell that she had been adopted, our understanding that Gerard Revell had been brought up by an aunt, our discovery of the grave of the child, Gerard Revell, and our suspicion that her father's name was not really Gerard Revell. She didn't give an account of why we suspected; she only said that an old friend of her mother's had given us information about him.

'You live in London?'

'No, we've come from Westmorland. My father inherited a house called Foulstone Manor in a place called Rawthdale. He was left the house by the father of a friend who was killed in 1918. I was born in 1922. My mother died in 1924 and I was adopted at the age of three.'

'What happened to your father?'

'He died in 1928.'

'Oh, and you were adopted before he died. That's a little strange.'

'He wasn't able to look after me. That's what I was told by my Aunt Mary. I don't remember him.'

We had decided not to mention Nowell or the war, or Gerard's suicide. That would make it all too complicated.

'How did you find me?'

'We met the churchwarden. We wanted to see the parish records in case there was anything about the child Gerard Revell and he directed us to you.'

'What do you hope I can tell you?'

'We're not sure,' I said. 'We wondered if there had been another Gerard Revell, or if another boy had been born at the same time — if there might be an address.'

'I don't know of any other Gerard Revell connected to my family. I never heard of a Gerard Revell brought up by an aunt in Chelsea.'

'Oh, then we are sorry for taking up your time.'

'No, no, I do have something to tell you. When you said that your father was brought up by an aunt, it made me think of someone. An aunt who brought up a little boy. We'll need coffee for this.' She looked at Joan and smiled. 'It's another long story. Come down and sit in the kitchen while I make it. I need to get my thoughts in order.'

We followed Miss Revell out of the drawing room. Joan lingered a moment by a table to look at some photographs. Then we went down to an old-fashioned kitchen — a much bigger version of Joan's kitchen at the cottage — with a red-tiled floor, a big wooden table, lots of shelves stacked with crockery and copper pans, a Belfast sink, a very old refrigerator, a cream Aga, and, of all things, a rag rug in front of a fire in the kitchen range by which there was a Windsor chair with arms where a cat lay fast asleep.

There was a kettle already on the hot plate and Miss Revell touched it. 'Won't be long. Is instant coffee all right? It will be quicker.'

She took some brown mugs from the hooks above the counter tops and spooned in some Nescafé. There was milk and sugar on the table where she motioned us to sit. When we each had our coffee and she had put biscuits on the table, Miss Revell sipped hers and we did the same. She would take her own time.

'You'll have to let me tell this in my own way. I shall have to start with my brother, Gerard. I was born in 1897, long after his death, though my mother never got over it. There was a measles epidemic at the time. Gerard was her first child. She was only twenty-three when he was born; my father was thirty in 1890. It is astonishing to think that we are talking about the last century. My mother was born over a hundred years ago — in 1867. I can hardly imagine that — when Charles Dickens was still alive, and now, the world so changed. Gerard was born eighty years ago — my brother whom I never knew, but whose death cast a very long shadow over my parents' lives, and mine, too, in a way. It is extraordinary.'

I thought so, too. Here we were in a stranger's house talking about two babies from nearly a century ago, yet their lives, one hardly begun, and one blighted by a terrible war, still had the power to influence our lives. Joan's, especially, Joan who was looking fixedly at Miss Revell. Lily Mountjoy-Smythe had called Joan "Miss Revell" and here was the real one. Strangely, they were not unalike — I could imagine Joan at seventy-three with the same white hair and blue eyes. I might persuade her into a pale blue cardigan and silk blouse. She would look good, I thought.

Miss Revell continued after another sip of her coffee. 'In those days, measles could be fatal. It could lead to infections of the brain as it did in Gerard's case. They couldn't save him. I should think the suffering was very great. However, you want to know about your Gerard Revell. I think he may have been Henry Simpson, brought up by his aunt, Mrs Alice Simpson. There was never a Mr Simpson according to my mother. She didn't talk about any of it until she was in her eighties — she died in 1957. My father had died in 1942.'

The same year as Emily Bate, I thought. All these connections — threads, really, not quite strong enough yet for us to stitch them into a whole picture. Miss Revell crumbled a biscuit on her plate, but she didn't eat it, only sipped her coffee again. This was bringing back memories, I thought, painful ones, too, and not just for Joan.

'I was the only daughter at home. My sisters are married, one in Edinburgh, and the other living not far away. Gerard was the first child and only son. That meant a lot to my father. He wanted an heir, I suppose. He was born in the middle of the Victorian age and that's what he was — old-fashioned and remote. I never really knew him. I don't think he was interested in his daughters, except as marriageable objects, or someone to take on domestic duties. It seemed quite natural to him that one daughter should remain at home to look after my mother. My fiancé died in the Spanish flu epidemic — he survived the war and succumbed to that. Well, time passed, and I got used to being the spinster daughter — and then it was too late to change.'

'I understand that,' Joan said. 'I looked after my adoptive father until he was ninety and I found myself suddenly forty with greying hair and no idea of what to do next.'

Miss Revell looked at me and smiled. 'We shall be a lesson to you, my dear, though this modern world will offer a good many more opportunities, I hope. Now, I've wandered from the point. Age does that, but the matter of a father's desire for a son shows how devastating the loss of Gerard was to both my parents.

'Sons, you see. There was no Mr Simpson, and my mother always wondered if Henry were really the child of Alice Simpson. Of course, she never asked. Alice Simpson worked for us — a sort of housekeeper and cook. We had maids, of course, and a laundress came for the washing, but Alice ran the house and took charge of the maids. She lived with the boy in the mews cottage behind the house.'

'How old was Henry Simpson?' Joan asked.

'A little older than Gerard, five, perhaps, a quiet, rather self-contained little boy, my mother remembered. She felt sorry for Alice, a woman on her own, bringing up a child — whether her own or someone else's. My mother kept those thoughts to herself — not ideas I imagine she would have shared with my father. I don't think they shared very much. Three daughters and no other son. He'd think it her failure. It was Henry Simpson who caught measles from the little school he went to. My father paid for that, and Henry sometimes played with

Gerard in the garden. That's how it happened, I imagine. Henry survived — he was older, less vulnerable, perhaps.'

'What happened to Alice after Gerard's death?'

'This is the difficult part. Remember, I'm telling you what my mother told me when she was an old lady. What happened had preyed on her mind, I think. It was a sort of confession. Alice did not love the boy. She regarded him as an unwanted burden left to her by a feckless sister — I'm not sure if that's true. You can judge for yourselves by what follows. Alice sent him away. And I'm ashamed to say that my mother didn't stop her. She couldn't bear the sight of him alive — and her precious baby had died.'

Joan looked too stunned to speak so I asked, 'Where did he go?'

'My mother didn't ask. She only found out when Alice was dying. They never spoke of him. Alice did her work. My mother had her daughters. I didn't know any of it until not long before my mother's death. It was something on her conscience. It was a secret between her and Alice, something shameful, never to be mentioned. My father never spoke of him. I don't remember them ever speaking of my brother, Gerard, either. It was like that then — there were always secrets. Do you know, I never spoke of my fiancé to them? They had no idea how I felt, or they didn't want to know.'

'But your mother found out something when Alice was dying?' I prompted her.

'Alice had cancer. She died in 1935. My mother said she spoke of Henry then. Her sister, Alice said, had been married to a soldier who was killed. She died not long afterwards, and Alice was left with her child. Alice sent him to The Royal Military Asylum —'

'Asylum?' Joan blurted out.

'It's not what you think. It's called The Royal Military School now. It used to be in Chelsea, on Sloane Street. The building is still there, but the school is in Dover now. It was for orphans, sons of soldiers — boys went from the ages of four to twelve. Somehow, Alice got him in there. She didn't say how, except that she thought he would have a career in the army, or he could have become a schoolmaster. They trained schoolmasters at the Asylum back then.'

'And she never contacted him again?'

'I'd never even heard of him until my mother told me. She was very ashamed and so was I. It seemed cruel to take it out on a small boy. He couldn't help catching measles. My mother told me that he came back once. She didn't know until Alice told her when she was dying. He was seventeen, I think, and about to join the army. He asked to see my father. I imagine to show him that he had made a success of the Military Asylum. He saw Alice, too, but Alice didn't tell my mother anything about those meetings — I don't suppose my mother wanted to know.'

'The photographs upstairs,' Joan said, 'is there one of Alice or the child?'

'No, Alice wouldn't have either of them photographed.'

'She didn't want him at all then.'

'No, I don't think she did. Still, it seems that he did have some good fortune, inheriting a country house, marrying, and having a daughter. What a pity he died so young. He was in the war, I suppose?'

'Yes, he was a captain and was awarded the Military Cross.'

'So, Alice, perhaps, did right by him in sending him to the military school, even though she and my mother did wrong by sending him away.'

'Why should he steal your brother's name, I wonder?' Joan asked. 'He must have been successful at the school. There must have been other boys who did well in the army and kept their own names.'

'That is true. There was a man called Archibald Nye whom my father knew. My father was a solicitor who did legal work for the Asylum. Archibald Nye started out at the school and rose to be Vice Chief of the Imperial General Staff. He went in as a non-commissioned officer and was commissioned as a lieutenant in the First World War. He never hid his origins which were quite humble, I believe. It is a mystery. I can only think that Henry thought our family owed him something. I suppose they did.'

'You can forgive him for stealing your brother's name?'

'It is so long ago, Miss Goss. Two wars have obliterated that wrong. My mother, to whom it would have mattered, is dead. And was it greater than the wrong done to him? No harm came of the imposture.'

Little did she know, I thought, as Joan and I left her at the front door. I was stuck again by Miss Revell's dark blue eyes. They made me think, but I didn't say anything. I thought about the silent and remote Mr Matthew Revell, who never spoke of the boy, and I thought of his connection with The Royal Military Asylum. That shadow cast over the Revell family by a son's death might be longer than Miss Revell knew.

We walked down to the embankment and stood staring at the river. I didn't want to say anything. I knew that Joan would want to gather her thoughts, as I did, too. What a story — and what a possible twist to it, though I had no idea how to broach that.

Joan spoke first. 'Have you ever looked at a face and seen another face there — just for a moment? When I saw you first, I saw your mother, of course, but there was just a fleeting impression of your grandma. And then I knew it was in your chin. Mrs Hill still lives in you.'

I knew what she was getting at. She could be very quick, Joan, and very observant, and she remembered what people said. 'Miss Revell's blue eyes?'

'Like his. Like mine. Do you think she noticed?'

'She didn't say. I don't think she ever thought that Henry Simpson was —'

'Matthew Revell's illegitimate child. I didn't think that at first, but when I looked at one of the photographs, I saw Gerard Revell's face just for a moment and then it was gone. It was a very old-fashioned wedding photograph — from the last century, I thought. Miss Revell's parents. I know I only saw Gerard Revell in my dreams, but that face in the photograph looked like his. I thought I was imagining things again, but then in the kitchen, I stared at her — her eyes.'

'No wonder Mrs Revell and Alice never spoke of it. No wonder Mrs Revell wanted him gone. Perhaps, she suspected. Her husband's son, and her son dead.'

'More secrets, more lies. What damage they do.'

'And,' I added, 'Matthew Revell paid for the little school, and he did legal work for the Military Asylum. That's how he got him in because there would be no evidence of a real father who was a soldier, but Matthew Revell's word would be good enough. A solicitor in a fine house in Chelsea. And our Gerard Revell asked to see him when he went back that one time. That all suggests that Matthew Revell thought he owed him something.'

'But Matthew Revell wouldn't go so far as to acknowledge him as his son, I suppose.'

'So, he stole the name. He thought it was his right to be Gerard Revell after what they had done to him. It really is quite horrible to think he was sent away. No wonder —'

'He lied about everything, even his age. He was two years older than the real Gerard Revell. He didn't really know who he was. Just as I don't know now who I am.'

'You are just as much Miss Revell as she is, Auntie Joan.'

'So, I am. Not that it matters much. I'm glad we didn't tell her everything. No use burdening her with his suicide and her father's illegitimate child. She felt bad enough as it was.'

'What do you feel about him now?'

'I suppose I understand him more. I know how it feels to believe you've been abandoned and rejected. But I can't forget his treatment of my mother and that thing Lily said about not believing in him. And the way he treated William and Mary, lording it over them, plotting to sack them —'

'What?' I saw her face, as if something had struck her.

'It still doesn't make sense. It was a year after my mother's death that William and Mary Goss left Foulstone with me. They bought the house in Kendal, yet they came from Highdale, and, as far as I know, they never went back, yet in Helena's account Mary Goss spoke so fondly of her life there — her brother, the cousins in Hawes, the Methodist Church. A community, Amanda, where they belonged.'

'It is strange, but we don't know what the war did to that community. Maybe her brother was killed. Maybe her parents died, and she had no reason to go back.'

'They bought a house in Kendal — a substantial house. It wasn't a cottage, a two up and two down in a back street. They must have had money for that. Did he pay them to take me?'

'Unless Arthur Dearlove left them something. He would have, surely, he was so fond of them.'

'Yes, that'll be it. I saw his will, but I only looked at what he'd written about Gerard Revell. I can see why they'd want to get away from Foulstone and him, but he sent me away. He did the same to me as was done to him. I don't suppose being a parent meant anything to him except that he wanted a son to inherit. It seems to me that having a son called Revell was to be a kind of revenge against Mr Matthew Revell.'

'We know where he got his grand ideas from — even at five, he must have taken in what it meant to be rich and have a position in society. That's why he took to being the country gentleman — and why he wanted rid of the Gosses. They reminded him that he wasn't the rightful owner.'

'So did my mother. She knew, and perhaps he sensed that she never felt she belonged. He didn't like that. He didn't like her getting too close to William and Mary and talking about Nowell and Arthur. People thought he was a cousin of the Dearloves. That suited him. Get rid of them all, including me, and who'd ever know?'

'So, what went wrong?'

Joan was puzzled. 'How wrong?'

'He became a recluse — the newspaper said so, Mrs Sykes said so. No more hunting and shooting, no more parties or balls. No new Mrs Revell and a son?'

'And then he killed himself. Guilt?'

'Over the lie, Nowell's death, your mother's death, abandoning you. We can only guess. Do you want to find out anything more about Henry Simpson? We could get his birth certificate.'

Joan looked weary suddenly. Too many revelations that didn't lead anywhere except to more questions. She thought about my suggestion. 'It would give us Alice Simpson's name or some other, and then what? I don't think I can face chasing after some other address after a hundred years or poking about in another graveyard in search of dead people who can't answer our questions.'

29

Amanda

Foulstone still loomed over us, but Joan didn't suggest going up there to search for any more papers. I wanted to. I wanted to open that locked room which had been Nowell Dearlove's; I wanted to open all those chests and boxes in the attic; I wanted an end to the story so that Joan could close the book and —

What? I wondered. Come back to London? Enjoy herself, see the sights, enjoy the company of my parents when they came north, come to Lancaster when I started there? Travel? Join the Women's Institute? Well, that was going a bit far, I know.

Sell Foulstone? That occurred to me. We should clear it out, make it habitable, burn all the papers, open every window and door, let out the ghosts...

I didn't say any of these things to Joan. I just suggested that we drive to Hawes.

'You mean to find out if there's still any Lunds, anyone who might have known Mary?'

'Well, we don't know exactly where Mary lived or what her name was before she married, but she did mention the Lunds and their daughters. It sounded as though she knew them well. It's worth a try. There might still be a grocer's shop —'

'And if not, that's the end of that.'

We stopped on the high moors and got out to look at the landscape — empty as far as the eye could see. Rolling hills and moorland, just sheep grazing. How they got up so high, I couldn't imagine. Snow on the tops, the sky a clear blue like glass, the colour of that bowl which meant so much to Helena's mother, Joanna Lovelace, the original Joanna.

The landscape was beautiful in an austere way. I thought about the people who lived in the scattered farms from where we could see faint smoke curling from chimneys, and who had inhabited that ruined farmhouse below us? I couldn't help thinking of Mary Goss's family. We had passed through Highdale on our way. Joan hadn't wanted to stop there. We didn't know the name of Mary's brother, or her family name, or the name of the farm. In any case, it was so small a place that Joan was reluctant to make enquiries. Somebody who knew someone, or had a brother, sister, cousin in Rawthdale would recognise William Goss's name and would gossip. Joan didn't mind my parents knowing, but the idea of becoming the subject of tittle-tattle — her words — worried her. Hawes was further away.

There had been a ruined house on the roadside in Highdale and then there was a sign to Highdale Head where there was a railway station and some railway cottages. Highdale itself looked cramped, the cottages lining the road leaning against each other, but we saw the little Methodist chapel and the tracks leading off to farms probably. Perhaps Mary Goss's family had vanished, their farm now a ruin. No one now to remember young Mary who had met William Goss at the tea party; Mary who had never gone home again; had never spoken of her brother or her parents to Joan; had never taken her there again after that time in the summer of 1923.

'I still can't understand it,' Joan said, echoing my thoughts. 'We probably passed a lane that led to Mary's old home. She never mentioned a name, a place, or any person, except the supposed sister, Margaret. And I've thought of something else. There were no photographs of any family in the Kendal house. If Margaret existed, then surely Mary would have shown me a photograph. Think of all those photographs in Miss Florence Revell's house.'

'Gosh, you're right. In Helena's diary, Mary mentioned only a brother. There was no sister, Margaret.'

'It's like Alice Simpson — there was no feckless sister married to a soldier. She sent away her own son, her disgrace, her shame. Not because of the measles, but because the boy was Matthew Revell's son, his shame, his potential disgrace, and Matthew Revell didn't say a word.'

'Because he was frightened that Henry Simpson might look very like him — at least about the eyes.'

'What was Mary frightened of, I wonder?' Joan asked. 'It's as if she and William were in hiding, as if they were frightened of something. It's fear that keeps secrets. Look at me — frightened to death of opening Mary's boxes, frightened to death of going into Foulstone — frightened I'd find out something terrible.'

'And you have,' I said.

'Well, it hasn't killed me, and I wonder, standing here with you, if it hasn't made things better. The things we've done, Amanda — I wouldn't change those. Visiting London, seeing your parents, doing things instead of just accepting things as they were.'

If we had not been to Foulstone Manor; if we hadn't read Gerard Revell's papers; if we hadn't read Helena's story; if Joan hadn't seen the three grey figures in the wood, we might have been very doubtful, possibly a bit amused even, by the woman we met in the small cottage behind Hawes Church. I think I would have laughed at the cat, especially. I think Joan might have had a very sceptical glint in her eye, but as it was, we accepted her just as if she had been an ordinary little old lady who remembered Mary Goss and was prepared to tell us all about the old days at Wardacre farm down in Highdale, a place she remembered vividly.

The sense of something not quite normal began with the lady in the grocer's shop in Hawes, still called Lund's but owned by someone else. We asked for Mrs Lund and were told that Miss Agnes Lund lived just behind the church.

The lady looked at us curiously. 'She doesn't do much in the healing line these days, but some folks still believe in the herbs an' that, fortunes, even. You'll have heard of her, I daresay.'

'Yes,' I lied, 'I'm researching the history of the dales.'

'Oh, well, Agnes Lund knows all the old stories, 'specially the ghostly ones. You should write 'em all down before she's gone. She's nigh on ninety years old, I think. Mind, that doesn't stop her. In that garden come rain, come shine. Mixin' up her potions, too. Readin' the cards for them as still believes. They say she's right more often than not.'

There was a long path through a garden where there were still a few late roses and a few straggling purple daisies and lots of beds. Herbs, I imagined, recognising a bay tree and rosemary. I recognised chrysanthemums, too, in a pot by the door and the crimson Virginia creeper climbing up the porch to the slate roof of the old stone cottage and I noticed how the little windows in their thick stone settings shone. Miss Agnes

Lund might be nearly ninety, but she obviously did her garden and cleaned her windows.

The front door was ajar, and Joan knocked this time. A ginger cat appeared on the doorstep to gaze at us while we waited, looking down into the green eyes. He didn't seem very impressed, but he didn't move. His stare was a bit unnerving. Ghost stories, I thought. I looked away first. Joan knocked again and a very little old lady appeared with a tea towel in her hand which she flapped at the cat.

'Shoo,' she said. 'I've told you, there's nothing for you. Get off home.'

He went with an insolent flick of his tail and made his way slowly down the path.

'Cheeky beggar,' the lady said, 'he's next door's but you'd think he owned the whole row.' She looked up at us properly now with a question in her eyes, very clear eyes in a little round, wrinkled face the colour of a russet apple. 'Now, let's have a look at you.'

She looked at Joan, seeming to study her face for a long time. We didn't say anything. There was something very penetrating about the little woman's gaze as if she knew all about Joan and why she was here.

'Not the future you're after, I fancy. It's the past you want to know about.'

'My name's Joan Goss. I've come to ask about Mary and William Goss.'

'You're that child, little Joanna Revell. I remember your eyes. I saw him once. Nigh on fifty years it's been, but I didn't forget him. I always thought I'd see you again. Time has no meaning where some things are concerned. I'll put the kettle on.'

Her voice was soft but very matter-of-fact. Time and the kettle — as if they were equal, as if there were nothing unusual in the idea that time has no meaning. Another strange encounter, but we were getting used to that.

There was no hall. We just went straight into a small parlour where dried herbs hung in bunches from the old black beams, and every shelf and surface were crammed with jars and bottles with handwritten labels. The room smelt of lavender and mint and something more pungent, something medicinal. There was a black pan bubbling on the old cooking range tucked under a huge stone mantel on which were more bottles and jars.

'Cough cure,' Agnes Lund pointed to the pan. 'It's aniseed you can smell and mint. Black treacle, too. Two teaspoons when you need it. We used to put laudanum in it in the old days. Can't get it now. You can use cherry bark, too, in a syrup.'

'Mary Goss used to swear by ginger for sickness, and chamomile tea when you couldn't sleep. Comfrey for bruises. I remember quickthorn jelly for heartburn.'

I was surprised. It was as if Joan knew her, too, as though they were continuing a conversation they'd had yesterday. But, after what we'd been through, I supposed, a wise old countrywoman was hardly a shock.

'She would,' continued Agnes. 'Raspberry leaves for the red eye. No need for all these new-fangled things. Mary's mother knew all the herbs, too, up at the farm. You've not been there.'

'No, I don't know what it's called.'

'Tea first. The kettle's boiled, dear,' she said, looking at me. 'Sit yourselves down and I'll tell you what you want to know. Mind, I don't know it all. Naybody can know it all — not where folk are concerned. Everyone's a mystery, my dears. You'll find that out when you've lived as long as I have.'

The water was poured into a brown teapot from the big black kettle. There were china cups and saucers on the table where we sat and sugar and milk. When our cups were full, Joan said that she wanted to know why Mary Goss had never been back to Highdale.

'We found some papers and Mary spoke very fondly of her home and her brother, and she mentioned the Lunds of Hawes. That was back in 1924, but when I was growing up, I had no idea where she came from.'

'Naught there now, my dear. Wardacre it was called. Mary's brother took it over when their parents died. He married my sister, Ann, so I was always about there. I mind very well the last time I saw Mary. 'Twere at her brother's funeral after that time when she brought you there. When John Ward died, Ann went to live with her daughter over Leyburn way. She's dead now. Naybody made much of Wardacre after that. It's hard country round here. You've to be bred to it and John Ward's heir weren't his own son — only daughters. Tom Oakley who took over were John's cousin's boy. It happened then, children sent to live with relatives, and no one asked any questions. You see, Tom Oakley's father lived in Lancashire. Poor as charity with five sons — one going spare and that's how it came about, but I knew Tom Oakley hadn't the heart for it. He were the wrong boy. His brother were meant to come, but he went off to war — and never came back.'

That war again, I thought, indirectly the cause of the ruin of Wardacre. 'What happened to Tom Oakley?' I asked.

'He went off to Manchester to work in a factory and no one heard of him again. 'T'were all over with Wardacre after the second war.'

'And you never saw Mary again?' Joan asked.

'I knew I wouldn't. On the day of the funeral, I could see she was troubled. Mary didn't hold with what she called my fancies. I saw things. I knew that John Ward would die. It were in his eyes — deep in them, a kind of darkness. Something shadowy that were always there. My brother, Jim, was the same. Merry as a cricket, but a darkness there. He went off to war. I were that fond of him and I knew he'd not come back. I saw him, though, on the day he died. He were up at the pinfold where the sheep are kept, sitting on the wall. In his uniform with the same smile he'd given us when he went. He waved to me then he were gone. When I went back home, the telegram had come.'

We couldn't answer, though I imagined that Joan thought the same as I did. Once I would have been very doubtful, but after what we'd seen at Foulstone and what I could see in that wise old face told me that she was telling us the truth. It was somehow in the scents of the herbs, the pot bubbling on the hob, in the quiet that fell between us, and in her eyes. She looked straight at us. Very pale grey eyes, almost silver, full of light in this dark little room. Far-seeing eyes, I thought.

'On that day, the day of John Ward's funeral, Mary and me went for a walk. Now, remember, Mary didn't hold with dreams and visions and seeing the future, but that day she told me that she'd seen something at Foulstone — something that couldn't be true. 'T'were in the twilight in the woods. She were coming along the path. Three figures was on that path, coming towards her. Three grey men, two in front and one behind them. Tramps, she thought, just for a moment, but she saw a face she knew. Mr Nowell Dearlove as had been killed in the war. And the face of Mr Gerard Revell who passed without looking at her. None of them saw her and then they was gone — just gone. The path were empty. But Mr Gerard Revell were alive, up at the house, yet he looked like a dead man then. Mary didn't want to believe what she'd seen — she never told anyone, not even William, but it stayed in her mind, and she had to ask. She thought I was the only one who might explain.'

'Who was the third?' Joan asked.

'She didn't know him. She asked me what it meant. I told her it meant death. Mr Nowell were dead, and Gerard Revell would die a young man. I saw him just the once when I went to Foulstone. He passed me in the hall, and I saw his face in the mirror there — very white and his eyes black in his reflection. Troubled eyes. Very blue like yours when I looked at him, but dark within like Mary's brother, John. And the third must die if he weren't dead already.'

'I saw them, too. They are still there, all three, haunting Foulstone.'

'Then there is something unfinished. I always thought so. Mary wrote to me that she and William was leaving Foulstone and taking you. She couldn't abide the place any longer. I were not surprised. That one time I went, I sensed it was a troubled house. Mary said that Gerard Revell was a bad man, and he couldn't stop them going. I saw his suicide in the newspaper — years later. I weren't surprised at that, either. Something he couldn't live with. Hereabouts, they say 'tis a judgement on a man who does not die in bed. But Mary never wrote.'

'And you didn't write to her?' Joan asked. 'You were friends.'

'I kept Mary Goss in my heart, and she kept me in hers, I don't doubt, but sometimes you have to accept that some things are not to be in the time on this earth. My lad was killed with our Jim. I knew that, too, and there wasn't to be anyone else. My heart was too full. But sometimes you've to wait for time to do what it will or will not. Time brought you here and time will finish the tale. Mary took you away from Foulstone. She had her reasons, and it were not for me to question them. I knew something were wrong about Foulstone when she came here with you, but she didn't say, only that your mother were poorly and then she did write to say that Mrs Revell had died in childbirth.'

'Something was wrong about Foulstone. Something still is. What can we do, Mrs Lund? Have we to accept, do you think, that it is a blighted place and leave it for time to sort out? I'm not sure I can — it's a burden. We think —' Joan looked at me. Should I tell her? That was the question in her eyes. I nodded — 'We think there is something terrible there.'

Agnes Lund's gaze was clear as glass. I thought she understood. However, she said, 'I can't tell you what to do. The answer is within you, but, if you wish, I can read the cards — not for the future —' she looked at Joan — 'it's not always clear and not always right to know, but there may be a sign and you, only you, must decide what path to take.'

Joan nodded and Agnes took out a pack of cards from her apron pocket. 'Choose,' she said, and when Joan had selected one card, Agnes told her to look at it and tell her the suit she had chosen.

'Spades,' Joan said.

'Change, my dear, a warning, sorrow to come, perhaps, and the number?'

'Three.'

Joan's voice was quite steady, but I felt a distinct chill at the back of my neck. Gerard Revell's words came into my head. "Who is the third?" Mary Goss had seen them, and Joan had just asked the same question. And we knew who it was. A man who had disappeared, a man last seen near Foulstone Manor. A man who would die if he were not dead already.

'You've asked the question, my lass, and in that number lies the answer. Mary saw three. She knew two of them. The third is the key. The answer is at Foulstone if you choose to turn the key. And one last thing to remember, whatever you find out, Mary Goss were a good woman, and William Goss were a good man.'

As we prepared to leave, Agnes took two bottles from her mantelpiece. 'Lavender oil,' she said, handing Joan the smaller bottle, 'good for the nerves. Helps you sleep. And take this — my blackcurrant wine. Go easy with it, though.'

30

Joan

Of course, Amanda knew as well as I did. I could tell when I looked at her as we went back down the path. It was a queer thing, though, that card. I'd not have believed it except I could believe anything now. 'Samuel Bate,' I said.

'I thought of him, too, when you said the number. It gave me quite a chill when you said it, and those words, "The third is the key." Do you believe her?'

'I do. I'm surprised at myself. Mary Goss didn't hold with fancies. Agnes was right about that. "Lot of old nonsense," she'd say if I read out my horoscope in the paper, and she wouldn't have cards in the house. Now I know why. But there was something about Agnes Lund. I felt as if I knew her the minute she started talking — I knew she was telling the truth about Mary. In any case, I saw them, too.'

'Mary and William left Foulstone Manor and Gerard Revell couldn't stop them, couldn't stop them taking you — his only child.'

'A bad man. They didn't leave after my mother went, after what he tried to do to her. It was a year later.'

That gave us something to think about as we walked back to Amanda's car. I stopped and looked over the graveyard at the old grey, mossy tombstones, some leaning to the side, some almost falling backwards as if the wind, which was strong and piercing in this high town, was pushing at them. The coarse grass looked yellow under the heavy grey sky and here and there I could see stone crosses, sometimes a more elaborate tomb surrounded by rusty railings, one with an angel pointing upwards.

Another graveyard. The dead — long forgotten, their bones crumbled to dust. No one to remember them now. I thought about the War Memorial in Rawthdale churchyard, those names, and how on Armistice Day in the town, there'd be wreaths of poppies on the memorial and a service to honour the dead and two minutes' silence. "Their name liveth for evermore." That poor boy in the cemetery who'd died just after the war was over. They were remembered. I thought of Gerard Revell. The dreadful memories he'd left behind and no grave to honour him. No grave. No stone to record Captain Gerard Revell, M.C. Because he wasn't Gerard Revell. Where was he? If you choose, Agnes Lund had said. It was for me to choose to act or to accept what time would bring. Leave it, William Goss had advised me. I hadn't left it. There was no choice.

'Mr Lamb,' I said to Amanda, 'the solicitor in Kendal in that newspaper you read.'

'I remember. What are you thinking?'

I pointed to the graveyard. 'Where is Gerard Revell?'

'He couldn't have a grave, maybe, not with the wrong name. I wonder if he left instructions with Mr Lamb. You know, about what was to happen after his death. He must have planned it. I mean he was found in the cellar —'

'You didn't tell me that.'

'I don't think I took it in at the time — I think I was so bowled over with him being a war hero and a poet, but — oh, heavens — the cellar in Helena's diary. All that stuff about the damp and nobody allowed to —'

'Go down there.'

I remembered again. The little girl outside a door — I'd never known which door, only that it was a forbidden place. And Gerard Revell seizing the child's arm. That furious white face. Blazing eyes. The terror and the smell. I hadn't told Amanda, but I told her then.

'The smell,' Amanda said. 'That's where it started, and it stayed with you.'

I thought of that other man without a grave. Samuel Bate who had vanished in August 1923 when Helena had her miscarriage. When the baby boy she wanted to call Nowell had been born dead, and when she had been in the nursing home and Mary and William Goss had taken little Joanna that one time to stay at Wardacre. And in the winter, there was a smell from the cellar and Gerard Revell had gone down because the steps were too rickety for William to manage.

William Goss who was fit as a fiddle, who had been as spry as a much younger man when he was in his eighties, who had only begun to fade after he reached eighty-five. William Goss who had told me to leave Foulstone to rot.

Rot — Amanda had picked up on that word. Foulstone had brought misery to William and Mary Goss as well as to Gerard Revell and my mother, and to me. I looked at the graves. Where was Samuel Bate? The third — the key to the mystery. And I'd had that third key hidden away for years.

I turned to Amanda. 'We think Bate was blackmailing Gerard Revell. Think what that would have meant. Gerard Revell in with the gentry, the war hero, the poet, the cousin of the Dearloves, the rightful owner of Foulstone Manor.'

'And Samuel Bate was by the bridge on the day that Helena had her miscarriage. Mary Goss remembered and then Revell sent them to Wardacre with you.'

It was obvious where our words were taking us. I couldn't say it. I looked at Amanda's face. She couldn't say it, either. We looked at the graveyard and felt the icy wind sweep down from the hill.

I repeated Agnes Lund's words. 'The answer is at Foulstone.'

'In that cellar,' Amanda said.

'A judgement, Agnes Lund said, a judgement on Gerard Revell.'

Amanda nodded, and that was as close as we got to uttering the terrible thoughts that we knew we both had.

31

Amanda

We drove back along the winding road, with the high, empty moors on either side and dark clouds rolling towards us, an ominous purple colour like great bruises on the sky, threatening rain. I couldn't help thinking of that dark abyss I'd imagined when we contemplated the idea of Gerard Revell having murdered Arthur Dearlove and how guilty we'd felt. I had the same feeling now as if we were standing on a precipice looking down into darkness, unable to see what was there, and terribly afraid. More afraid than last time because we knew more now. We believed that Gerard Revell was Henry Simpson, the illegitimate son of Matthew Revell and his housekeeper. We knew how much Gerard Revell had to lose.

I thought of Chelsea, just across the river from Battersea and Searle Street where Samuel Bate had lived. Suppose he had found out. He might have known that Gerard's account of Nowell's death was untrue, and now it seemed perfectly possible that he knew that Revell was an impostor. What might that knowledge have meant to a man who was himself a liar and a crook?

I broke the silence. 'Samuel Bate's letter was to Mr Dearlove, but it was only a fragment that Mrs Bate showed to Helena. Was he writing to tell the truth about Gerard Revell? I mean we think he met Gerard Revell in the park and Gerard gave him something. Maybe he didn't send that letter because he found out somehow about Gerard inheriting Foulstone Manor from Arthur Dearlove and guessed that he had lied. It must have been possible. Maybe he watched him, followed him —'

'Bate knew that there would be a lot of money to be had then. He wrote to him at Foulstone demanding more and more — but wait a minute, that doesn't work. Mr Dearlove was dead. Who would Bate tell?'

'Oh,' I said, 'we hadn't thought of that. Other men from the regiment? Officers?'

'Would they believe him? It seems he was a bad lot and a deserter. His word against Captain Revell's.'

'Mr Crabbe said he was clever, clever at exploiting people — a sort of low cunning kind of intelligence, I reckon, and he was in with all sorts of criminal types. Suppose someone mentioned the newspapers. Might he have threatened Gerard that he would sell his story? War hero's lie — that kind of thing.'

'Wouldn't the threat to tell his wife and his wife's family be enough?'

The rain spattered on the windscreen and then it came down in one of those great rushes of drumming rain that you get in the Dales. The sky was black as we drove down into Rawthdale.

Joan got out of the car by her front door, and I parked the car and ran back to find Joan already lighting the fire.

'Kettle,' she said, and soon we were sitting by the flames, nursing our cups to warm our hands. Still, we didn't say the word. It was true, though, I thought. What Joan had said about Bate threatening to tell Helena and her family rang true to me. He wouldn't know that her parents were dead. He might have thought she had relatives. Just the kind of thing Bate would think of — a sneaking, low-down threat. It wouldn't matter to him what damage he might do to an innocent woman. He'd beaten his wife, abandoned her, even stolen her rent money.

Was blackmail worse than what we thought Gerard Revell had done? Imagine living with that threat hanging over you — like having a gun to your head and not knowing when it might be fired. Torture. No wonder he lost his mind. Every time he went to London, he must have thought it was the last time and then Bate turned up at Foulstone and Helena saw him in the woods and by the bridge.

Joan spoke. 'We worked it out before. William saw him by the bridge at the time Helena had the miscarriage. Mary couldn't remember exactly when and she didn't know if William had told Gerard Revell. Suppose he had.'

'Suppose Bate told Gerard that he'd seen his wife, that he'd be seeing her again to tell her.'

'And Gerard Revell put two and two together. Samuel Bate had frightened his wife and she had lost their son — the son who was going to secure Foulstone. He hated that man already. "Good Lord, deliver us from battle and murder." That's what he wrote.'

I thought about the shadow in the dark corridor near that cellar. 'Did I —'

'What?'

'When I saw — that movement in the corridor, was it him? Bate? Had Gerard Revell seen him?'

'Oh, Lord, Amanda, he saw a dead man rise — Bate coming out of that cellar to —'

'That's why he couldn't go on. Bate, Nowell, haunting him — two deaths on his conscience.'

'Three, if you count my mother.'

'What shall we do?'

'If he's up at Foulstone in that cellar. I don't think I could bear…'

I didn't think I could either. Go down into that cellar and find Bate. A ghost or a skeleton. I didn't know which was worse. I had no idea what he would be like after fifty years. Just bones. I thought of a skull with sightless sockets staring at us. A nightmare. And then what would we do? Would we just lock the door again and walk away? Or would we have to tell the police?

Joan was staring into the flames. Was she seeing what I saw in my mind's eye? I thought of what she'd said about burning the place down. I was tempted, but they'd find out it was arson and suppose the cellar did not burn and a body was found. They'd come to Joan first — it was her house. They'd suspect her. Could we lie our way out of it? I felt sick at the thought. And I had no idea what to say.

'Not knowing,' Joan said, 'or knowing, which is worse? Forever thinking that there's a body in that cellar. And when I'm gone, he'll be found, and it'll be all over the papers. My name, my story.'

'But you won't know.'

'You will. You'll have had to keep my secret for years. Suppose you have children. Would you tell them? Oh, Amanda, what have we said about secrets? How they ruin things. This is my fault — dragging you into all this.'

'I started it by getting you to talk about it. I was curious — it was an intriguing story. I didn't think at first —'

'Neither of us could have imagined that we'd be sitting here frightened to death, not knowing which way to turn and nobody to help us. Just us.'

'Sherry,' I said. 'I'm still cold.'

'I feel as if I'll never be warm again. I'll put more wood on while you pour. Make them big ones. Driven to drink, we are.'

Getting the sherry bottle out of the corner cupboard where it was hidden from prying eyes — though whose, as Joan had said herself — and getting glasses out and pouring gave me time to think and after we'd taken our first gulp — a really necessary gulp — I told Joan what I'd thought.

'Bate was under that bridge, hanging around. You saw, and Mary saw, three in the woods. Gerard Revell killed himself in the cellar. I'm wondering if Bate is in the woods.'

'Buried there? I've a couple of spades in the barn.'

Admittedly, our laughter was shaky, but it was laughter which for a moment dispelled the terror and we drank more sherry and felt at last the heat of the fire.

'The cellar, though, Amanda, your idea doesn't explain his fury when I was jumping up at the door handle and why he wouldn't let William go down there.'

'No, I was clutching at a straw, hoping that we wouldn't have to contemplate again the possibility that Bate is in there.'

'We really think Gerard Revell —'

'I think we do.'

'Mary and William knew? That's why he couldn't stop them taking me. That's why Mary wouldn't ever, ever talk about the past. She knew I was the child of a murderer. There, I've said it. They kept that secret for all those years. It spoilt their lives — cut them off from their families, sent them in hiding to Kendal, made them lie. Agnes Lund said they were good people.'

'They did it for you.'

'A terrible burden. To know that and to hide it. I can't ask you to do the same, Amanda, you're a good person. We have to know — even though my heart goes sick to think of opening that door.'

'Mine, too.'

'Then I'll have to do it.'

'Not on your own, Auntie Joan. No, no, we've come this far together. What if —'

'What?'

'We're wrong and he's not there. I mean it's all speculation. We're piecing together the things that we know from Helena's diary — the dates and that, guessing that Gerard Revell saw him at the bridge. Mary didn't know that William told him.'

'But we can't find out anything more. There's nothing in those scribblings of Gerard Revell's except that we know he hated Bate. That's the only real evidence.'

'I was thinking again about where Bate was the night before he saw Helena under the bridge. Where had he left that suitcase that Mrs Rudd spoke about? A leather one. It looked new.'

Joan looked doubtful. 'But we said we couldn't ask about the town. We don't know who let rooms fifty years ago.'

'We do. Mary Goss told Helena. In the war, out of work men slept in the barn at Mrs Gibson's. It's just up the road. You can see Foulstone from there. Bate could have watched them.'

'Old Mrs Gibson's long gone. Her daughter-in-law is still alive. But would she remember that far back? I don't even know if she was there then.'

'How old is she?'

'Seventies, I should say, but very spry.'

'1923 — she'd have been in her twenties.'

'She could have been married by then, of course, to one of the Gibsons. How do we go about it?'

'Research, Auntie Joan, woollen industry, farming, unemployment in the First World War and just after. I could ask her if she remembers what kind of men came looking for work.'

We were putting it off, of course. Whether Samuel Bate had stayed at Mrs Gibson's farm or not didn't make any difference; we'd have to face that cellar eventually, but if he had stayed there and left his suitcase then that might help us come to that dreadful decision. We could be more certain that Samuel Bate was the man under the bridge.

32

Amanda

I went up to the farm on my own. Joan didn't want to face the Gibsons' prying eyes. They'd want to know why Joan was there but using my alibi as a history student would deflect their attention away.

The door was opened by the elderly Mrs Gibson. She lived with her son and his family at the farmhouse. Her daughter-in-law, Patricia, wasn't there. She was away to Kendal with her daughter. Her son, Mr John Gibson, and her grandsons were out in the fields.

She invited me into the kitchen, a lovely old farm kitchen with rough stone walls and a great big black range where a fire glowed — though there was an electric stove as well — and a huge, scrubbed pine table marked by years of use, a variety of chairs, including Windsor chairs with arms at each end. On the table there were brown Denby mugs and a teapot in a woollen cosy. I could smell new baked bread and bacon had been cooked for breakfast.

It all looked very comfortable — a happy family lived here, I thought, three generations of them. I had tea and fruit cake and told her about my studies. I was interested in agricultural work between the wars.

'You see,' I said, very seriously, 'it's what my tutor calls primary research. I'm not supposed to get it all from books. He wants me to come up with original research, talk to people, find out what life was like after the First World War; for example, what kind of work people did, whether they moved around. He was talking about soldiers, really, saying that there was a lot of unemployment and men travelled all over the country to find work. I wondered if that happened round here.'

I even convinced myself and I had a notebook and pencil to prove my credentials, so to speak, and Mrs Gibson was such a kindly soul that she was quite ready to believe me, to pour me more tea, and to think back to the old days.

'I were nobbut a lass then, not married long. James Gibson, my husband, were the eldest son. I had my first son, John James, by then — in 1923. He's been a good lad to me, our John. No question that I'd to leave when his father passed, and Patricia, that's Mrs Gibson now, she's a good daughter-in-law. Never still, Patricia — always on the go, but that's farming. Dear Lord, my dear, I can hardly believe I've been here nearly fifty years. It's a hard life, that's what it be, and harder then. That first war — I mind it all very well. I weren't married then, but my folk was farmers, too. All those lads havin' to go. Dear me, my father had to apply for exemptions — lot of old paperwork an' questions. What did they think we'd to do without farmworkers? How'd there be any meat or milk? Fools they was. But there was them as had to go — my husband's brother had to. Never came back. Grandmother Gibson — that were James's mother — never got over it. Youngest, see — just a lad...'

I had to let her talk. Like Miss Florence Revell in Oakley Street, she'd tell her story in her own way. I'd learnt a lot, I thought — being patient, listening, and how much older people had to tell, and what they had been through, and how resilient they were, how brave. I thought of Lily Mountjoy-Smythe, Jack Fournier, Hettie Rudd, Mr Crabbe — soldiering on, as it were. And Joan — she'd rallied. That joke about the spades. Not much of a one, but it had calmed us down. I made a note in my book about exemptions. Paperwork? I wrote while Mrs Gibson waited. I'd seen how her face changed when she'd mentioned her brother-in-law.

When I looked up, she continued, 'James's brother. That were a blow, but there was plenty of others. You should have a look at the War Memorial up at the church — James's brother's name is there. Michael Gibson. His best friend, Frank Pinch, killed, too. His name's up at Dent; a cousin of mine up at Cowgill — fancy, six men gone from that tiny place. Only sons, too — Mr Dearlove at Foulstone Manor. You know the ruined house?' I nodded. 'His only son, Nowell. A nice lad he were, always friendly. Fine looking lad, but so was they all in their uniforms. King and country, eh? And we'd to do it all again.'

'What happened to Foulstone Manor?'

'Oh, some cousin came an' lived there, Mr Revell. I didn't know him. Mixed with the gentry then his wife died in childbirth. Pretty lady. That'd be 1924 — I remember because I were expectin' my boy, Michael — named after James's brother. It gave me a fright, I can tell you. Showed it could happen to anyone — gentry or ordinary folk.'

'And what about the farms when they suffered losses? Did other workers come?'

'Oh, yes, you asked about that. In the war, there was tramps — deserters sometimes, but we never told. You'd sometimes know a fellow had lain in the straw, taken an apple or two, but after Michael were killed, we felt sorry. "Let 'em be," that's what James's mother used to say. She'd not turn anyone away. You didn't know what they'd been through, and sometimes we'd find 'em work here or at some other farm.'

'Where did they come from?'

'All over — mostly the north, though, roundabout here, o' course, Lancashire, Yorkshire, Cumberland, even. There's a queer story about a fellow from London. Somethin' about him Grandmother Gibson didn't like. Told her he'd been in the war and thought he could get work up north. Nothin' doin' in London, he'd said. She let him sleep in the barn — she didn't want him in the house. It weren't like her. She were a real generous soul, but him, she said, something shifty about the eyes.'

I wrote down the names of the counties and London. I wanted to think about what I might ask next. It was Bate; I was certain. 'When was that?'

'Must have been 1924 because I was expectin' our Michael — summer, I should think. It were hot, I know that. Terrible swollen feet I had.'

'Did he give his name?'

'Simpson — Henry Simpson.'

I nearly dropped my pen at that name, but I managed to ask, 'Oh, what happened to him?'

'It were a queer do. I remember him because he went off one morning and never came back. Never said he were goin', but Grandmother Gibson were glad to see the back of him, an' I remember William Goss — he were gardener at Foulstone — askin' James if there'd been any strangers about an' James told him about this Henry Simpson. William Goss had seen some fellow on the bridge an' didn't like the look of him. I don't know if it were Simpson and William didn't mention him again.'

I had to ask, though I wondered if Mrs Gibson might think it strange. 'Did he leave anything behind?'

'Funny you should ask. Grandmother Gibson didn't trust him an' I mind why now. He weren't like any of the others that came — not well-dressed, but not too poor, neither. Suit and tie — shabby, but, well, lookin' for farm work? That's what Grandmother said, and he had a leather case that looked new. I haven't thought of him for fifty years, but, gracious, I remember him now. I remember his shifty eyes. There was others that came. You felt sorry — there were a sadness about them. Somethin' haunted about the eyes — what they'd been through, but that man. Looked like a crook. We was glad to see the back of him.'

I'd learnt something else, too. How to dissemble — not lie, exactly, more how to get the information I wanted. I'd been an art historian on the telephone to Lily Mountjoy-Smythe's brother, Peter. Now I was a historian in search of primary sources.

'What happened to his suitcase? I'm thinking if there were papers in it — that would be very interesting for me. A primary source, you see — a case study.'

'Naybody mentioned it. Mebbe still in the barn where he slept. We never throw anythin' away. We've never any time. It'll all be there in a hundred years when we're all gone and the farm's a ruin like Foulstone. Mind, there's all sorts in there. Tools, old farm machinery, old chairs, chest of drawers, an old cot, I mind — cradle. From the last century, I should think. Not fit for any babby now, but you can have a look if you want, but I shouldn't get your hopes up. James's dad might have chucked it out when he knew that man weren't comin' back. They didn't like him. And no need to come back in, my dear, I've my vegetables to do.'

Joan was waiting when I returned. The kettle on as always, sandwiches on a tray. It was long past lunch time. I'd been gone for three hours.

'That's his case,' she said, looking at the mildewed thing in my hand. 'Oh, my Lord, he *was* there.'

'He was.'

She fetched the tea first and made me eat a sandwich and then I told her what Mrs Gibson had said and that Bate had called himself Henry Simpson, and that William Goss had asked about strangers, and that James Gibson had told him the name.

Joan supplied the conclusion. 'William Goss told Gerard Revell and Gerard Revell knew what that meant. Samuel Bate knew who he really was.'

'I wonder how.'

'Made it his business to find out. You said he was cunning.'

'Mr Crabbe told me that Bate was eager to get back from the war — he said it was time for a reckoning. He wanted Gerard Revell to pay for what he'd done. Bate had been left to die in that shell hole. He found him — in that park. Maybe by chance and then he knew that money could be made. Not that it matters how. He did it.'

'What's in the case?'

'I haven't opened it. Mrs Gibson told me not to bother to go back into the house. I came away as quickly as I could. I didn't want anyone to see me.'

'What did you tell her?'

'That I thought any papers in the case might be useful in my research.'

'Oh, Amanda, what have I done to you? Fancy you having to lie — again.'

'I wasn't lying to cheat them — not really, only to find out something that couldn't harm them.'

'That's true. We've done no harm to Mrs Gibson or to Lily's brother. White lies, I suppose. Nothing compared to Gerard Revell's lies.'

'Exactly, nor to Samuel Bate's. Mrs Gibson said I was welcome to keep anything I found.'

We looked at the case, the case that Hettie Rudd had seen Samuel Bate carrying away down Searle Street to the railway station and the north from where he would never return.

It wasn't new now. It had lain in an old chest of drawers in the Gibson family's barn for nearly fifty years. The chest was probably Victorian. The beautifully carved cradle was much older — what a shame, I thought, to leave it as a receptacle for old paint tins and useless brushes. I couldn't help wishing I could have that, but I'd made myself concentrate on the drawers, and I found it buried in the deep bottom drawer under a roll of cracked oil cloth, old ledgers, rusty trowels, hammers, boxes of nails, rotted string, a rake without its handle, an old Thermos flask. Things that had just been chucked in — things which might come in useful one day. The Gibsons would never have guessed which of those things would be the one.

33

Joan

I once heard a bit of a play on the wireless. Someone had left a bomb in a house — a time bomb, they called it. Not my cup of tea and I turned to the Light Programme, but I did listen for a moment or two to the ticking. It sounded really frightening and I imagined innocent folk in their beds, not knowing and the bomb thing just going on. No one to stop it.

Well, I thought of that as Amanda and I sat staring at that leather case on my table. A timebomb. I wished it was in a way. Only at Foulstone. It would blow the place sky high. Nothing to do with me. But it wasn't. It was just a suitcase, and we were going to have to open it. I reached over and pulled it towards me. I heard Amanda's sharp intake of breath. Her eyes were very big in her suddenly pale face.

The catches were rusty, but I managed to lift the first of the metal clasps which held the catches in place. The click sounded like a gunshot in the silence. Amanda slid the case across to her and lifted the second clasp. Another shot.

And we stood up and lifted the lid together.

The smell — more hideous than I'd ever experienced before, rank, earthy, sick-making. The smell of Foulstone. I slammed down the lid.

I felt even more panic than when I'd woken that time in the dark. 'We can't have it in here. It'll poison the place — put it outside — Oh, God, Amanda, someone might see — what'll we do?'

Amanda seemed frozen for a moment, her face whiter still, then she said, 'I'll put it —'

'No, don't touch it — it'll poison you — don't —'

'We've touched it already. Get an old towel — we can wrap it up —'

'We can't leave it outside. I know — in one of the old outhouses by the mill. We'll hide it.'

'We'll have to open it — I can't stand the thought of it —'

Neither could I, but I couldn't bear the thought of it in my parlour, tainting my house. I'd never be able to live here again — it'd spread to Amanda's cottage, and we'd never escape it. But we couldn't just stand there looking at it. I fetched an old towel and Amanda got a couple of torches. Though it wasn't quite dark outside, the outhouses would be.

I left my door open. We picked our way along the lane like two thieves in the night, me holding one of the torches to light our way and Amanda holding the case before her. I kicked open the door of the first outhouse and shone the light in. Amanda threw the case onto the stone floor and the towel unravelled itself, showing us the case. Of course, the lid had flown open, and the contents had spilled out.

We slammed the door shut and stood outside. I could feel Amanda shaking beside me and I could hear her ragged breaths. I was shaking, too. We both took great gulps of the freezing night air, and we stood there watching the dark fill the lane, watching the stars come out one by one. We could hear the river rushing on its way and somewhere an owl hooted. The silence and the cold eventually calmed me, and my heart resumed a steady rhythm. I heard Amanda breathe out — a breath of relief, I thought, not panic.

'He's there, isn't he?' I said. 'He's part of it. The smell, hauntings, murder. I don't understand it, but he's there, I know it.

Amanda took my hand. 'I think so, too, but we'll have to open it, or we'll never be sure.

34

Amanda

We went back to Joan's cottage — she wanted to check, but we couldn't smell it. There was only the smell of woodsmoke from the fire and the faint whiff of oil from the lamps. Her parlour looked just the same, just cosy, as if two ordinary people had had tea there — the brown teapot, the china milk jug with its pattern of roses, the matching sugar bowl with its silver spoon, crumbs on the plates. Only my chair pushed back from the table as if someone had stood up quickly suggested anything amiss.

'Did we imagine it?' Joan asked as we stood staring at the things on the table. 'It's not a real smell — it's a ghost. I mean the ghost of a smell — if such a thing can be.'

'It's gone, anyway. Perhaps it won't be as bad down there when we — we'll have to. We can't wait until morning. I mean all night, thinking, imagining.'

'No, you're right, we've had enough sleepless nights, and, do you know, I don't care if they're here, if they've come down from Foulstone, the three of them — I just want to know. I've had enough of being terrified. We'll do it.'

I could still smell something in the outhouse, but it wasn't as strong or as sickening, more the smell of damp and disuse. We shone the torches on the case and its spilled contents. They looked pathetic rather than terrifying. A man's belongings — all that was left of him. Thrown on the floor.

Something greyish white, folded up which looked like a shirt. We stared at it. Samuel Bate's shirt. It didn't look very clean.

Perhaps he had put on a clean one to go to Foulstone. He was going to go back to the farm for his case and when he had his money he'd be leaving.

There was a grubby looking collar underneath. It looked as if it was made from cardboard. Perhaps Bate had put on a clean collar, too. We stared at the packet of cigarettes which had fallen a bit away.

'Woodbines,' Joan said, 'I remember them.'

I thought about the man under the bridge who had tossed his cigarette into the water. A man who had made a decision, perhaps. And Helena had smelled the smoke. That figure had been no ghost.

'He was smoking,' Joan said, 'under the bridge.'

I could see a little book, too. It looked like a Post Office savings book. There was a cut-throat razor, a dirty looking comb with some teeth missing, and a pair of dark-coloured socks, darned at the heel. I thought of Mrs Bate and the hungry face that Helena had described, her bewilderment, and her poverty. He'd taken everything, even the socks she'd darned for him. I felt less pity for him then. He'd been a horrible man.

There was a small bag shaped like an envelope which looked as if it was made of canvas. Joan picked it up. 'I don't suppose I'll catch anything,' she said with a flash of that dry humour. She put it on the rickety old table, undid the button, and shook out the contents. Coins spilled onto the table and notes. A wad of greasy looking notes with an elastic band round them which crumbled as she touched it. Pound notes and five-pound notes in another roll which also crumbled. I pulled that towards me and picked up a note.

'George V, issued by the Lords Commissioners of His Majesty's Treasury. From years ago.' I looked at the coins in the torchlight. 'Florins, half crowns, shillings. It seems a lot for a man who slept in a barn.'

'Ill-gotten gains,' Joan said.

'How much?'

'A lot of pound notes. I'll have to count them.'

There were forty pounds in one-pound notes and there were four five-pound notes. Old-fashioned, big ones, printed on one side with big black letters.

Joan touched the five-pound notes, 'I remember these from when I worked in the bank. Five pounds was a lot of money even then, never mind in the 1920s.'

'Stolen, perhaps, or blackmail money.'

Joan picked up the little booklet from the floor, 'It's a Post Office Savings Book. I had one of those, too. It is him — look.'

She showed me the signature on the front: *S. Bate*. And then we looked inside at the list of deposits. Samuel Bate had first deposited ten pounds on September 24th, 1920.

'The anniversary of Nowell's death,' I said. 'He had seen what really happened in that shell hole. 1920 — when Helena saw him with Gerard Revell in the park, do you think?'

'Very likely, and Helena wrote that Gerard went to London in September 1921 — you remember, after he got a letter. It's here — twenty pounds this time.'

I looked a bit further down, 'November 1921. Helena saw the man in the woods. Gerard Revell guessed it was Bate, found him, and paid him off. Fifty pounds this time.'

'After I was born, he went to London then. On May the 6th, Bate pays in fifty pounds and he's asking for more and more. In the September Revell went to London again. A hundred pounds in that September — a hundred pounds, Amanda, a fortune then.'

'Oh, goodness, Auntie Joan, five hundred pounds in the November. Five hundred pounds.'

'More than a fortune. And then nothing.'

I thought for a moment. 'Because that's when Gerard Revell met Sir Anthony Gresham — on the train coming back from London, and then he got in with the hunting people. Helena said he was happy in that winter and spring — he must have thought it was over. That five hundred pounds was to be the end of it.'

'And then Bate turned up in the August and Helena lost her baby. No wonder —'

We were silent then. Here was the evidence of blackmail. And all that money. Bate had made withdrawals over the years, the last one being for seventy-five pounds in August 1923. He wouldn't have left his sixty-odd pounds behind, at the Gibson's farm, nor his savings book in which there was still two hundred pounds.'

'Think of it,' Joan said. 'All this money and Mrs Bate left with nothing and I'll bet she and that Mr Crabbe didn't have much.'

'Mr Crabbe is still alive. He should — oh, heavens, Auntie Joan, what on earth do we do with all this?'

'We can't — I mean, we can't give it back. We'd have to — but we don't know yet if — that cellar. What would we do if we found — would we have to tell someone? The police, I mean. I can't cope with this, Amanda, and yet, to leave it... We can't do that, either. Me thinking forever about a body in the cellar up there.'

'And there might not be. He — Bate — could have, I don't know, fallen in the river...' Me, clutching at straws again. 'No, of course not. He'd have been found. He was smoking — waiting, watching. Perhaps he'd seen the ambulance with Mary and Helena in it and William Goss followed in the car. He could have gone to the house then, and —'

'I was there. In the nursery, probably. What does it matter? It all adds up and we don't know what to do.'

'We need help. What if I ask Dad to come? He could come with us up to Foulstone. We've got to do it, Auntie Joan, we've got to know. And we can't do it by ourselves. Dad was a doctor before he retired — he'll know about — well, bodies. What people do. I'm sure he'll give us good advice.'

'We need someone. I can't face the idea of police — just us. Yes, ask Richard to come.'

We shoved the stuff back in the case and hid it under the table behind some boxes and empty petrol cans, but we took the Post Office book.

I don't think I can really convey the fear and dread we felt that night while we waited for Dad to come. I had to tell him why we wanted him — we thought Samuel Bate might be in the cellar at Foulstone Manor, but we couldn't face going to investigate and we hadn't a clue what we would do if we found something.

Dad was very calm. He said he'd find out what usually happened when human remains were found. I shuddered at that word "remains". Dad could tell by my breathlessness that I was frightened. He said I could tell him the details when he arrived.

Joan and I talked about searching for more papers that evening while we waited, trying to find the key to Nowell's room, going into Helena's sewing room to see if her pictures were still there, going up into the attics to look at Arthur Dearlove's will or to see if Mary Goss had left anything, but the spectre of Samuel Bate's bones loomed before us, and we hadn't the courage. That corridor which led to the cellar door. The place where I'd seen that shadow move. The cellar where Gerard Revell had shot himself. Ghosts. Gerard Revell or Samuel Bate? Or both?

We felt guilty, somehow, as if we were concealing something dreadful, which we were in a way. We were certain that Samuel Bate was there in the cellar. We felt guilty about the money, too. We left the suitcase where it was — no one was likely to be rummaging about the outhouses and Joan certainly didn't want it in her cottage. Nevertheless, we couldn't forget about it.

We tried Agnes Lund's blackcurrant wine — a bit strong, Joan thought. We should keep our wits about us. We didn't want to be falling downstairs. Joan found a tinned Fray Bentos pie in her larder.

'Two and ninepence,' she said, 'I don't know why I bought it — I could have made my own. It'll do, I suppose.'

It did. We ate it, though without much appetite. After that, Joan knitted. A black scarf for me. Why black? I didn't ask. Useful for a funeral, I thought. We might be going to one. I mean I had no idea what happened if a skeleton was found. Would they do tests to find out the age of the person, the time of death? Inquest. The word popped into my mind. Surely, there would have to be one. Questions for us. And then I thought, would they bury the remains in a churchyard at some secret ceremony? Would we have to go? And the most dreadful question of all. Would they know he'd been murdered? I could hardly bear to think that word, never mind say it.

Joan — mind reader — suddenly asked, 'How did Gerard Revell kill him?'

That brought the heat to my cheeks. Not a question we'd thought about until now. I thought of the gun found by Gerard Revell's body. Had he shot Samuel Bate? And would they find a bullet in his skull?

And who would "they" be?

35

Amanda

'The police, there's no choice, if he is there,' Dad said when he arrived at my cottage. He wanted to talk to me and think things through before meeting up with Joan. I nodded and then I told him everything, including the finding of the Post Office book with Samuel Bate's name in it, the sums of money, and the dates.

'Though he gave the name Henry Simpson to the Gibsons at the farm,' I added.

'Gerard Revell's real name. Bate knew that Revell was an imposter.' Dad nodded his understanding.

'We think he might have known that Revell's account of Nowell Dearlove's death was a lie.'

'Yes, Mr Crabbe told you that Bate had been left to die in a shell hole.'

'He hated the officers.'

'Blackmail then — you were right. Bate was a scoundrel, but we can't cover up the finding of a body.'

'I know. Joan knows. It's just so awful for her. She'll have to tell them all about Foulstone Manor and Gerard Revell — we'd have to tell them we suspect he murdered Bate.'

'Not so fast, Holmes, I've been doing a lot of thinking. We'll talk it all over at Joan's.'

Joan had made vegetable soup and there was new bread to go with it, and Wensleydale cheese. While we waited for Joan to bring in the soup, Dad looked at the Post Office book.

'It looks pretty clear to me. Bate was a blackmailer.'

Dad ate everything he was given. Joan took a few sips of soup, looking at him anxiously. I ate most of mine — it was something to do while we waited for Dad to finish. Then Joan made tea.

'Delicious soup, thank you, Joan. I know you're both anxious and I have been thinking. First, if Samuel Bate is there, then we do have to report the finding to the police — you've accepted that?' he asked Joan who nodded. 'I'll tell you what happens next. The local police will report to C.I.D. in Kendal — a detective will come, and the bones will be looked at. They'll obviously check that they are human —'

The word "human" made it worse somehow. Bate had been a living, breathing person. A scoundrel, as Dad had said, but a human being left in a cellar to rot away. I thought of William Goss telling Joan to leave Foulstone to rot. They had known or guessed.

Joan was asking a question, 'You'll know that, though?'

'I will, but the police will need to confirm it. A report will be sent to the coroner's office. The bones will be sent to a laboratory — Carlisle, I should think, the sex and approximate age determined. The coroner is obliged to hold an inquest — not necessarily with a jury, but the pathologist will give his findings, as will the police detective, and any other witnesses.'

'Us,' I said, feeling sick at the thought.

'So, you have to decide what you are going to tell the police — or how much. You have to decide what to omit. I was thinking about the name Henry Simpson which Bate gave to the people at the farm. You haven't mentioned the name Samuel Bate to anyone?'

'Not round here,' Joan said, 'only to you and Sheila.'

'Hettie Rudd and Mr Crabbe knew he'd been here,' I put in.

'Hm — it was fifty years ago nearly. I doubt a story about a Henry Simpson would make the London papers and the name Henry Simpson won't mean anything to them. Henry Simpson, a man who disappeared from a farm in Westmorland — a man looking for work — a disreputable looking man whom the Gibsons didn't like or trust —'

'The suitcase,' Joan blurted out.

'No one knows you found it, Amanda?'

'No, I didn't tell Mrs Gibson.'

'If the inquest can't determine the cause of death after fifty years — and they won't be able to determine an exact date — then they won't be able to say if it is the mysterious Henry Simpson and there are no living witnesses from Foulstone Manor — only you, Joan, and you were a little child then. You can't tell them anything about Henry Simpson.'

'You mean conceal everything about Gerard Revell and Bate?'

'I do,' Dad said. 'Now, I know you spoke to me in confidence, but I confess that I've talked to Sheila about all this. I had to — I needed her advice. And I couldn't lie to her about why I was coming.'

Joan looked relieved. 'I want her to know, and I'll take her advice,' she said.

'Well, she doesn't think anything is to be gained by exposing the whole story. Only food for tabloid newspapers and Joan hounded by reporters about her father, the suicide and murderer. And, Joan, about Mary and William taking you away, and, perhaps, concealing the murder — their reputations in shreds. Changing your name, your mother leaving you, her death — it might all come out.'

Joan went white. 'I couldn't stand that.'

'I know. We weighed it all up very carefully. We agreed that you couldn't leave the body — if there is one. Samuel Bate was a human being and he should be buried, not just left, or his bones thrown away, but there is no family left. There is no need for his story to be told, either.'

'What does Mum think we should do?' I asked.

'Her advice, and mine, is that you two don't know anything. There's nothing incriminating in the suitcase — except that Post Office book, which would have exposed his identity. We thought about anything with his name on, but we concluded that it wouldn't matter as you, Joan, wouldn't know anything about him, even if the old story about his disappearance came out. But now the name Henry Simpson has come up, Bate is out of the picture.'

I had a thought that might mean that murder was still in the picture. 'We wondered how he died — I thought what if Gerard Revell had shot him? There'd be a bullet. Gerard Revell had a service revolver.'

'That would complicate things, of course, but there'd still be no evidence of who did it or when. Yes, Revell's suicide might come out, but no one could say definitely that he killed Henry Simpson, or even that he knew him, or probably even if the body was there when Revell lived there. There's no evidence that William Goss mentioned the name to Revell so there's no evidence that it is Henry Simpson. I think it would be an open verdict. The coroner would direct the burial of the bones — up in Carlisle, I imagine.'

'I'm so grateful, Richard,' Joan said, 'and to Sheila. You really think it will work?'

'It depends on you two. Can you be sure to keep to your story — that you know nothing about Gerard Revell or Henry Simpson?'

'How did we come to find the body, though, Dad? What were we all doing in the cellar?' I asked, thinking of a stern-faced detective asking us those very questions and none of us able to answer.

'Very good, Holmes,' Dad said rather drily.

Even Joan gave a weak smile. 'What on earth would we be doing down there?'

'Well, first, I've got to go down to see if there is really a body, and I can't report that that was the first thing I did when you showed me the house. We're going to have to plan this.'

36

Joan

The plan was that Richard and Amanda should go about a bit
— walking by the river, up the fell, through the woods and so
on. If anyone local saw them, Amanda would introduce him.
Nothing suspicious about her father visiting for a holiday. Just
a holiday with his daughter

As Richard and Sheila were old friends, there was no reason
I wouldn't show him around Foulstone if he came to stay with
Amanda. Richard came up with a good idea — that I wanted
his advice. What to do about Foulstone? I'd say I'd been
worrying about it. I'd told Amanda so. Then they'd go by
themselves to have another look. That was when they'd say
they had looked in the cellar. If asked, Richard would say he
wanted to see what condition it was in — whether it was safe.

I knew I could hold my nerve when the police asked
questions. That talk of newspapers frightened me. If the whole
story got out, I couldn't bear the thought of nosey people from
papers wanting to interview me, having to talk about Gerard
Revell, and about my mother. What would the papers make of
all that? And Lily Mountjoy-Smythe telling her story to
London papers.

Richard had said that such a story might well gather a sort of
momentum — body in cellar for fifty years, tragic wife of war
hero, suicide, murder, that kind of thing. It was a dramatic
enough story for national papers to pick up from the local
Westmorland Gazette. They wouldn't be interested in a probable
tramp called Henry Simpson, but an unexplained death and a

267

suicide in a manor house would be just up their street. Nationals — the local paper was bad enough for me.

And nosey parkers from town all knowing about me — thinking I was the queer one — the woman whose father had been a murderer. People whispering, pointing me out, folk coming to look at the house. It was terrifying.

Truth to tell, I didn't care much about Samuel Bate — he'd been a bad lot, hanging about the place, blackmailing Gerard and frightening Helena. I thought it was partly his fault that Helena had lost her son, and if he hadn't been standing by the bridge, my life would have been different. Gerard Revell wouldn't have killed him, and my mother would have lived, perhaps.

I was more angry than anything about him, but I understood that we'd have to report the finding of the body. He could be buried in Carlisle or anywhere for all I cared about him. I think I'd have dug a hole in the woods and put him there if I'd found him on my own.

He was there. The third. Of course he was. In that cellar. Richard found him. He didn't think I needed to see him, but I knew I had to. I had to face it, not just leave it to them. The smell that had haunted me for all those years. It hadn't been real. It had come from that moment of terror when Gerard Revell had found me by the cellar door. It had come from him. He smelt of death because he was a murderer. It had come from that suitcase because of Gerard Revell.

I know you'll maybe think it's daft, but it's what I believe. And I'm not afraid that I'm going mad anymore. It was nothing to do with me. It had come from the war. From that shell hole where Nowell had drowned and Bate had seen. Where it had all begun.

So, I went with them through the break in the fence that second time. I went down the kitchen corridor with them. I had given them that third key. I knew somehow that'd be it. Mary Goss had left it in her box. Maybe she'd thought that if the old bones were ever found, they'd be chucked away. She'd hope for the best. That was Mary. Turn a blind eye.

Amanda and Richard left me in my cottage when we came back from the house. They knew I wanted to be alone, and they had to go up to the police station.

Turn a blind eye. So, Mary Goss had. Even when she was very ill, she didn't tell me anything. I could remember her in that hospital bed, only half conscious with the drugs. Morphine it was. They kept increasing the dose. It was all that they could do for her. She looked like a bag of bones, but she opened her eyes once and said, 'You're a good girl, Joanie, love. Don't fret none. It's too late. All over now.'

I'd thought she'd meant her life, but perhaps she meant that it was too late to mend all that had gone before. She had loved me in her fashion. I knew that. And I was grateful. William and Mary had done what they thought was right — for my sake. For the first time in a long time, I wept for them. Good people. Young Nowell Dearlove had said so. And old Agnes Lund.

I thought about William's death, too, and my mother who had loved her little girl, Joanna, and Gerard Revell who was really Henry Simpson whose mother had not loved him. I couldn't forgive him, but I sort of understood him. People are complicated. Agnes Lund had said that everyone was a mystery. Time will or will not, she had said. Some things we'd never know, and we'd have to put up with that.

Even Samuel Bate. My anger passed. I wondered what made him what he was. He'd been a child once in a cot with a mother looking down at him. It's a funny thing, I thought then, that we should all have been innocent once. What life did to people — if they let it. I knew all about that. Well, we'd bury Samuel Bate, no doubt. He deserved that, at least.

I heard voices outside. Amanda and Richard were back and someone with them. Losses, I thought, I'd lost so many, but I'd reconnected with those two and Sheila. Friends. I shoved my hankie in my pocket. 'Shape yourself,' I said aloud, and went to put the kettle on.

The police might like tea.

37

Amanda

Detective Inspector Carson from Kendal made me feel guilty by just looking at me, though it was hard to tell what he was thinking when Dad showed him the skeleton where we'd found it in the farthest room of the cellar.

I was glad Dad was with us. Joan and I could not have gone through that third door alone. Damp had swollen the wood, anyway. I don't think we'd have had the strength to open it, and I remembered the front door and how I'd had to push it open to close it again and I'd seen that movement in the shadows.

I felt the cold seeping into my boots, travelling up my legs which were shaking. It was difficult to breathe. Of course, I thought I could smell something rotten, but maybe it was just my imagination. I don't know. I only know that I felt sick with apprehension. I didn't know if I wanted Bate to be there or not. I held both torches, and the light shook as I watched Dad try to turn the key in the rusty lock. Naturally, he'd thought to bring a can of oil, and eventually the key turned. I still held my breath, but Dad just went in.

There was a sink, blackened with mould, the taps rusty, but evidence that water had dripped down at some time over the years. It did smell of damp and rot. The skeleton had been covered in what looked like the remains of an old coat, perhaps the coat I'd read about in that old paper from 1923.

I hoped to God that it didn't have a London label on it. But we had seen the skull and the bones through the tatters of cloth and the remnants of the clothes he had worn. Gerard Revell had been found in the first room. Perhaps, he had intended to die with Bate, but had not been able to face unlocking that third door. I'd felt a distinct sensation of ice at my neck when I thought of Gerard Revell, but there was no shifting shadow there in our torchlight when we went back.

Sergeant Roberts from Rawthdale police station was there with Inspector Carson. He had been sympathetic — sorry for the shock we'd had. The inspector looked down at the bones, his face grim in the shivering light of our torches. He had not been very pleased to know that there was no electricity. He played his torch along the skeleton, lingering on the skull. I looked away. The skull was the worst thing. It had horrified me when I saw it the first time, very white in the gloom, its jaw open and grinning, showing the irregular teeth with black holes where the gaps were — that was dreadful to look at. And those empty eye sockets full of shadow like dark eyes staring. Accusing, it seemed to me. I hoped the inspector wouldn't think that.

Joan had been very calm, almost matter-of-fact about it, when she came with us to see the bones, but I guessed she wanted to be by herself for a bit while Dad and I went to the police station. Now she stood further away, looking like a woman who was very much bewildered by a skeleton in her cellar. She had certainly dressed for her part — an old grey beret pulled low over her forehead, an overall under her old grey cardigan, her gardening coat with buttons missing over that and wellington boots.

I looked back at the inspector who was playing his light on the window. 'No catch, Sergeant,' he said, 'someone could have got in.' He turned to Dad. 'And the skeleton is just as you found it?'

'Yes, I didn't touch anything. I knew it was human, of course, by the skull. Then I reported to your sergeant.'

'Right. I'll inform the coroner in Carlisle and the bones will be sent up to a lab. See what we can find out. From the remains of the clothes, I'm guessing a man.'

'Tramp mebbe,' Sergeant Roberts offered. 'Looks like it's been down here for years — lot o' tramps about in the last war an' the one before that.'

'Perhaps,' the inspector said. I wondered if he wanted it to be something else. He had a predatory look. He turned to Joan. 'You own the house?' He sounded sceptical, but I thought Joan would be a match for him. Even if she didn't look it.

She pulled her coat together. 'My father left it to me. He took his own life in 1928 and I was adopted and taken to Kendal when I was three. I've never lived here since. No one has for nearly fifty years. It's too big for me on my own, and I never fancied living here. My father, you see.'

'How long have you lived down in the cottage?'

'Ten years — after my uncle died. I lived with him, and my Auntie Mary, but she died years ago.'

'And you never came down to this cellar in the ten years?'

'I come to the house from time to time, but I don't need to come down here. I mean, it's a bit dangerous — those steps. I didn't fancy it at all. On my own — my legs are not what they were, I can tell you.'

I kept a straight face — Joan was hardly elderly and she whipped up and down her narrow staircase like a spring lamb. Inspector Carson kept a straight face, too — for a different reason. He had a suspicious mind, no doubt.

'But the doctor came down here yesterday. Why was that?'

Joan was ready for that question. 'Amanda and Richard had a look round the other day. Amanda's studying history. She was interested in the old things and there's a lot of books I thought she might like. And, I'll admit I have been worrying about the place. It's all a bit too much for me — on my own. I know I've let things slide, Inspector, but, well, time goes on and you ignore things —'

'And?'

'Well, I asked Richard for his advice and Amanda took him to see what needed doing. He thought there might be water in the cellars, so I came back with them to have a look. I must say that skeleton gave me a turn.'

'You have no idea who it could be?'

'I can't tell you about anybody from the old days. I can hardly remember my father.'

'And your mother?'

'She died in childbirth in 1924 — I don't remember her at all.'

'Inspector, do you think we could go upstairs? It's very cold down here. The ladies have seen enough of that skeleton,' Dad said.

'Certainly, sir, but there may be more questions once we have found out how he died and when it might have happened. We'll be asking around the neighbourhood. I need to know if anyone went missing, say, around the time of the last war, as my sergeant said, or before.'

38

Joan

They did find out about Henry Simpson, but, of course, I couldn't tell them anything. I was only two years old at the time and the people who had lived at Foulstone Manor were all dead.

The inspector came back. I didn't like him at all. Very hard eyes, he had, looking at you as if he was trying to catch you out, but I kept my simple country bumpkin's face, even though he gave me the impression that he thought I was a bit soft in the head. He kept going on about Foulstone and why I'd just left it to rot. Amanda was scared that he might dig so deep that he'd find out something about Bate, but I had the measure of him. Young and ambitious, wanting to turn the story into something sinister. Well, it was, but that was not for him to know. Those newspapers were always on my mind.

They went up to the farm and Mrs Gibson told them about Henry Simpson, the bad lot, and how he'd disappeared. He'd left a suitcase behind, but she couldn't say what had happened to it after fifty years. They were welcome to search in the barn, but it was that full of rubbish, they'd be there for a week. She didn't mention Amanda's visit, but then the inspector probably gave the impression that he suspected them of something. That was his manner. I bet she wanted to get rid of him. He was an off-comer anyway — from Stoke or somewhere down south. Mrs Gibson wouldn't have liked that.

They searched Foulstone Manor, but we had Helena's diary, Gerard Revell's papers with Bate's name on them, and that blasted suitcase. I did have a fright about that, but Richard said the police wouldn't have any grounds for searching the mill sheds, or my house, for that matter. 'Even if —' He'd stopped then and my heart lurched.

Amanda turned pale. 'If what?' she asked.

'Well, it might depend on how Bate died.'

I knew what Richard meant. 'You mean if they find out that he was murdered — that someone shot him.'

You can imagine how we felt in the days before the inquest. Fortunately, Sergeant Roberts came to tell us what the pathologist had found. There was no bullet.

We all repeated our story at the inquest. The coroner questioned me about my parents and the house, but very kindly. I wore my old black hat and grey coat, thick stockings with a darn in them, and black lace-up shoes. I didn't have to try very hard to look like a simple country woman whose life was a bit strange, granted, but who really had no idea about a skeleton in her cellar, and I must admit I was nervous. The coroner realised that. I think he thought it was because of the court — well, it was, but only because I was hiding the truth.

Anyway, he seemed to accept my story that I did sometimes go up to Foulstone Manor, but I had no reason to go down into the cellar where my father had shot himself nearly fifty years ago. That came up, of course, but the coroner had read the account of his death and the verdict of temporary insanity — no doubt caused by the effects of his experiences in the First World War. He expressed his sympathy for me, but he understood that I had never really known my father or mother and, having been adopted at three years old, I could have no idea as to the identity of the skeleton.

The pathologist reported that the deceased was a male, aged between twenty-five and thirty-five, five feet seven inches in height, shoe size nine. He was of slight build; some teeth were missing and those that remained were in poor condition and there was no evidence of dental treatment. The remains of the hair were mid-brown.

The remnants of the clothes showed that they were probably from the 1920s or '30s, but there was nothing to tell where they had been purchased. He did not think the deceased had been the kind of man to have a Savile Row tailor. The worn condition of some of the remnants suggested that the clothes might well have been second-hand when acquired.

He estimated that the body could have lain there for between thirty and fifty years. He couldn't say how the injuries to the skull and arm were caused, but he had examined the scene and thought that if the deceased had climbed in through the window, he could have fallen and cracked his head. If the house had been uninhabited then, it was reasonable to suppose he had died there.

The coroner recorded an open verdict. There was no evidence to connect the deceased with the name Henry Simpson, the man who had stayed at the Gibson's farm sometime in the 1920s. The persons at Foulstone Manor in Rawthdale who might have remembered him hanging about the house were all now dead. The condition of the deceased's teeth and clothes gave credence to the idea that he had been a tramping man, but, of course, it was impossible to be definitive about that.

What a relief. I felt a bit shaky, I must admit, when we all left the court and Inspector Carson came up to thank Richard for his assistance and said he thought we must be glad it was over.

'Bit of a mystery, eh, sir? Ah, well, I don't suppose we'll ever know who the poor devil was. What a way to go. I should do something about that cellar, Miss Goss, if you don't mind me saying so. Dangerous place.'

The cheek. I did mind, but I only nodded vaguely as if I didn't know what he was talking about. I didn't like that hard look in his eye.

'Don't mind him,' Sergeant Roberts said kindly. 'He was after a nice little murder to make his name. He has some daft ideas. As if.'

Samuel Bate was buried in a pauper's grave, so Richard told us. He went with Detective Inspector Carson and Sergeant Roberts. Richard thought he should — he didn't want Carson thinking we had something to hide. A plain elm coffin with a plaque which read: "Unknown Male. Date Unknown. About thirty years." Public plot 29783.

An unmarked grave. Like poor Nowell Dearlove. At least his name is on the War Memorial. Honoured, not forgotten. Bate hadn't been a hero. He didn't deserve his name on a memorial.

That led me to think about Gerard Revell. Where was he?

39

Amanda

The story appeared in *The Westmorland Gazette*.

BODY IN CELLAR

The coroner at Carlisle recorded an open verdict on the skeleton found at Foulstone Manor in Rawthdale. The pathologist reported that the skeleton was of a male person and that he had probably died between thirty and fifty years ago. Miss Joan Goss who owns the empty house said that she was shocked by the finding, but as she had been taken away by her adoptive parents at the age of three, she had no idea who he could be. Her parents had died nearly fifty years ago. Sergeant Roberts, the local policeman, said he thought the man had probably been a tramp who had injured himself when trying to get into the empty house. The coroner agreed that this was a possibility.

When the reporter came to see us, Joan just said that we didn't know anything, and Dad told them that the police were looking into it. The open verdict put paid to any ideas about murder or suicide.

There had been some gawpers, as Joan called them, people who, for some reason, wanted to see the house where the skeleton had been found.

'Do they think it'll be on display at the gate,' Joan said. 'Silly fools.'

They gave up eventually and Foulstone Manor was left still brooding under the dark winter skies. We'd have to do something about it. Joan knew that, but she didn't know what.

'You should start by clearing out any private papers — and burning them,' Dad advised. 'Then you could get a company in to take away any old stuff you don't want. Get someone to see to the damp and get cleaners in to give the place a thorough going-over. Make it habitable at least. You could let it, you know, Joan, or sell it.'

Joan looked doubtful about the last two options. I knew that the idea of strangers looking down on her wouldn't be welcome, but she did agree that we should at least see if there were any papers. The fear of anyone finding anything after she'd gone was stronger than her desire to leave well alone after all the trauma of the skeleton and the inquest.

Of course, Joan and I had talked about Gerard Revell and Bate. We had no actual evidence that Gerard had murdered Bate and what haunted us was the idea that there might be something to prove it. His study where we'd found that bundle of papers in his desk. There were a good many books on the shelves — suppose he had left something. Letters, for example, or even a diary. The thought appalled Joan. She couldn't help imagining those newspapers again, digging it all up.

'Let's do that then — look for any papers,' she said, 'while you're here, Richard. I'll not rest until we know that there's nothing there.'

I didn't say anything then, but I wondered if the answer to where Gerard Revell was buried would be found up at Foulstone Manor.

The Bible on Gerard Revell's desk. We hadn't paid attention to that the first time we'd been in his study, but then we had been anxious to get out of the house. I picked it up. The paper was very thin and gilded on the edges. Inside on the flyleaf there was a name: *Nowell Arthur Dearlove. April 1910.* When Nowell was thirteen. His confirmation, perhaps. It had once been on his bedside table. Arthur Dearlove had held it and prayed for acceptance, for something to ease his agony.

There was a thin silk ribbon in between two pages. I turned to them as Dad and Joan watched. At the bottom of one page was Psalm 23. Nowell's favourite, the one that Arthur had read aloud when his son was dead. Perhaps, Gerard Revell had sought comfort in the words about goodness and mercy. Then I saw the pencil marks on the next page in the margin of Psalm 24.

Something must have shown in my face because Joan said anxiously, 'What is it?'

I read out the words: 'Who shall stand in His holy place? He that hath clean hands and a pure heart; who hath not lifted up his soul to vanity, nor sworn deceitfully.'

'Oh,' Joan said, 'oh, gracious — clean hands. He hadn't got clean hands.'

'A confession?' I asked. 'Perhaps he read the verses before he killed himself. He couldn't believe in Psalm 23 — it was the Psalm Nowell loved most.'

Joan didn't answer but I saw her lips folded into a tight line.

I put the Bible down and searched through the drawers of the desk. In the bottom one I found Gerard Revell's handwritten papers from 1928 that finally gave us the answers we were seeking.

The old lie. Of course, it was. Owen was right. Was my lie any worse than theirs? Those whom Sassoon called the scarlet majors at the base. Watching the men go up the line. For another show. Scarlet swollen carnage. The old liars.

There was no truth out there. That raid to capture the bulge. We all lied. Right oh, sir. Nothing easier. Good show, boys. He lied. What a stunt. He'd come. Fearing but dishonour's death — that's what they taught us. Lied for fear — to be thought a coward. We all lied. Our bowels turned to water, our hands shaking until the rum stopped them. Cheerio, boys. Back in a tick. One. Two. Three. Up we go, lads.

Bate lied. Turned his ankle, he claimed. I ordered him at gunpoint. He hated me for that. Useless swine — a rat — worse than a rat. We knew the rats, insolent, swollen with eaten flesh, corrupt. They knew what we were — carrion. Their red eyes calculating. They didn't lie.

Matthew Revell lied. My father, I knew it. He denied me. I am Gerard Revell. Alice lied. My mother. There was no feckless sister. Two bodies in a filthy embrace — in some cheap hotel, in greasy sheets, under a blue light. She was no better than the whores in the French brothels. Blue Lights for officers. Red for other ranks — little runt Bate was a Red Light man. I was never a Blue Light Man. Matthew Revell was guilty, all right. A coward. It was in his eyes when I saw him that once after he'd got rid of me. She denied me to the end, but I saw the guilt in her eyes, too. She was only sorry that I'd come back. Born of two liars. Two liars who left me nothing but corruption in the blood.

Helena Lovelace. She had secrets. Liar. She stayed too long in the sun. And the blood gushed onto the carpet. I lost my son. Gerard Revell, heir to Foulstone Manor. She spoke that other name. Liar. She didn't know him.

Goss lied. He said the name Henry Simpson. There never was a Henry Simpson. I am Gerard Revell. Goss's wife lied. They knew where she had gone. Three liars in my house.

Three lines of trenches, reserve, support, front. Shell holes out there. One man awake. One asleep. One dead. Man, beast, thing. The white, the red and the green, the smoke, the blood, and the gas.

Truth, fiction, lies. Old lies seeping like smoke, or gas, or blood, turning everything rotten. Coward, shirker, blackmailer, his greedy eyes in my house, my hall, taking it all in. Louse. I'd paid enough. He wouldn't stop. It would be the last time. Liar. Off to America. A thousand pounds would set him up. Liar.

Until the next time. Not America. He'd crawl back to his whore in that filthy little dug-out in Battersea. I knew what he was. Cowering in that shell-hole, playing dead, but those mean eyes watching Sergeant Corley bringing him in. Sergeant Corley who staggered away to die of his wounds because he'd brought him back. Nowell. He should have died out there. What difference would it have made? I left them. One I thought dead. And one asleep. Three-quarters dead. Blood on his ruined face. 'Home,' he said and smiled. I had no home. The mud would take them. Their pauper's grave. The smell of earth and death and of those who lay beneath. It was my duty to go back. Captain Gerard Revell, M.C., did his duty.

I saw a dead man rise. He should have been dead. Saved for what? To lie, to thieve, to destroy. I had killed. It was nothing. All the dead men, smashed to pieces, carrion flesh, lying where they had fallen, food for rats. I hit him and he fell. A curse on his lips. I heard the crack of bone on the stone flags. It was nothing. I have heard the crash of metal, the burst of steel, the scream of shells, the monstrous anger of the guns.

He weighed nothing. What might the other have weighed if I had carried him? I left Bate there to rot in that little room. Food for rats. He cannot come out of his grave.

But I smell him. I taste him in my mouth. Trenchmouth.

Three walk in the woods. Two dead and one awake. From my window I see one in the garden under the moon. I see his wounded face and the reproach in his eyes. He knew. 'Come,' he says, waving his arm. 'Come,' he says, walking ahead in the twilight, 'it is time.' The other is with him. Come from his grave. They look back, unspeaking now. I follow.

Three dead men. Homeless, home.

40

Amanda

We made an appointment at the firm of Lamb and Greenwood in Kendal. We hadn't spoken much of the papers we had read, but what a tangle of emotions they'd left me with. It was complicated. I didn't know what to feel really. Sorrow for them all, I suppose, and a sense of waste. All those lives spoilt.

I couldn't tell what Joan really felt — her emotions would be even more complicated. Gerard Revell was her father and he had called her mother a liar. He had hated her. But Matthew Revell and Alice Simpson had made him — and the war. It was impossible to judge, as my father had said. Impossible for outsiders, I thought, but I was worried about her. She seemed to have withdrawn from us — from me. Dad had said nothing to Joan once we'd read Gerard Revell's paper, but we continued to look through the drawers in the desk. There was nothing else of note.

Joan simply said that she wanted to know where he was buried. I hoped that perhaps that would be the end of it — at least as far as the story of the events was concerned. Some things would have no end.

Joan mentioned Arthur Dearlove's papers, his will in the box in the attic. She remembered that Mr Lamb's name and address had been on the envelope. It had been this Mr Lamb's father who had spoken at the inquest.

'Oh, I remember it well,' young Mr Lamb told us — he was probably older than Joan. 'Not that I was involved, of course. My father dealt with it. He told the story later — when I started work here. He only spoke of it to me, Miss Goss. He had a great respect for confidentiality. Confidential matters remain so, Miss Revell. It —'

'Goss,' Joan said firmly. 'Mary and William Goss brought me up and gave me their name. Gerard Revell gave me away.'

'Yes, I was told that he wasn't able to look after you... Mr Revell's instructions, though, it was the oddest thing. That's why I remember. He didn't want... I have the papers here. My father thought his mind was unbalanced. The war, you see. He said so at the inquest. You know about that.'

'I read about it in the newspaper archives,' I added. 'Auntie Joan didn't know anything except that he had shot himself. She doesn't know where he is buried.'

'And you wish to pay your respects, Miss Goss.'

'I would like to know what his instructions were to your father,' Joan said.

Mr Lamb blinked. He must have thought Joan rather odd, too. 'Yes, well, do please bear in mind that my father had a duty to his client — to respect his wishes which were signed and dated. Even though my father would have preferred something more ... fitting, I suppose. Do you wish me to read them to you?'

'No,' I said. 'We'd rather —'

'Quite so.' He took out a folded paper and handed it to me. 'The grave is in the town cemetery. Unmarked, I'm afraid, but you can find out exactly where it is from the authorities. There is a plot number.' He looked down at his other papers. '28649.'

'A pauper's grave,' Joan said. I thought of Samuel Bate, too.

'Not quite, Miss Goss — simply that Mr Revell wished for the barest — er — rites. The grave was paid for out of the estate. My father attended and Mr William Goss. My father thought that someone should be there, even though... Well,

anyway, may I help you with anything else this afternoon —
you might wish to talk about Foulstone Manor. I understand
that you have not lived there.'

'No thank you, Mr Lamb, not today.'

I did not want Joan to read the paper in the street. When we
got back to the car, I handed it to her.

'Old Mr Lamb thought him mad. This is another example, I
suppose.'

'You'd better read it.'

She read it and handed it to me. I recognised that spidery
black handwriting. It was painfully austere. A man who hated
himself.

Mr Lamb,

*I intend to make my will and will send you the details later. It is time
for me to consider how Foulstone Manor is to be disposed of after my
death. Not that I foresee it in any immediate future, of course, but it is a
duty that must be done. It is a great pity that Mr Arthur Dearlove, the
previous owner, had no relatives to whom I might bequeath the estate.
Your enquiries in that direction were not fruitful, as I recall. It would have
been most fitting for a member of that family to inherit.*

*I wish you to carry out the instructions for my funeral which follow —
when the time comes, naturally.*

*I stipulate that my burial shall be in the municipal cemetery in Kendal.
My grave shall be unmarked. There shall be no clergyman to conduct any
Christian service, nor any prayers or flowers. There shall be no mourners.
If there must be words, they must be as plain and simple as you can devise.*

Gerard Revell

Foulstone Manor

Rawthdale

September 23rd, 1928

A man who thought nothing of his daughter — he had forgotten her existence. That was heart-breaking. I looked back at Joan. Her lips were folded in that old tight way, but her eyes were dry. Mine weren't.

'Well, we know everything now. We know where he is.' She looked across at me and pressed my hand. 'Don't cry, love. He paid for what he did. I am sorry for him. I'm sorry for all of us, but not for myself anymore. What'd Mary Goss say, eh? Spilt milk — that'd be it…' She was quiet then for a moment. 'You won't let it spoil things for you, will you? Don't fret about it all. You've your own life to live.'

I squeezed her hand and we sat for a while, watching the people come and go in the car park, carrying their shopping, their briefcases, their babies, looking at their watches, carrying on, hurrying into their futures.

EPILOGUE

Amanda

We cleared out Foulstone Manor — with help, of course, as Dad had advised. First, though, workmen came to clear out the cellar, to scour it clean, to repaint it with white, damp-proof paint, to replace the windows and the door. The door to the room where we found Samuel Bate was taken off and thrown on the bonfire — we didn't replace that one. The corridor was replastered and painted white, too. We opened every window from attic to cellar to let in the wind and we left them open, night and day, until we were sure that we could only smell fresh, spring air.

We employed a house clearance company from Lancaster and a cleaning company. We left it as we thought Helena had first seen it, shining, polished, scented with lavender and flowers. Hyacinths in the spring, roses in the summer. New curtains, copper in the kitchen, the pink plates and tureens as Mary Goss had arranged them on the old dresser, the silver shining in the dining room sideboard — the silver with the Dearlove monogram. And the photographs in the tarnished silver frames we found in the boxes in the attic. We polished those ourselves. The photograph of Nowell in his uniform, Nowell in his cricket whites, Nowell at school, with his dog, a photograph of Arthur Dearlove and his wife holding Nowell as a baby.

And in Helena's sewing room, there were her pictures, and on her marble-topped desk the photograph of her parents, and one of Lily and Helena in a park in London. The photograph of Helena as a girl in a white dress with her hair piled up, we put on the mantelpiece with a photograph of Nowell with his parents.

We put Arthur Dearlove's books back in the study. Nowell's room still contained his bed, his table, and the sarcophagus. We put his Bible back and his poems of Walter de la Mare, but nothing else. The photographs were enough to remember him by.

Gerard Revell's bedroom was cleared out. We didn't open the box in the attic which was labelled *Revell War* nor did we open Nowell's kit bag. Dad burnt them. Helena's bedroom was cleared out. Joan preferred the nursery to be left as it was.

But it was Arthur Dearlove's house again, and Nowell's, and the house Helena thought she would love.

Dad and I burnt Gerard Revell's papers, though I kept that poem about the three in the woods and the copy of *The London Mercury* with Revell's poem 'The Ghost' — the historian in me, I suppose. I think now that I should have let them go. We burnt the suitcase, too, the money, and the Post Office savings book. Mr Dearlove's diaries and papers were locked in the safe. Mr Lamb had the deeds of the house. Joan did make that appointment.

Dad tried to persuade Joan to let the house, but that, she said, was a step too far. Strangers looking down on us. No thank you. And so it stayed empty. But she gifted me Mrs Sykes's cottage and I found myself returned to live there full-time once I completed my doctorate.

I went up regularly with Joan to Foulstone Manor to keep the house clean and to air it. We lit fires in the winter and a gardener came to do the heavy work, but Joan kept it tidy. She wouldn't discuss what she intended to do with Foulstone and I didn't pester her. She would take her own time.

Joan was different from when I'd first arrived. She was chatty and lively with my parents when they visited, but there was still something of the old Joan — she didn't want to go out much. Just an occasional pub lunch and the cinema. She was still wary of strangers, and she kept her distance from her other neighbours.

She often went up to Foulstone Manor on her own. She'd tell me the garden needed doing and she planted bulbs and new bushes and flowers, but there was something else, I thought, some legacy of what we'd been through, which I couldn't quite share. I caught her expression occasionally — her eyes darkening and her mouth tightening. That old, closed look. Pain and loss, I thought. She was still haunted. I was, too; I couldn't forget those last words of Gerard Revell — such torment that we could not bear to speak of it. Such bitterness. Such suffering that could not be made sense of.

The daffodils are out now. I can see them, great swathes of them, bright as coins in the spring sunshine. I live alone at Foulstone now. Joan left it to me after her death in 1988. She died at Foulstone. She had fallen down the stairs. It was I who found her in September — you'll know the date — when the light was fading and there was no sign of her, and Foulstone was in darkness.

I took my torch and went across the field. I think I knew what I would find. Joan had asked me a question once, long after the events at Foulstone.

'Is there a darkness deep in my eyes?'

I knew that she was remembering Agnes Lund. 'No,' I said, 'you've lovely eyes.' But I was thinking how Agnes Lund had stared at Joan. And that she had said that it wasn't always right to know.

'They're his, though,' Joan said. Her eyes darkened then.

The front door opened easily because we'd fixed everything, but in the dark, there was still something inimical about Foulstone, something I thought we had banished — the smell. Faint, but unmistakable underneath the familiar, comforting scent of lavender polish. I knew it because I'd smelt it the very first time I'd been to Foulstone, something damp and something rotten which caught the back of my throat, sort of gaseous and sickly.

She was there at the foot of the stairs where Mary Goss had found Arthur Dearlove nearly seventy years ago. Not that I mentioned his death at the inquest, which found that her death was an accident. I didn't mention the army cape that covered her either. What good would it have done? I took it away and hung it by the back door on the hook from which Helena Revell had taken it on the day she had walked in the woods, the day she had met Samuel Bate. Nowell's cape, I think now. It's still there.

I saw them. I went out the back way through the gate which had replaced the rotten fence. Three walked in the woods.

One lost in Belgium, his bones turned to dust in that earth where blood red poppies grow; two in unmarked graves where no mourners come. Joan, not forgotten, in her grave in Rawthdale cemetery where I take flowers, the roses she loved and the daffodils from the bulbs she planted every year. I think about her, too, when I walk in the woods and sometimes catch a glimpse of those grey, silent, oddly fragmented figures drifting in the mist and rain of Autumn afternoons in the descending twilight, or just shifting shadows in the falling snow in freezing winter dawns when the light is only the colour of dim pewter. Sometimes three, sometimes four.

HISTORICAL NOTES

This novel was inspired by a house called Foulstone, not far from where I live. The name has always intrigued me because it sounds rather sinister, the implications of the word 'foul' suggesting somewhere haunting and derelict, smelling of damp and decay. It is not an uncommon prefix in my part of the world, its origins being, as Gerard Revell explains in the book, the Old English 'fugol' meaning bird. There is a Foulsyke farm not far away, though the origin of this name appears to be 'ful-sic' in Old English, meaning a dirty stream. Foulmart Hill is up on the moors overlooking Lower Soursyke, another dirty stream, I imagine. Foulmart seems to be linked to 'marten', a kind of weasel. There is a nature reserve called Foulshaw Moss, this 'foul' coming from 'fugol' again and 'shaw' meaning a small wood.

The real Foulstone is a rather grand house dating from 1655 and there's nothing derelict about it, so I'm guessing that the name is more to do with birds than dirty streams. It was too grand for me, though, so I stole the name and based the house in the novel on Thorns Hall, another house nearby in Sedbergh, which has some chilling tales attached to it, and dates from 1584. Near this house is the magically named 'Merlingstremefeild' in Tudor deeds, and Great Abbot Syke, another parcel of land.

Thorns Hall has an interesting history which is where the chilling tales come in. One John Mayer, who owned the house, assisted King Charles I against Parliament. He died in debt and the house was sold to Mr Posthumous Wharton, a poor schoolmaster, who married three times. I stole his name for my

Charles Dickens mystery, The Redemption Murders. All the wives of Posthumous were wealthy and died young, rather conveniently. He had two sons, one called Lancelot – to match Merlin and his field, perhaps.

However, Thorns Hall was inherited by one of Posthumous's daughters and her heirs, the Batemans who eventually died out; the house was then bought by a sea captain, who brought with him a black servant, Jenny, who gave birth to his child, Maria. That story gave rise to all kinds of legends about black slaves in the cellars at Thorns Hall – legends given short shrift by serious historians, though the tale of a little slave boy who starved to death in the cellars appears in various publications. He is said to haunt the gates of Thorns Hall. There is also the story of the black dog which at midnight on New Year's Eve howls his ghastly howls at Thorns Hall. And there are tales of ghostly figures seen on the moors and old roads, but the tale of the vampire of Dent is the most bizarre and gruesome – a man reputed to drink sheep's blood died at the age of 94 in 1715, was exhumed, found to be uncorrupted in his grave, and buried again with a brass pole driven through his body.

I don't know whether there are vampires at Thorns Hall or indeed if it is really haunted and I can't say I felt anything particularly chilling when I visited, but the stories made me think about a haunted house and what secret might be hidden in its cellars.

The Sedbergh War memorial with its seventy-six names gave me the idea of setting my story in World War I, and in a fascinating book, *Sedbergh and District 1914-1918* (2016), edited by Diane Elphick, I read about the soldiers missing in action.

The story of the soldier who disappeared after the war came from the British Newspaper Archives where I was browsing for information on World War I. The Lakes Herald and Westmorland Gazette gave me missing cats, a missing monk, a missing millionaire, several brides and bridegrooms, and a lady teacher who disappeared after being terrified by reading Wilkie Collins's *The Woman in White*, a book which her headmistress had abandoned because it was too disturbing.

That story led me to an account of a missing soldier, and I found more, advertised for by families desperate for news. The war cast a long shadow for those relatives who were still advertising in 1920 and beyond. One soldier returned three years after he had been posted missing in action in 1917; another, reported missing in 1916, found his way home to Cardiff in 1928. Astonishingly, he was served by his sister in the first café he went into. Some soldiers went missing because of amnesia or shell shock, or they had deserted, and some, it seems, simply vanished in search of employment, leaving their wives and children to the workhouse, and some took to crime, including blackmail.

Samuel Bate's story which Amanda reads in *The Westmorland Gazette* is based on the true story of an ex-soldier whose wife went to Bow Street to report her ex-soldier's husband's disappearance. I also read of a man last seen at Oxenholme Station who was presumed to have arrived on the London train. No trace of him was ever found, so the two stories came together and became the story of Samuel Bate who travels to Foulstone to blackmail Gerard Revell.

Gerard Revell's story is based on much of the reading I did on the history of the First World War, notably the books of Lyn Macdonald, the poems of Wilfred Owen, Siegfried Sassoon, and Walter de la Mare. There are hundreds of minor poets who served in the war and there are two soldier poets from Sedbergh School who are mentioned in a volume entitled, *Soldier Poets Who Have Fallen in the War*, (1918). Robert Sterling (1893-1915) was educated at Sedbergh School and Pembroke College. He enlisted and went to France in February 1915 where he wrote of 'the storm and bitter glory of red war' and his 'grief's infinity' at the death of a friend, killed in action in March. Robert Sterling was killed in April 1915. The few poems of Robert Sterling can be read at archive.org.

The kind of raid carried out by Gerard Revell and Nowell Dearlove was very common; one of the most vividly described is that in R.C. Sherriff's play, *Journey's End*.

Gerard Revell's poem, 'The Three', discovered by Amanda and Joan, was written by me, and much of the information about the significance of the number three came from *The Great War and Modern Memory* by Paul Fussell (1975).

A NOTE TO THE READER

Dear Reader,

I thought it was time I left Victorian London for a while and, looking out of my window to the hills one day, it occurred to me to use my own territory as the setting for an entirely different kind of book, but I have invented some places, and all the characters are fictional.

Rawthdale, the setting for this book, is based on the town of Sedbergh which is actually in Cumbria, though the town is situated in the Yorkshire Dales. The nearest big Cumbrian town is Kendal which used to be in Westmorland and since Joan and Amanda go to Kendal, I placed my fictional small town in Westmorland where Sedbergh is in one sense because it is now in the newly created Westmorland and Furness government district, though in the Yorkshire Dales for planning and it was in Yorkshire at the time of World War I. You can see why I wanted to simplify matters and why I gave up on geography and made up a name.

The details of the church and its war memorial belong to Sedbergh, but I invented Foulstone Manor, though Joan's cottage is real, and the old mill existed and is situated by the River Rawthey from which I invented the name Rawthdale. Highdale from where Mary and William Goss came is based on Garsdale, a remote village up in the Dales, and I couldn't resist the place called Fee Foe, on one map spelt, Fea Fow. Poring over my 1913 map of Garsdale, I very nearly went off course following the river Clough by a place called 'Stephen's Wives' – how many did he have? Could I send Joan up there for a walk just so that I could mention it? Or to Michael's House or

Hugh's Moss? Very territorial these old farmers, clearly. I was tempted by Mouse Syke, too, but I resisted and went on to Hawes where Agnes Lund lives and is actually Hawes and Dent is Dent, another remote village which is unchanged and was home to the 'terrible knitters' of Dent, who knitted, as Mary Goss does, with a knitting stick tucked into a waist belt so they could knit with one hand.

Although I invented places and characters, I did a lot of research into life in the Dales at the time of World War I, so I found out all about the snowstorms, trains, hunting, sheep farming, milk deliveries, knitting, preserving, recipes for the home-made medicines which Agnes Lund concocts, and I found a lot of intriguing place names. I loved the poetic 'Old Hush', 'Fell End Clouds' and 'Raven Thorn' but how about 'Hangingstone' for another haunted house?

Reviews are very important to writers, so it would be great if you could spare the time to post a review on **Amazon** and **Goodreads**. Readers can connect with me online, on **Facebook (JCBriggsBooks)**, **Twitter (@JeanCBriggs)**, and you can find out more about the books and Charles Dickens via my website: **jcbriggsbooks.com** where you will find Mr Dickens's A–Z of murder — all cases of murder to which I found a Dickens connection.

Thank you!

Jean Briggs

Sapere Books is an exciting new publisher of brilliant fiction and popular history.

To find out more about our latest releases and our monthly bargain books visit our website:
saperebooks.com

Made in the USA
Las Vegas, NV
15 February 2024